WAITING TO LIVE

WAITING TO LIVE

A NOVEL

MEWA RAMGOBIN

AVENTURA

The Vintage Library of Contemporary World Literature

VINTAGE BOOKS
A Division of Random House
New York

AN AVENTURA ORIGINAL, May 1986
FIRST EDITION

Published in the United States by Random House, Inc., New York, and simultaneously in Canada by Random House of Canada Limited, Toronto.

Library of Congress Cataloging-in-Publication Data

Ramgobin, Mewa, 1932–
  Waiting to live.

  (Aventura)
  I. Title.
PR9369.3.R28W34   1986   823   85-40972
ISBN 0-394-74432-2 (pbk.)

Manufactured in the United States of America

Text design by Robert Bull

To all the justice and freedom-loving people of the world who received only in giving their all.

ACKNOWLEDGMENTS

The publication of this book would not have been possible without the intervention of my friend Verna Hunt. She pushed me on. She was, especially during the period of my imprisonment under South Africa's security laws—I was detained without trial and later charged with treason—the link between me and the outside world. The original draft of *Waiting to Live* was completed before my detention. Verna assisted me in preparing the final draft while I was still in prison.

I am also indebted to my friend Advocate Ismail Mohammed, Senior Counsel, who kindly read the final draft to avoid any "treasonable" references while I was charged with treason.

WAITING
TO LIVE

"I don't want to be you! I don't want to be like you! I should hate to be like you. You show me what it is to be naked, to be barren, to be dispossessed. I hate everything I see in you! You, Father, the whole world walks over you—your white masters, the men in this cesspool of a place, even your wife! I know what she does in the other shacks here: she's a slut! She's a whore! Nothing is yours, not even your wife. Oh, to me this shack stinks of shame!"

The young man turned away, his face contorted with grief and rage.

CHAPTER 1

One day Elias and Nomsa were playing in the fields near his village. Elias was twenty years old. He was tall and slim and lively. Nomsa, who was seventeen, had beautiful deepset black eyes; her body shone with youth and innocence. Their families had been friends for generations.

The huts were methodically grouped together. The groups were neatly spaced and protected a whole family of families. They were a community. They belonged together. Their cows and their goats, their chickens and their pigs, their horses and their mules were nearby in separate areas. These were very important possessions of the household. Beautiful tropical trees abounded. The tilled areas provided mealies* and sweet potatoes. There was plenty of fish in the Umgeni and the Umzinyathi, and game to hunt in the unspoiled bush.

For many years the community had been visited by the "visitors" who had looked, at first, strange in their white skins. The folk of Umzinyathi were curious for a while, but they got used to the presence of these foreigners. Elias and Nomsa were

* mealies (from Afrikaans, *mielies*): maize plants; corn on the cob

also curious when they saw them, but they were not disturbed. Their parents would entertain the strange-looking visitors.

On this day Nomsa and Elias were playing in the mealie fields, chasing each other, singing to each other. They reached an untilled area where Elias plucked a few sweet-smelling wild flowers. He beckoned to Nomsa and she came closer to him. He turned her around and decorated her hair with the flowers. They laughed aloud and they laughed softly. Then they heard a distant call from Elias's father, headman of his village. They stopped laughing and obeyed the summons.

Near the huts a huge fire was burning. A motor vehicle was parked a little distance away from the fire. An ox had been slaughtered and chunks of meat were being distributed, and in customary style these chunks were being braaied* on the open fire. Dancing and singing had begun. Elias could not understand the reason for all the merriment. More meat was distributed, and these bleeding pieces of meat were held to the flames to be roasted. The flames were suddenly fanned by an unexpected wind. Those nearest the fire moved back, but the flames still shone on their damp black faces.

Fingers and hands of visitors and hosts were blood-stained. They were soiled with the ashes from the burning fire. They were soiled with the fat from the meat. No one minded. With their hands stained with blood the visitors talked about the book and the pamphlets they were handing out. With hands equally stained the hosts were receiving them. It was being explained to the hosts through a translator that knowledge of the contents of the books and pamphlets would lead to a different world. A world full of promise and hope. A world not only new but replete with wisdom and worldly goods. The testament that they were distributing was, they urged, a witness of love, of brotherhood and of charity. For many moments, in the

---

* braaied (from Afrikaans, *braai*: to roast, grill, fry or braise): barbecued

midst of eating, roasting, giving and taking, there was a strange empathy among all who were present.

Gifts were produced, and just before they left, the visitors handed out adornments in the simple form of a cross hanging from a fragile beaded chain. On being shown how to wear them the hosts put them on without any assistance. The chains hung securely around the black necks of these robust people.

For days after this event there was great talk of the new wisdom, and consultation among the elders. Nomsa and Elias were indifferent to the commotion. Later, on Sundays, Nomsa, Elias and all the other youthful ones from the neighboring households were sternly told to tidy themselves. Then they were taken to a formal gathering under a huge tree, which had a cross carved out in the bark of its trunk. The incision had not cut deeper than the bark. The carved sectors were filled with what appeared to be whitewash. After it had rained the whitening left the incisions and overflowed to run messily down the tree trunk. The villagers had to pray together; this was compulsory on Sundays. Nomsa and Elias did not understand, but they did not question too many things.

One Sunday afternoon, after the new kind of meeting, Nomsa and Elias decided to spend the rest of the day together. Holding hands, they left the open parish and began walking the trails that led to the encircling willow trees. The scent of wet grass was overpowering. Without a care they walked and walked. They saw the hundreds upon hundreds of strelitzia plants with their pointed buds. Most were still half-opened. Cattle, goats, mules and horses were grazing untended, as they always had; it was Nomsa and Elias and their kith and kin who were beginning to change. Chirping and crying, birds of all colours and sizes flew around them, over them and towards them. It was as if the creatures were teasing them, mocking them. Nomsa and Elias chased them. They ran in vain but it was fun. They plucked a blade of grass here and another blade there and tickled each other with the pointed tips. They laughed. Suddenly they began singing. Both had clear rich voices.

Clasping their hands tighter in each other's, they continued walking. They walked and walked as if this were all they had to do. From a distance they heard the monotonous sounds of the Umzinyathi River. Without any warning to the other each began running towards the river. When they reached the bank they were both out of breath, but they became enchanted with the soft, tender flow of the water. Through the pure water, they saw on the riverbed little pebbles of many colours and shapes. Leaves and branches of the overhanging willow trees licked, without respite, the untainted surface. The lush green growth on the banks of the river had remained unspoiled.

Elias jumped into the knee-deep water and without a moment's hesitation shed his hide pants. The cool, clean water tingled against him. In sheer joy and satisfaction he shouted out to Nomsa, who had already entered the river. She, too, was stirred by the water, and by the thrill of seeing her Elias naked. Her muscular little bottom contracted as she gazed at Elias and his bow-like erect penis. She had not seen this before. Almost without knowing it and unasked by Elias she slowly undid the band around her waist and her own hide skirt slid down into the water. As if magnetically attracted, they were drawn into each other's arms. They sucked each other, they kissed each other, they rolled together in the water. In their wetness the realisation came. It was like magic. They didn't exchange a single word. They clasped each other and then it began happening. Nomsa found herself lying on her back, with her head resting on a smooth rock. She drew Elias closer. And he, although already in her arms, seemed as if he were running into her. Digging his fingers into her body, tugging at her nipples with his mouth and then kissing her with bites on her lips and then tugging again at her nipples he tried to pierce the entry into Nomsa's body. It was difficult. But the waters of the Umzinyathi helped. He tried, tried and tried harder. Then suddenly it happened.

Nomsa had Elias where she wanted him and Elias was where he wanted to be. They shared the greatest moment of their young love. Their oneness was sealed. There in the waters of the Umzinyathi no other baptism was necessary.

After that, not a single day passed without Elias meeting his Nomsa. They had become the talk of all the neighbouring villages. The elders in the community anticipated a formal announcement of betrothal. The air, for Elias and Nomsa, was full of Nomsa and Elias.

Elias and Nomsa were down at the river again. The sun was hot. In the western corner of the distant sky a cloud was gathering. Suddenly, countless ants appeared on the pathways, in the grassy fields, in the cultivated fields and almost everywhere. What were they running from? Could they be harnessed? Nature planned that they never be harnessed. Their glory lay in their community and their indifference to danger. They sprang from the soil and they were holding fast to the soil. And yet, they were moving. They moved in ignorance—or was it the knowledge?—of the fact that the strength, the bigness and the power of man could not harness them. The power of man could not destroy these ants, but could only, momentarily, scatter them. Their fearlessness, or foolishness, was boundless as their numbers.

On the distant hill clouds of dust were raised by a fast-moving machine that seemed to be heading towards Elias's village. It was a four-wheel-drive, a landrover, and appeared to be making its own path. There were no roads for motor vehicles, but there were many tracks and trails. The landrover, with its wheels, cut deep trenches into the soil, deeper than those trodden in by the weight of all the humans who had walked these trails with each other and behind each other for decades. Even the tracks made by roving cattle were shallow in comparison. A landrover could flatten more grass and tear away more budding trees from their roots in just one trip than the local folk had done in years. On hearing the burring sound of the engine, men and women, boys and girls ran out of their huts and wondered what its presence heralded. The young lovers ran back to the village.

Two white men in khaki safari suits and boots jumped down from the jeep. A black man, barefoot and also dressed in khaki, but in floppy shirt and short pants, jumped from the back of the vehicle. In the hand of each white man swayed a thinnish but strong-looking cane. They had revolvers holstered to their waists.

They shouted to the headman, who was easily distinguishable. Mzimande came forward and with the customary salutations invited the visitors into his hut. But the visitors preferred to stand outside. The barefoot, half-naked men and women and boys and girls stood outside with them. Quietly they speculated on the purpose of the visit of these official-looking men. The new visitors, the villagers were convinced, were different from the meat-sharing, present-giving, singing ones who had come and spoiled their Sundays. The locals wondered what was going to be spoiled by these two strangers.

As the white men took turns to talk through the black interpreter they had brought with them in the back of their landrover, Elias's father sent young boys running to the nearest neighbours to fetch the headmen. The listeners looked at each other in disbelief. The visitors looked pleased with the response on the faces of the older men, but a discomfort was irritating them. The ants, hundreds of them, had already reached beyond the upper edges of the heavy leather boots, and several had fallen into the boots of the two white visitors. The creatures were swarming up and up and up. Angrily, the visitors began to swear in a language known only to them and their interpreter. With their bamboo canes the two men began beating their boots in the hope of clearing the ants already there and warding off others. They tried and tried but they managed merely to spread them. The ants were divided, for short moments, into little groups. While many of them were killed, they seemed to regroup, and their numbers appeared, to the naked eye, to remain the same. The visitors jumped around and scratched their tender skins. The sight of the jumping and scratching aroused a giggle and then a hilarious laugh among the barefoot adolescents. After reprimanding the young ones for the indiscretion of laughing at the visitors some of the headmen offered to help rescue the men from the ants. With grass switches and sand, they broke the unity and power of the ants.

As soon as the visitors' comfort had been restored, they resumed their negotiations. The two men eyed the youth and virility of the local men. These were their requirements: they wanted strong young men as labour recruits for Durban. Arrangements were made between the two visitors and the headmen that one hundred young and healthy men be loaded into large motor vans that would come within hours to take them to the city. Several hundred had gone before this batch from other areas, and there was a suspicion among those that remained that there would be several hundreds to follow.

There was little resistance from Elias's father, who had recently acquired implicit faith in the jewelled cross and its donors. The instruments of this new testament must be trusted; they must be listened to and followed, and above all they were here to deliver the people.

Old man Mzimande, in his patriarchal fashion, tried with the full authority of his position as headman to allay the fears of a few of his tribesmen. He asked, "Are we not happy that new frontiers are being opened up for us?"

"It all depends what the new frontiers are and what will become of us there. Have we thought about this?" asked Nomsa's father, who had just arrived.

"What do you mean, what will become of us? I think these white people, who have already been so long in our land, should be given all the help and labour for the things they want to achieve and create. We have an abundance of labour and they have an abundance of new ideas, and knowledge that we don't have. Don't you think we should be partners in what they wish to do?"

"That's all right. But are you sure we are going to be partners?"

"Why not?" Mzimande paused. "They will be useless without us: we have the labour, we are the people. They have the money and the knowledge and the power. For us, they are the key to the outside world. Yet they cannot do without us. Do you understand that? Do you understand that in recognition of what they are doing for us the least we can do is to mix our sweat and our blood with the mortar they want to use in building this new and brave world. For too long we have been timid, and too far away from everything that has happened and is happening in the world. This area, according to their judgement—and I agree with them—will not hold out and feed all of us and our children and our children's children. These pieces of land are being used up too fast by too many of us. We increase in numbers all the time but the land area is fixed. And the demarcation is done by them. Thus far our survival has depended on our land. Don't you agree that they make sense? So far we have not thought about the problem of our survival. They have. They are going to move us from these things that we are accustomed to, and include us in their society."

A convoy of trucks appeared in the distance. As he spoke, they approached slowly along the track the first landrover had cut. Old man Mzimande saw the cloud of dust, and went on with his speech.

"They will teach us all about money and what it means. We will be educated by them and with the help of this education we will learn to buy their things and we will learn to keep some of the money for ourselves."

He had the attention of all those around him and, in order that the females in his audience might not be embarrassed, he said softly to the males, "At least we will also learn from them to buy the things they make to cover our entire bodies, not just our genitals. You know even our *lobolo** could be settled partly in cash and partly on terms, and with money instead of cattle. Come come my people, all these things are new to us. Don't you feel a kind of adventure in all this? Imagine the new life! We will be able to buy our meat with the money we earn. We will not require to be equipped with bows and arrows, we will not need to be more cunning than the wild animals. We will not have to herd our sheep and goats; we will no longer need to plant our crops. They will be doing this and we will be working the farms for them; we will no longer need blades of grass and wild blooms to give to our beloved maidens as tokens of our love—we will buy gifts for them: beautiful scents made from the petals of flowers. Of course, we will have to work hard, perhaps very hard."

He paused, paced the ground a little and then pleaded, "We must join them. We must go and join their new world. This new world is going to be ours, too."

Elias, being his father's son, was one of the first hundred to go.

Nomsa, who had heard everything Elias's father had said, stood motionless. She looked as if she were in a dream. Where her Elias was going, she did not know. Elias did not know either. She saw Elias through wet eyes. But she kept a brave smile. Then her eyes, which had been for just a few days the fount of many joyous tears, became the mirror and repository of this, their new pain—their separation.

As the vehicles bumped away, the clear skies were marred by clouds driven by the western winds. Suddenly the sun was

---

* *lobolo* (Zulu): cattle, or cash equivalent, handed by the bridegroom's people to the bride's guardian to secure the right to call the woman and any offspring of the marriage by the bridegroom's name.

blocked and it became dark all around. Peals of thunder; the sky opened its gates and let loose the rains. Nomsa began invoking her ancestors. She never gave a thought to the pendant that she wore. The cross was there. But she knelt and invoked her ancestors. The lucky ones who were left behind watched Nomsa, and joined her in her invocations. She looked up to the skies and whispered, "I wonder if your grief is as deep as mine."

Her tears flowed. It seemed to her that her tears for Elias were flooding everything around her. The dust in which she and Elias had crawled together as infants had turned into muddy murky water. Slowly she walked, and cried while she walked. She talked to herself and taunted herself and her new emptiness. She wondered about the well-being of Elias. She had forgotten about the others. She cried again. Her body shook with a fever-like anxiety. In a stupor, but steadfastly, she walked. She stopped and grabbed a mealie stalk and with practised ease tore a mealie from it. Nomsa unravelled layer after layer of thickly embedded leaves until she came to the shiny grains of corn, neatly arranged in rows upon rows. Reassured, she looked at the simple fruit of her land.

The same afternoon, Elias and his ninety-nine companions were ushered into a long, cold, empty room. Crushed mealies, boiled with beans, and a piece of meat with some gravy were served to them in greasy little aluminum containers. Most of the men were hungry and they ate. They were tired from the uncomfortable journey. Elias was in no hurry to eat. He was lonely. With his dish of food in his hand he sighed, "Oh Nomsa, I miss you, I want you." He walked a few paces away from the crowd and squatted on the floor. He ate as much as he could.

Some time later, official-looking men, both white and black, entered the room. The black men carried in an old table and some chairs; the white men sat down. Someone shouted instructions, and the men began filing towards the table. Thumbprints of the new recruits were taken. Papers were issued to them. Photographs were taken; the instant photos amused the men. These photographs were for their passes, prepared with methodical care—the sign of their usefulness. More details were solicited from them, including the names of their headmen, chiefs, tax areas and tribes. To Elias it seemed like madness. But he was here in the city of Durban. . . . With each man's papers was a parcel containing two blankets, a billy can, a spoon and a plate. These were tied up in a hessian bag, which was to become his bed sheet. All the men were led to a hostel, specially prepared for them. Some managed to get beds but most had to do without. The black man who took them to the hostel helped the newly arrived to cross the road safely; but he appeared to be a brother only in language and colour and hair texture.

Elias and his fellows soon came to realise that the pace of activity was much faster in Durban than in Umzinyathi. The black city slickers were quick to discover the arrival of the new folk. They did not delay in coming to make their acquaintance. They came to say that they were and always would be around to look after their needs. Good clothes, secondhand, were always available through them at reasonable prices. Payments for these and any other negotiated items could be deferred to the day of their first pay packet. There would be no problem . . . and there was no hurry. In equally unhurried manner, but very soon after their arrival, came the queen of them all. For money she negotiated many essentials. These new city-dwellers had to be properly informed, or else they would negotiate somewhere else. She was the cheapest in the area and she was easily accessible. Her establishment was open twenty-four hours a day. And the rules of her book had it that no customer should ever be turned away. Her customers' gratification was her total preoccupation. Nobody was to challenge her on that. She knew her business and she made it known in styles learned from the port area of Durban. Now she had both the know-how and the means. It was easy for her. For as long as they remained harnessed in this city she was assured of her returns. She realised that sooner or later she would have to use her expertise in other hostels and compounds. At the rate this flow of human custom was progressing she had to plan ahead. And Elias was in the midst of all this.

A great number of forms had been filled in at the compound. Registration of the migrant workers had to be completed, all of which baffled Elias. He did not want to migrate from Umzinyathi, yet he was categorised as a migrant. He had his own home, his own people, his own loves and hates in Umzinyathi, but here he was called a migrant. At one stage while being registered Elias had pleaded to be allowed to remain with the group he knew best. He thought he would feel secure in their company. But by this stage Elias was a mere number. At a sign from one of the black officials Elias moved forward, and looked over his shoulder to see whether he was being kept company by those he knew, who would care for him. None of them came forward or followed him. It was not that they did not care and worry about Elias. They too had become mere numbers. The inevitable happened: all the men from Umzinyathi were scattered.

A commanding voice ordered Elias to jump into the back of a truck. Elias obeyed. Meekly, he sat in a corner. The van bounced forward. Soon Elias was told that he was to join a gang on the railways. The van stopped with a jerk. He discovered that a great number of blacks, just like him, were already at work. Many of these people looked satisfied and some seemed to be old hands at their jobs. A large group just a few yards away was lifting a length of railway track. They were singing in unison. They lifted in unison. Their singing was led by the chief of the gang. This singing, thought Elias, was just like way back home. He remembered how he and the others of Umzinyathi sang as they moved the boulders to clear a space for their open-air church services. But the lifting, here in Durban, and even the singing were not quite the same as in Umzinyathi. There everybody worked together. Here there was one man standing and he stood as if enthralled by the tenacity and willingness of the toiling blacks. And this man, who didn't sing, who didn't carry, was white. His duty was to watch and guide and not to work. This was his destiny, they were told.

Railway sleepers had to be carried some distance. It was not difficult to explain to Elias and those with him that they must do this. His language was spoken, so he thought. But it was being spoken with a difference and by somebody who was different. He chuckled in the knowledge that it was *his* language that somebody who was different was trying to speak. What amused him was the fact that this different kind of man tried.

Elias soon discovered that the singing was not required. What was required was pure, simple effort. The shifting of the sleepers went on for some two hours, and then a rest was announced. The experienced blacks made for the billy cans. They sat on the remaining pile of sleepers, placed their billy cans to their mouths and tipped their heads backwards. The sour mealie porridge just slid down their parched throats, satisfying and refreshing. The white "guide" and a colleague who joined him took out some sandwiches from a stainless steel box and opened a flask of hot tea. They too looked satisfied. Their satisfaction was sealed with deep puffs of a sweet-smelling cigarette. Back at Umzinyathi the homemade reed pipe and the home-ground tobacco snuff were passed around and shared among all who cared for them. They relied on these and took their turns. Here in Durban it was different. Even those who looked like Elias wrapped their own tobacco in pieces of newsprint and revelled in their independent smokes. They also sealed their satisfaction, but each one his own.

Fifteen minutes had passed and the respite was over. "Back

to the rail and the sleepers" was the order. Nobody squealed. In perfect obedience the blacks resumed their work. Elias was no exception. They worked for the next few hours and then at the sounding of a gong the old hands made their ways in different directions. Elias and the other day-old recruits were smiled at by the supervisors and beckoned into the van. They had to be trained. Their labour was vital. But equally vital was the patience required to train Elias and his like.

They were driven back to the compound. All the black workers took their turns at the communal tap. They stripped unashamedly and washed. The sight of many black naked bodies shocked Elias. They were, all of them, indifferent to each other's nakedness. There was nothing personal about their bodies. It was all so different from the breezy valley of the Umzinyathi, where the river flowed snake-like and got lost in the Umgeni, where the course of the river provided so many secluded spots just to bathe and wash. Elias was accustomed to seeing half-naked males and females, but the nakedness that he saw in this compound was different. The men seemed to be caged and yet they were naked. Somehow, for Elias, this kind of nakedness was not proper.

For those who had to rise early next day, there was, in the new scheme of things, an early supper. "Please, sir, may I have some more," they dared not say. The employers who had brought them to Durban knew exactly how much food should be handed out. But the decision-makers did not eat there in the compound. They only rationed the food that the inmates of the compound had to eat.

An alternative was available. If the food was not plentiful enough or not good enough, more could be bought from private suppliers within the precincts of the compound. The vendors did not insist on cash: credit facilities were available. The customers' credit-worthiness was guaranteed by the closed compound itself. Chunks of meat and boiled mealies, just like Mother's, presented no problems. The inmates and their tastes were well known. The contents of the *khamba* could also be obtained, but not, here in Durban, a whole big khambaful—there was no sharing and passing around of the wide-mouthed earthenware pot. The thick beer they were used to was sold in small tin mugs.

At night the pimps, the good-for-nothings, began their work. These black men and women of leisure went to work when most of mankind went to sleep. Elias, who was only just twenty, and his comrades, the new ones in the marketplace, had to be taught the techniques and the terms could follow later.

CHAPTER 2

In Durban, Elias and his comrades worked every day except Sunday, when they rested. It was, they were told, the Sabbath. Elias had decided that at the end of the fourth week, he would go home on a visit. On the first three Sundays, after an early wash and in clean clothes, he sought out a compound mate and they went out together to explore their surroundings. They had to be careful to be back at the compound before the appointed hour, the curfew. They had been told that blacks were prohibited from being outdoors after 10 P.M. The more humorous in the compound had observed that the young madams and the young baases* must not be disturbed and frightened by the sight of black aliens like Elias late at night.

On the third Sunday, Elias and James Mazwai walked along concrete pavements flanked by tall fences made of bricks or stone or cement. Elias was amazed. Jammed close together were many houses, inside which were people who looked like the baases who gave orders along the railway lines. Elias wondered what they were hiding, behind their high walls. From inside their houses the people peeped and gave the black pass-

---

* baas (from Afrikaans *baas*): boss, master

ersby disapproving looks. Elias and his guide, Mazwai, passed
on. To whom did all these things in the city belong? It was
exasperating for Elias not to know. They saw a woman dressed
in city clothes, but she looked very much like the women Elias
had left behind in Umzinyathi. She was black, she had crinkly
hair and she had a child tied to her back. She told them she was
taking the baas's child for a walk. The child's parents were
not to be disturbed early in the morning on the Lord's Sabbath.

Elias marvelled at the fact that this part of the city was so
different from the compound yard, and so different from his
own Umzinyathi. Within the fences surrounding these houses
there grew lovely flowers of so many colours and shapes. The
high walls that enclosed the flowers seemed to hide them and
to keep the joy of their beauty from the people outside. It was
funny, and intriguing. But what was funnier was that there
were hundreds of blacks who were not observing the Lord's
day. They watered the flowers, they swept the yards, they
carried refuse and they minded their baases' babies. He wondered where all these people, his black brethren, lived. He soon
found out: there were lodgings at the back of these houses.
There were rooms underneath some of the bigger buildings.
Other buildings, he was told, had compounds for them on the
top, nearer the sky. These were the lucky ones, the ones that
slept on top of their baases and madams. Black men sleeping
on top! Where did the black women sleep?

Mazwai said his friend Sibiya worked in one of these huge
buildings. He suggested that the three of them get together for
the day. They entered the building through the yard at the
back and took the goods lift up. The lift at the front entrance
was reserved and not for the use of blacks, said Mazwai. Elias's
stomach lurched with the sudden upward jerk of the noisy
goods lift. But Mazwai was unperturbed. The lift stopped at
the seventh floor and they got out together and walked along

a passage. Mazwai stopped in front of a door and pressed a button. The bell resounded. The door opened and there, right in front of them, stood a full-breasted white madam in a shortie pyjama top. Just like Nomsa! But before the madam could be told how beautiful she was or greeted with a "good morning," the door was slammed in their faces. They heard the sounds of the door being bolted. Elias was baffled and wondered what the madam was frightened of and why she had locked them out. He knew that Mazwai had business there. Mazwai pressed the button again and this time there was no immediate answer. A little while later a baas opened the door, shaking his finger at them and demanding to know what they wanted. Both were terrified at the sight of an angry, threatening baas. Mazwai tried apologetically to explain that they had come for Sibiya, who was apparently, to Elias's amazement, inside where the madam had hidden herself. But the baas said Sibiya was busy making the madam's bed and not available. They should enquire from the caretaker later in the day. The two left without Sibiya.

Coming down in the lift Mazwai suggested they make for the suburbs. Elias was fascinated by the fine houses, each set in its own garden. He observed that each house was beautiful in itself, but not as a part of a total beauty. Each was heavily fenced in. Entrances were tightly secured by gates with large signs indicating that the public should "beware of the dog." Entry into the precincts of these houses, Mazwai explained, was very difficult by day for all blacks who had no business there. At night those who worked there could easily bring in their black friends. Their blackness could not be distinguished from the blackness of the night. There was almost a singleness in blackness. It was their security and their identity. While they themselves experienced their blackness as all these, everything around them indicated that their blackness was other people's insecurity.

It was past lunch hour. From all directions black "umfaans"*—clothed in short pants and thick white shirts edged with red—were converging on an open, wide, breezy piece of ground. It was evident they were in the habit of gathering here. The ones and twos arriving had soon merged into a large crowd. Elias and Mazwai, though they were dressed a little differently, soon found themselves in the midst of the singing and drum-beating, the chantings and wavings of gaily decorated knobkerries** and of sticks with chicken feathers stuck on one end, so that they looked like tall flaming altar candles. Before long they were all in a frenzy of merrymaking and jubilation. For all of them it was their time off, their time to be together. The rest of the week, in the city, their time was not theirs. They had particular roles to play that were defined and scheduled by others, others whose aspirations in life were different from those of the "migrants" to Durban.

Carried away by their own vigour and vitality, by the power of their songs, by their sense of oneness, they were invoking their ancestors and remembering their loved ones across the land. The invocations, the lyrical love songs, intensified Elias's longing for Nomsa. His stomach churned. His head reeled.

Almost telepathically the crowd moved. In unison and with compelling rhythm they moved up and up and up the hill, away from the open ground. They took the hard, tarred road that had been designed by their white baases and built by their black brethren. As they climbed, they went into further frenzy. They were leaving behind them the fenced, enclosed, divided houses. They wanted to look out from the top, in the hope of seeing the distant plains with their sprawling fields of maize, perhaps even a familiar collection of huts, a village. Their mood was joyous, and that sight would have crowned their joy.

Even the ear-splitting noise of a passing aeroplane could not

---

* umfaans (from Zulu *umfana*: boy): derogatory kitchen Zulu as used by whites; umfaan = black man of any age = "boy"
** knobkerrie: short, stout wooden stick with a knobbed head, all carved in one piece; traditional weapon among black South Africans

drown the sounds of joy. The aeroplane passed and was heard no more. The men beat harder on their drums. Their sticks clattered against each other.

They were on top, on the Berea, from where they had a clear view of that ever-changing sea that separates land from land, and men from men. These black men saw, down between themselves and the sea, the houses and some of the people in them, and these were as separate from the black men as any chunks of land divided from each other by the mighty sea. Some of the men on the hill thought that the separation had its origin in the baases' inability or unwillingness to obey the commandments they themselves had brought to the hearts of the black men. They felt that the separation of land from land was the effect of the machinations, good or bad, of the One they did not know.

It was from over the sea that these others, with their pale skins and their Ten Commandments, had come. Here was that sea, sometimes pleasing, sometimes cruel, the sea that had brought their baases and the Indian to this, their country. Elias had heard his elders tell how black men had once fought and killed each other; how tribe had fought against tribe and all had been weakened. He remembered how the story continued: how in their weakness they had had their land filched from them by the strange white men from across the sea. The sight of the sea filled him with these thoughts, yet it exhilarated him. His elders had talked around their fires about the new spirit that was born among them after the filching had taken place. They had begun shedding their tribal loyalties and started working towards the creation of a new kind of association. But, they said, the leaders who were working towards the new order were the very blacks who had been admitted into the church and the schools of these foreigners. Elias found it all very muddling. For those who had already been admitted to the schools and churches, life, said the elders, had become somewhat intolerable. They had formed a national consciousness and new ideas of nationhood. The couriers who had carried the seeds of these ideas were men and women from across the seas, and they had brought new tidings for the black men on almost every aspect of their lives.

These black converts to the cloth and to Western learning became aware of certain facts: once the whole sky had been their roof and all who were beneath the sky had had the right to be where they were. Now there were demarcations about where one lived and how one lived, especially if one were a black person. These black men of the cloth and of learning turned to the Book, to the testament, for an explanation. But all they found was that they should not steal or covet or hate or envy. They did not understand why the Book said "the poor shall inherit the earth." They did not understand because they had just lost their own land, not to those who were poorer than they were, but to those who were stronger.

Elias and his comrades were still high up on the hill. Suddenly the smoggy air below them was filled with the simultaneous ringings, clangings and thumpings of bells, all kinds of bells with all kinds of sounds. The city had come to life in its heavily built churches with their shepherds and flocks, standing or sitting, praying or listening to the tunes of the bells on that Sunday.

The knobkerrie-waving, drum-beating crowd made its way down, down through the hard streets among the steeples that were equally hard. These exuberant black men were returning to the backyards and the compounds.

Another week passed and Elias was on his way to Umzinyathi for the weekend. He had his new possessions bundled ready for his first visit home. Vendors in the compound had talked him into buying a string of beads, a headscarf and some chocolates. He was going home to his Nomsa. He had some money in his pocket. The money was for his father and mother. But somehow he believed that his father would use most of the money for the roof that was being planned for the new church. Elias smiled and talked incessantly about anything and everything. He knew about the "ticketing out" for the weekend and the "ticketing in" on Monday morning at the compound. The bus route was explained to him. From the bus stop near Umzinyathi it was a mere two-hour walk to his village and his people. This, for him, with Nomsa in his soul, was nothing. For those who had taken him away from Umzinyathi it was also nothing, though the reason there was different.

CHAPTER 3

At the bus rank for the black men Elias awaited his turn in an untidy queue. He boarded an Indian-owned bus and was bound for Umzinyathi. He was happy. The ride lasted little more than an hour and it cost him one shilling and six-pence. When he got off the bus he started running. He ran as if his shadow, which grew longer and longer behind him, were a monster pursuing him. Occasionally he looked back, but he pushed on towards his destination. Sometimes he called out from the deep valleys hoping that Nomsa might hear him and make the distance shorter by meeting him on the way. This was the lover's hope and his prayer. It remained a hope and a prayer. But he knew that his Nomsa was there, beyond the hills.

Like everybody else in Umzinyathi, Nomsa was of course unaware that Elias was returning that Saturday. She was steeped in her loneliness and resigned to his absence. Passion-ately running his way home, Elias stumbled and faltered, but kept up his pace. The visiting landrovers had made some kind of a trail for him to follow. But they had had to make some detours and deviations, and Elias was in no mood to waste his precious time. He scaled the hills. Trail or no trail, he jumped the rocks and pushed through the weeds. Dripping with sweat he reached his home.

His little sisters and brothers, his father and his mother, his uncles and aunts and cousins, his neighbours and his friends came running out from their homes and their gardens. They came and swamped his tired sweating body with their greetings. They kissed him and hugged him. They shouted and sang. They danced and jumped. They cried with joy and thanked their ancestors. Their son was home. Elias had arrived. Elias kissed and hugged and danced and jumped, and his folk realised how much he had changed in only one month. He was wearing short khaki pants and a singlet. They did not know what could be in the packages he carried. They did not ask. They were happy that he was there. Some of the elders were arranging the slaughter of a beast for the following morning. It was too late for that evening. While his folk discussed the slaughter, his father came up to him and asked, "Elias, do Nomsa and her parents know that you have come?"

"No, Father."

"Then it would be nice if you went to her and her people."

"If my mother and you don't mind I will—"

"Go now, my son. I know a woman's heart," encouraged his mother.

"Go!" commanded his father.

Elias ran towards Nomsa's household and from hundreds of yards away he shouted and called. Nomsa heard him. Suddenly for her, too, the air was full of music and a hot thrill ran through her. The early evening birds broke into peals of song. For these two even the setting sun seemed to still its course. The orange halo shone into Elias's face. His face in turn shone into Nomsa's. They cried to each other and they cried with each other. All things seemed to be in sympathy with them; they became indifferent to everything around them. And before long they were sealed in a oneness of love and passion.

They walked away from her home and into the fields where they were happiest. And the heavens became shy at the sight of these lovers, and receded into night.

In the darkness, joyfully he drew from his pocket the string of shining beads that he had bought in the city for Nomsa. He walked behind her and with gentle love fastened the lustrous beads around her neck.

A full moon had made her way from behind the fast-moving clouds. The stars had begun to twinkle here there and everywhere. There was a new heavenly joy up above. But the majesty of the joy of the lovers was unchallenged by the heavens. The two sat on the dew-gathering grass, oblivious to the damp.

"I missed you so much in the last four weeks."

"And I missed you too, Nomsa."

"Elias, I can't live without you. You must take me with you. Elias, I would die without you."

"My love, I too wish and long to have you with me."

"Then it is settled. When you go back to the new place, you will take me with you?"

"I didn't say that."

"Oh, you have already learned to mix your words?"

"No, no, Nomsa. It's not that."

"Then what is it?"

"You see where they make me stay . . . it is a huge room. It's in what they call a compound. Dozens of men like me, more than dozens live there. That is no place for my beloved."

He looked pensively at the moon and wondered whether he should relate all the happenings in his compound.

"Why have you suddenly gone quiet?" Nomsa asked.

He decided to tell her, no matter how disturbing for her. "You see, Nomsa . . . out there in the compound, the place where I live, there, there, only men live. And what strange things our men get up to in that compound. I . . . I never thought . . . they fight and swear at each other. They swear at anybody. They do everything that we have not yet seen here. You know Nomsa, they . . . they for a price, and not much at that, and, when not for a price then through sheer bullying, yes by bullying, the fellows, our own people do it standing. The big fellows bully the smaller ones and the smaller ones because they are afraid give in to them. Yes Nomsa, this is just part of the life that I see in the city."

"Then I must come with you. I don't want to lose you to one of those men, let alone another woman."

Elias laughed. Nomsa did not think it was funny anymore and in her naivety she begged to go with him. But Elias said, "Nomsa, I think I will go back alone this time. And, as soon as I have a few free moments I will look for a place where you can live. Then if we can't live together, at least we will be able to see each other. I have seen quite a number of our girls working in the kitchens and the gardens of the baases. They even carry the baases' babies on their backs. That looks like nice work. I will see if I can get such a job for you."

"I will do any work . . . just so that I can be with you."

"We will have to get married first."

"I don't mind how or where, as long as I am with you."

She paused a moment and then asked, "When will we get married?"

"On my next visit—" Before he could finish what he wanted to say Elias was smothered in Nomsa's kisses. New clouds came and moved on. More clouds came and smacked the face of the moon. In a short while the clouds had blanketed almost all the twinkling stars. Nomsa's eyes were half-closed, and then closed with agony and pleasure. For a while, she was unaware of the palpitations of her heart. She drew Elias closer to herself and asked in a tired whisper, "Do you think I will be able to give you babies?"

"I know you will."

They clung to each other. And when they did release themselves from each other's hold they found that the moonlight was yielding to the dawn. They didn't care. Their parents knew and loved their children. Their parents knew about their love for each other and they had, in their own ways, approved. They knew that their children would not disgrace them. They felt that their children would be like them. So, their spending the whole night together under the sky, with the cover of darkness as their only privacy, was something their parents would understand. When Nomsa awoke, Elias was still sleeping. She hurriedly tidied herself and, standing, she gazed at her tired, youthful man. She smiled. She woke him up, and with pride, she walked with him to her home.

Elias met Nomsa again for a brief moment on the Sunday. He had to leave Umzinyathi early in the afternoon to catch his bus. He had been warned that the Monday morning bus might not get him to Durban in time to start work. The bus stop seemed much farther away than it had the day before, but he knew he would not be running, and left himself more time. He reached Durban about five o'clock. He walked, alone, to the compound. The streets were quiet. The few baases who were around went lazily about their Sunday afternoon pursuits. Elias had wondered how it felt for them to have their homes, their places of work and their amusements and pleasures all within easy reach of each other, even though these homes were clustered together and had high walls around them. He walked in awe.

On his arrival at the compound he was surprised at the sight of a fellow black man who spoke his own beautiful language but was resplendent in foreign-looking attire. Elias was dazzled. Entries, numbers, accommodation, food requirements, ticketing in, all were being checked and supervised by this new man. Elias's entry number was checked. It was in order. His checker smiled but Elias, being dazzled, just stared. Thinking of nothing but the splendour and brightness of the clothes and the authority that emanated from them, he walked into his section of the compound.

No sooner had he sat down in his damp, dark corner than he was confronted with these words, firmly spoken: "You did not greet me!"

"Eh, what did you say?"

"You did not greet me!" shouted the new black man in the splendid clothes.

"Oh, I am sorry." Elias gathered himself and continued, "You baffled and dazed me with all these clothes; your authority and your manner of speech frightened me—"

"You too can wear these. You too can be in authority like me. You have to work hard. You must follow instructions and you will be paid well. Then, if you are liked and if you are obedient you too will stop digging trenches and carrying sleepers. You too can become an *induna** like me. Right now you do not understand what the baases want. I do. And from now on I will tell you what to do out there in the compound. Therefore, from now on you must greet me. Do you understand that?"

"Yes, sir, I do."

The new black man, satisfied, walked away. He swayed his bulk from side to side. He pulled out his snuffbox, inhaled some snuff and let out a deep resounding sneeze. In moments he was gone but behind him he left his stench, compounded of sweat and snuff.

* *induna* (Zulu): foreman

CHAPTER 4

The Monday morning bell rang. Its piercing sounds not only woke the workers in the compound, but also sent back into hiding the vermin that thrived in the gutters, in the roofs of compounds and houses, in the alleys, in slits in the walls that enclosed shops and factories. At seven o'clock Elias, in the company of a gang of black men, was driven away to begin the week's work. The gang did not know their destination. They only knew work had to be done.

Some of the men at the back of the truck felt drowsy enough to go back to bed. Many had half-shut eyes, after a sleepless, restless night or a night of heavy drinking. In the railway yard the truck jerked to a stop. The black men jumped out and some stretched their arms in an attempt to break their tiredness. Others yawned deeply and seemed to be revived by this involuntary impulse. Elias and the others awaited their orders and before long they had all been told what the day's work was to be.

Picking up their shovels the gang walked across to the bull-dozed, levelled area where they had to mix stones with cement, sand and water. As they mixed, sweat dripped from their bodies into the mortar. Trenches were neatly dug. These were the foundations for another warehouse. One of the older men, greying at the temples, pointed to an existing warehouse and boasted to Elias that he had built it from foundation to roof.

"But that looks just like the compound we live in!"

Another new warehouse, planned for the harbour authorities. Merchandise, goods from different lands, would be stored here. Their origins were in distant lands, but the agents of the manufacturers, in some cases their kith and kin, were here to take delivery of these goods. The goods would be housed for as long as necessary. Then other gangs of black men would take them to their destinations. Sooner or later people would buy the goods. These purchases would eventually reach valleys like Umzinyathi. The gangs of black men had to learn fast, learn more so that they might earn more, and earn more so that they might buy more. They had to buy more because there was always plenty on the way.

The concrete mixture was loaded onto wheelbarrows. One after another these were pushed to the building site. And soon the energetic movements of the gangs of black men gave rise to spontaneous songs. The black men worked and they also sang. Architects, quantity surveyors, supervisors and contractors, none of them black, were on site. With a mug of tea in one hand and a lit cigarette between the fingers of the other, the contractors were amused by the singing that kept time and rhythm with the movements of these black men. The noise of the offloading and reloading of the wheelbarrows was the only jarring sound to spoil the rhythm of the songs.

Elias had become one of the many in the gangs of black men. He could sing and swing his pick or shovel with the best of them. He was younger than most of his group, and more agile. He thought often of his new compound induna and the image of the man made him more willing.

Soon after tea break on this Monday morning, the rhythm of work was rudely interrupted by shrieks and yells. Everybody, including the baases, was running towards the shouts and cries. A short distance away, streaks of smoke were turning into sheets of flame. A common danger threatened them all. A fire was engulfing everything within its reach. Instinctively every man and woman, everybody in the vicinity, made towards the fire. They all tried to help. The latecomers to the scene shouted in horror. Each person tried whatever he could think of to help smother the flames. But the fire raged on as if nothing would stop it. All the mechanisms that separated man from man were suddenly forgotten in the common danger, the common fear. Together they must act to extinguish the fire. Hosepipes were dragged out and connected; buckets, dishes, any containers handy were used to pour water onto the flames. This did not help. Sand and soil were thrown onto the flames. The men used their shovels, and those who had none used their hands. But they were unable to put out the fire. The fire engines had been called but had not arrived. The loose sand on the site was almost used up. In their panic the men did not realise that it was an impossible task to smother those flames with their shovelsful of sand. Yet no one gave up.

Until the firemen arrived, it had seemed to Elias that this must be the end of his life, for the flames were threatening to consume everything. He was tempted to run away, but he had heard the screams and shrieks of the people caught in the burning building. His stomach felt empty and he wanted to vomit. Ambulances had also arrived. The firemen were doing everything their training and equipment made possible, and still the fire raged and spread. The sheets of corrugated iron, now twisted and buckled, that had roofed the warehouse adjoining the building where the fire had started collapsed into the flames that were eating up all those goods from distant lands.

Like most of the others who had helped before the fire engines came, Elias stayed to watch. They were now mere spectators. The firemen seemed to be everywhere, not all of them in the front line of the battle where the hoses were directed at the fire. More ambulances, sirens blaring, screeched their way to the burning buildings.

The sky was full of smoke, dirty black smoke that was being licked by the ever-rising flames. The sight was colourful, exciting, frightening. All onlookers were cordoned off. Together, regardless of who they were, they were all cordoned off. Shouts and loud cries for help from the upper storeys of the building filled the air. There were people still up there. Sudden explosions drowned the cries and shouts: bursting motor tyres, gas tanks exploding their vicious contents added to the volume and intensity of the flames, and to the terror in the cries. Pandemonium broke out. The crowd began moving forward together. Some prayed, some shouted encouragement and hope.

One man, Peter Evenmore, the architect, ran towards the fire. He had seen a panic-stricken man jump from several storeys high. The man had not risen after his fall to the ground. The man was bleeding from the mouth, and blood was streaming from his ears and nose. He was engulfed in the thick smoke. Peter Evenmore ran into the smoke; he heaved the unconscious body onto his shoulder and ran out again into the open area. There was no immediate danger here and he began fanning the injured man's face, which was covered with soot and sweat. While waiting for the ambulance men, Peter wiped away the dirt from the nostrils of the injured man, and tried mouth-to-mouth resuscitation. The crowd watched. Elias was enthralled. The flames behind Peter leapt higher. The ambulance men were taking their time, and, impatient, Peter tore off his shirt and made strips with the cloth to bandage the man's bleeding head. Elias stood watching in wonderment that one man could do this for another.

Peter cried, "Please give me a hand to carry this man to the ambulance. Please somebody, come and help me!"

Elias was nearest to him. Instinctively, he ran forward and

held the injured man on one side. Peter held the man on the other side and together they carried him to the ambulance. The stretcher was pulled out and they placed the man on it. The ambulance men took over now. But before the injured man could be lifted into the ambulance he gasped for air and his limbs jerked involuntarily. Peter tried mouth-to-mouth resuscitation again. But the man was bleeding profusely and a blood transfusion was urgently needed. The ambulance men had stood watching as if Peter were engaged in a pantomime, even though the man was bleeding to death. Peter battled, but in vain.

"I knew from the start—" one of the ambulance men began.

"I bet you did!" said Peter, as he pulled up the blanket and shrouded the tortured face. Elias stood aghast. He wondered who the dead man was. Nobody knew. All they knew was that he had jumped from high up, that he was wearing his "kitchen boy's uniform" and that he was a young man. The ambulance took the body away to the hospital, to be certified "dead on arrival."

Slowly, Elias and Peter walked back to the crowd of onlookers. The firemen had succeeded in controlling the fire, but it had taken its toll of dead and injured. Yet for Elias and Peter, particularly Elias, there seemed to have been a mysterious fulfilment. In the midst of the fear, damage and grief this fulfilment blew about and thumped in their hearts.

The gangs of black men had scattered in the confusion. They now returned to their positions and dejectedly resumed their work. Their singing had stopped, but the work continued. For everybody, the baases and the black men, the day had become a heavy one. Much was destroyed—by what was later discovered to have been an electrical fault in the air conditioning system in the building—yet something was born.

At the end of the day's work, as Elias was waiting to board the truck to return to the compound, a gentle tap on his back attracted his attention. He turned round and faced Peter Evenmore. For a moment nothing was said between them. Then Peter smiled and asked, "Can I take you home?"

Elias was stunned by his partial understanding of the question.

"I am also going home and I thought that having shared an experience . . . we saw somebody die, didn't we? Well . . . well if you don't mind leaving your friends . . . I mean, if you wish to go back with them, then you must. But I thought you might want to join me. You could come with me to my house first and then a little later if you agree, I could drive you to your house."

Elias appreciated this baas's attempt to communicate with him in his own tongue, and, having understood the gist of the request, he smiled and his milky bright teeth shone. He stammered his thanks. It occurred to both that spoken language had not been necessary.

Elias and Peter told the black induna about their arrangement and walked away together. They had one thing in common in their hearts: they had shared the naked sight of pain, and of death. Peter's car was locked. As they opened the two front doors fresh air poured into it and cleared the stuffiness inside. It was hot in the car. After the day's work and the extra heat from the fire, Elias smelled of dirt and sweat. But there was a new sweetness about, a sweetness that even the sweltering heat could not subdue. As Elias sat beside Peter Evenmore, he realised that this was the first time he had sat beside a white man.

Peter sighed with relief and took out from the glove compartment a packet of cigarettes.

"Cigarette?"

He turned his head towards Elias and held out the packet, at the same time starting the car.

"It does me good at times, like today."

Elias shook his head and smiled. He didn't smoke. Peter lit his cigarette and inhaled deep, soothing streams of smoke. The smoke made a haze in the car and the tobacco aroma engulfed them both.

"You are new in Durban?"

"Ya, baas."

"Don't call me baas, call me Peter."

"Eh! Baas!"

"Please, just Peter!"

"Ya, baas."

Peter Evenmore sighed in disappointment and helplessness, for he hated the word that in his mind created such a gulf between him and the passenger sitting beside him in his own car. Then he said, "When did you come here and from where did you come?"

"About one month ago and I have my home in Umzinyathi."

"Where do you live in Durban?"

"At the railway compound . . . that's my home in your city."

"Are you happy there?"

"Well . . . "

"What do you mean?"

"Well, here we sing while we work and for a while we sing on Sunday afternoons. I have not heard anybody else sing. Not even you. In Umzinyathi we are forever singing. In Umzinyathi we sing not only while we are working but in our grief and joy too. Oh, it's so different there."

Peter slowed down and out of the corner of his eye he looked at Elias, who had by then made himself comfortable on the thick leather seat. Peter was afraid for a moment that he had lost his sense of ease. But Elias smiled.

"I guess, you must have left your wife in Umzinyathi?"

"No."

"Then your girlfriend?"

"Yes. Nomsa must be counting the days to my return. You see, last weekend when I visited her, I promised her that I would bring her here, so that we could be together . . . always."

39

"Then why don't you?"

"Oh, baas, I am so new here. I don't even know how to get along myself."

"You will learn."

"And until then Nomsa must remain at home."

"But didn't you promise her?"

"Yes, yes, I did. And I won't see her again until I know that I can keep that promise."

Peter lit another cigarette and then looking at Elias he asked, "When you bring her here where will you live?" Not intending to hurt Elias, he said with some hesitation, "You won't— I hope you won't—keep her in the compound."

"No! No! Never there."

Elias began sweating and became very edgy. "You see as soon as I have found a place here for Nomsa I will bring her here. She is willing to work. I am told she can come and stay in Durban, but I have to find work for her first. Then I will go home and marry her."

"What kind of work could she do?"

"Anything baas . . . anything."

The car purred ahead. Moving smoothly it passed the regularly spaced lamp posts, lamps already lit, although it was only late afternoon. The breeze gushing in through the open windows freshened the two tired faces in the car. Peter's relaxed expression revealed that they were not far from his home. He hoped there would be hot tea ready when they arrived. They drove along tree-lined streets; masses of multicoloured flowers were everywhere. For Elias it was breathtaking. Both men fell silent.

Peter turned into a driveway, and leaving the engine running, he jumped out to unlock the gates. Elias saw the beautifully laid-out garden surrounding the large, well-built kind of house a white man lives in. It was like heaven, he thought. Peter drove carefully up the driveway, the car wheels on two parallel paved strips set in the grass, and took deep breaths, as if he were taking in the fragrance of his garden, where his wife was waiting. She ran up to the car and impatiently kissed her husband through the window. He put his arms around her lovingly. Elias was overwhelmed. In peasant style he turned his gaze away from the embracing couple. He, being embarrassed, thought he might embarrass them.

"We have a guest, darling. May we please have some tea? Oh my, I am forgetting my manners. Elias, this is my wife, Mary, and darling, this is Elias."

Mary and Elias exchanged smiles and before Elias could say "Good evening, ma'am" Peter gestured to him to get out of the car. Mary ran indoors while the men strolled towards the house through the garden. It all seemed unreal to Elias. There were so many strange things and people in the city. But he was young and keen and above all willing to learn.

As they entered the house Elias heard a melodious voice, accompanied by musical instruments. He was fascinated to hear a song in the baases' language and apologetically he approached Peter. With a broad smile he said, "I see the missus can sing. I haven't heard you singing."

Peter chuckled.

"No, no, it is not Mary who is singing."

He walked across the sitting room to the far end and pointed out to Elias the high-fidelity system and the record on the turntable.

Mary entered the room with a tray of tea and some biscuits.

"Sit down you two and stop looking so serious."

Elias did not understand the request and only sat down after Peter did. Elias discovered that Mary was wearing a sweet smell, which helped to drown his own sweaty one. The scent comforted him a little, though not for long.

Mary poured tea for the two men and gave a cup to Elias. For the first time since their arrival she scrutinised him, and with some misgivings she looked at Peter. She was horrified.

"Whose is that blood on your clothes, and Peter, your shirt! What happened?"

In moments Peter related the day's experiences to her. More tea was drunk, and Mary's anguish, her concern and her doubts about the blood and Elias fell away. She was full of pride in her husband and his newfound friend.

"So, your Nomsa lives away from you?" she asked.

Peter translated and Elias nodded. The couple's hospitality overwhelmed him. What all this meant, he did not know. He was getting more and more confused.

"I do hope to meet Nomsa some day."

Elias indicated as best he could that her desire to see Nomsa could not be greater than his own. He smiled.

"People like Elias and his wife-to-be can't move into the cities, seek work and sell their labour on the open market as they please," Peter explained to Mary. "Even if they themselves are employed, the men can't bring their wives and children here. Their wives have to be employed too. I don't really know the ins and outs of it."

Mary bit her lip and looked at Elias. Peter cut short the tense silence.

"It is tricky, isn't it? The ways of the city are different."

But Peter did not know to whom he directed these remarks. Elias had lost his sense of time. He was enchanted. The luxurious sitting room with its glass light fittings and pretty white table lamps, the soft comfortable settees, the manner of having tea all together fascinated him. Abruptly, he rose. Peter rose too, and said, "All right, I will drive you home."

The three walked out of the house. In the garden they saw the housemaid, who had the Evenmores' child tied piggyback. Peter went over to the maid and lifted the baby's chin with one hand. With the other he tickled her behind the ear. He introduced the baby Pam to Elias. Elias, who looked puzzled, didn't move or say a word. Before he could sort out his thoughts, Peter crossed the lawn to where Mary was standing, and said softly, "Darling, remember the other day we were discussing the need for some more help around the house? It occurs to me, if Nomsa is as hard a worker as Elias, we could . . . . Both of them, Lucy and Nomsa, could stay in the *khaya*. * What do you think?"

Peter was thrilled with himself. Mary also looked pleased but she wondered what Elias would make of the proposition. Joining Elias and walking on with him towards the car, Peter put his hand on his arm and tried to be persuasive: "Listen Elias, we are asking Nomsa to come here and stay with us, in our khaya at the back. Nomsa can work with Mary in the house and you can continue with your own work."

Elias had understood the gist of what was said and he had gone numb. He wondered whether he was dreaming. He thought, this is not true, it is too quick; these two are different from the other whites. He could not suppress his enthusiasm even though seconds before he had been full of doubt.

"Is it all right with you, Elias?" demanded Peter.

Elias smiled and smiled.

He thanked Mary for the tea and said goodbye, and Peter drove him back to the compound.

---

* *khaya* (Zulu): house, home, inhabited place; used by whites, especially in Natal, to designate the room, separate from the main house, where domestic servants are housed

CHAPTER 5

At the building site the next morning Peter Evenmore, the architect, had spread out his drawings and plans in the makeshift quarters known as the builders' shed. The contractor was there. The site supervisor looked in to make sure of his instructions. This was a government project and the work had to proceed in an orderly manner. A lot of money was involved, from sources both local and international.

Elias and his gang of black men arrived and were given their heavy picks and shovels. Peter came out of the shed and looked for Elias. Without much difficulty, as Elias was looking out for him too, their eyes met. They walked towards each other. With few words they exchanged a greeting.

Abruptly Elias and his gang were called. With Peter Evenmore's plan in his hand the supervisor shouted out the day's work. Elias did not know that Peter had designed the warehouse. Today they were going to dig up the hard tarred road that led to the railway yard. This part of the road had to be dug out by hand. Elias and his gang of black men were going to use their hands, their picks and their shovels with the precision required by Peter's plans, until the huge pay-loaders, that were operated and driven by the baases, carried away all the tar and mortar reduced to rubble. A new edifice was going to stand where the road had been. Peter, who was standing there in the company of those who were not required to dig, smiled in anticipation of his new creation.

Weeks went by, and now the road and its verges had been transformed into a large, precisely levelled area. It was time for work on the new edifice to begin.

Elias sought out Peter during a break in the work and suggested that he was ready to go home, for a week or so, to marry and then return. "Lobolo could be settled partly in cash and partly on terms." He remembered the words of his elders back home, the day he and his contemporaries had been recruited to work in Durban. He thought his city earnings might suffice for the cash portion.

"Have you saved enough money, Elias?"

"I really don't know how much is enough."

"Never mind. I could help you with your expenses. You can have a loan from me you know!"

A loan! This again was new to Elias. He wondered what this loan could be.

"I don't understand, baas."

"What I mean is that I will give you the money, all the money that you need and then when you can afford it you can pay it all back to me."

Elias wondered. Unable to comprehend the new suggestion, he did not answer.

"Elias, you see I want to help you. If you think that you will not be able to pay me back, then you can keep it as a present."

Much to the astonishment of Peter's colleagues and Elias's gang of black men, Peter embraced his new friend. Elias smiled, and then grinned. Looking around, he saw that everybody present was staring at him and Peter. He grew purple with embarrassment. He looked Peter straight in the eyes and said, "Baas!"

"I am going to do everything I can to help you to succeed here. There is a better future here for Nomsa and you. You know Elias, you must learn my language, and many other things as well. You and the other black men can go to night school. The churches have started these classes. And the more you learn, the more you will earn."

For Elias the new bond with Peter was one of joy and strength. He was already beginning to feel different, and in many ways he was becoming different. He went about his work in harmony with those around him and with those above him. Often he stared at the horizon. For fleeting moments his silent cries went out to his father, his mother, his brothers and sisters, his uncles and aunts, his fellow men in Umzinyathi, to all those who together had been his anchor in life. He was going to leave them. He wanted to cry, as he was seized with the urge to forget Umzinyathi and to seek, to reach out to what stood before him and beckoned. Everything and everybody seemed different now. And he was leaving in two days to fetch Nomsa. Peter had arranged a week's leave for Elias. During that week Nomsa and Elias would be married.

On Saturday, Peter and Mary drove Elias to Umzinyathi in their own car.

This visit after weeks of absence was different for Elias. This visit did not attract the children from the huts he passed on his way home. They only noticed another machine going by. Elias did not shout out his greetings. He couldn't. He was just passing by in a motor car that raised enough dust to block him from his neighbours' view. Some of the people of Umzinyathi stood in awe; some of the younger ones, in Elias's age group, were jealous, but mostly they were just astonished that Elias had come home in a motor car. This was another kind of opening into the hearts of the men and women of Umzinyathi. With the passage of time these openings would become ruptures, just as the little openings that were once caused by erosion had become the Umzinyathi River. Elias guided Peter to the home of Gumede, Nomsa's father.

The car stopped and Elias struggled with the door handle. He tried and tried again, but he was unaccustomed to the mechanism. Peter flicked the door open. Elias said, "Instead of doing it why don't you teach me how to do it?" He jumped out of the car and ran towards Nomsa. All the children from the neighbourhood had gathered. The elderly women with their thick leather kilts and sagging naked breasts gaped in astonishment. On this visit Elias was wearing long pants, right to his heels, and a shirt and a jacket, not just a singlet. On closer inspection they discovered that he was wearing shoes too. These shoes hurt his toes a bit, but he wore them and they looked good and clean. Elias's broad grin, a grin of self-satisfaction, intrigued Nomsa. Shy and confused, she gathered herself slowly and took a few steps towards Elias. On his previous visit she had run into his arms with total abandon. Now she was wondering. She looked deep into his eyes, where she had read the power of his love for her. Elias was beaming; she was wistful.

"Nomsa!"

"Elias, what have you done to yourself?"

"Nothing. Why?"

Elias noticed her looking at him apprehensively.

"Oh, these!" He brushed his clothes with an alien gesture and laughed. "These are my new clothes. They do make me look new, don't they, Nomsa?"

"Oh! Elias, I am frightened. Who are these people in the car? Why have they come with you? Are they going to take more of us away from here? Tell me, Elias, who are they and why have they come?"

"Nomsa, my love, I have kept my promise!"

"Who are they, Elias?"

"The man is a good baas, Nomsa. And the girl with him is his wife. They have come to help us."

Peter and Mary stood next to their car not knowing what to do. Elias had for some moments forgotten them though

Nomsa kept enquiring about them. Grabbing Nomsa by the waist Elias jerked her towards his friends. They, who had once been his hosts, had now become his guests. Elias in his own simple way introduced Nomsa to Peter and Mary. Nomsa, who was still frightened, tried to smile. Mary tried to speak the few Zulu words of greeting she had learned, but her attempt at reaching out to Nomsa was a failure. Peter saw the confusion and suspicion on Nomsa's face.

Elias, holding Nomsa's hands tightly and lovingly, explained to her that the guests were in fact his friends, who had come from Durban to help speed their marriage, and if possible also to be present at the ceremony. He explained that they too belonged to the new congregation, the new community, that they were going to build together, where black and white would live and worship together. Nomsa relaxed a little and made an attempt to smile. Peter noticed, and moved away to open the boot of his car and take out the boxes and suitcases containing the new clothes and other presents that he and Mary had brought for Nomsa, the parents and other near relatives.

From among the onlookers stepped Nomsa's old father, and he was soon introduced to the guests. He was more amused than amazed at the new Elias. Silently, he surveyed the situation and reassured himself: my Nomsa is a lucky girl. And I, her father, am lucky too. Now I do not have to worry about her future and her happiness. Elias already has good connections on whom he can depend. Gumede walked towards the back of the car and wondered what the boxes contained. In his urge to know, he offered to help carry them into the house.

Entering one of the many huts that were clustered together with a peculiar unity and interreliance, Peter and Mary looked around and marvelled at the clean simplicity. Nomsa hurried to follow them in. She picked up two stools and placed them near the guests, indicating with shy gestures that they should be seated. She drew a grass mat from behind the door and spread it on the floor for her father and Elias. All of them seemed to be seated in a new kind of brotherhood. But Nomsa was thinking of the dew-drenched grass, the clouds and the skies that had been their only physical comforts on Elias's last visit to Umzinyathi. She yearned for these and for the Elias who had shared them with her. She was happy that he was here, and she was sad that, in a way, he was not.

She withdrew to a nearby hut and brought forth an earthenware pot of home-brewed beer. She handed the khamba to her father, who took a deep draught and in simple friendliness held out the pot to Peter. Being new to such customs, Peter and Mary were taken aback for a moment at this kind of—to them, unhygienic—hospitality and friendliness. Peter looked up and saw the ironic twinkle in the old man's eyes. The old man jerked the pot towards him, as if to say "Come, let us seal this newness." Peter knelt on the ground and put one hand on each side of the evenly rounded container. With some reluctance, he drew as deeply from it as the old man had done. For him, whose drink was whisky and soda, the stuff had a very strange tang. Mary sat there wondering if her turn would come next. In her anxiety she held the edges of her skirt and was trying to make little knots in them. She dug the manicured nails of her left hand into her palm. Her forehead was damp and there was a slight quiver at the corners of her mouth. Nomsa was watching Mary closely.

Wiping his mouth with the back of his hand, in borrowed native fashion, Peter winked at his wife and whispered, "The stuff tastes nice—"

Before he could say more, Mary retorted, "Please have some more and pass it back to THEM."

Peter, amused at his wife's response, understood her misgivings and in deference to her wishes handed the pot to Elias. When Mary saw Elias hand the beer back to the old man, she sighed with relief. A moment later she asked, "Peter, shouldn't you get your business over so we can leave?"

"But darling, we have just arrived. Please don't fret and worry. You'll soon feel all right. Elias is depending on us. We have to give these people a hand."

Elias, who had understood the exchange, if not all the words, turned to Nomsa and said, "You may leave. I want to finalise our wedding with your father."

The old man was shocked at Elias's forthright manner. He knew he was a fortunate father. Elias was moving upwards and that augured well for his daughter's security. But he also realised that Elias had changed and acquired a few strange habits. He was forgetting his elders. The old man thought he should be reminded, and he stood up. He towered over all of them. In silence he surveyed them all, and then announced, "No, no. This will not do for me. I know Nomsa is my daughter. Nobody has to remind me of that. But Elias, I want to remind you that you are your father's son. It is not your task to plan with me about Nomsa and yourself. Go and fetch your father. I will talk with him about Nomsa and you."

He turned to Peter and Mary and continued very firmly, "This is how we do it here."

Elias translated the gist of this statement for Mary. Then he rose and stiffened: he had been chastised. He had forgotten his duty to his father. He tried to mumble something in his own defence but the old man stood firm in his authoritarian politeness. Peter, Mary and Elias prepared to leave. Outside in the yard, Nomsa had busied herself in gossip with the neighbouring girls. She was surprised to see Elias leaving the hut with the guests, the boxes and suitcases and all. She, too, confused by everything that was happening around her, had forgotten the traditional ways.

Elias, his arms heavily laden, walked up to her; they smiled at each other and parted.

.   .   .

It was already late on this Saturday afternoon, and Peter, Mary and Elias had to drive the few miles of subtropical bush to Mzimande's village.

"What's happening, Elias?"

"We have to go to my home. Let us go now, this minute, Peter."

"But why all the sudden changes?"

"We must go to my home, to my parents' place. Oh, all this . . ."

"But Elias, you are not telling me why. You have just talked to Nomsa and her father."

"Did I?"

"Didn't you?"

"Did we?"

"Elias, what's all this? Does the old man disapprove of you?"

"Oh no, he doesn't. But let us go to my home."

Peter was now quiet and Elias continued, "I have been a little forgetful. I have been impatient. So much has happened to me in the past few months. My work, the compound, my being away from Umzinyathi, Mary and you coming into my life, these new clothes, the new ways of thinking and all the rest."

Nobody spoke as the car bumped away from Nomsa's home. Elias turned round and tried to see through the rear window if Nomsa was still standing in the crowd that had gathered to see them off. He could not distinguish her from the other girls. The dust raised by the moving car further blurred his vision and though he strained his eyes he could not see her. But she was there, that much he knew.

Mary, who had kept quiet since they left the Gumedes' household, turned round and saw Elias sitting uncomfortably and looking more than agitated.

"Peter, poor Nomsa couldn't be alone with Elias, not even for a minute. She must be feeling very disappointed."

Peter nodded, sucked on his pipe, which was filling the car with a soothing aroma, and asked, "Which way, Elias?"

"Eh?"

"Which way?"

Elias leaned forward and spread his elbows along the back of the front seat.

"I am sorry."

He lifted his right arm and through the space between Mary and Peter he pointed to a distant hill. He showed them the tracks and trails the landrovers had made. It was quite a distance for the car to cover on these winding tracks. But on foot it would have taken less than half an hour.

Disturbed by the sound of the car engine, swarms of birds fluttered hither and thither, and their nestlings gave out little calls. In the trees nearer the roadside the birds in their swaying, pendant-like nests took fright, except the mother birds, who remained with their young.

Mary was peering out through the window. She was captivated by the sight of a single file of young people, not more than ten or twelve years old, boys and girls, with long bundles on their heads. They were singing as they walked.

"Ask Elias what those young people are doing," she said.

Peter translated.

"They are carrying bundles of grass and reeds and bamboos."

"What are they going to do with all that?"

"They are not going to do anything themselves. It's for the aged, the weak and the disabled. And some of our womenfolk."

"What will they do with it?"

"They make things: baskets and floor mats mostly. You see they keep our aged and our disabled folk occupied with something useful to do."

They drove by a cluster of huts before which sat groups of elderly men and women, some stripping bamboos, some weaving the grass into baskets and mats, some plaiting strips of reed.

"So in Umzinyathi there is no fear of old age or disability?"

"All our people belong to us, and we care for them always."

Nearly an hour had passed on that bumpy, uneven, uncertain drive. To herald their arrival at Elias's village Peter pressed his horn.

Old man Mzimande came forth from his hut. He looked at his son and gave a cry: "You have come at last! And with friends. How are you, my son? Your mother had word from the neighbours that you were at Nomsa's place. Oh, you are young and hot-blooded!"

Embracing his broad-shouldered son he continued, "So impatient!"

Elias embraced his mother, who looked younger than her real, unrecorded years; there was no method, besides certain memorable events, to record dates of birth. Her son was home from the city. She caressed his face and then looked at the guests, who had come out of the car and were standing next to her husband. Elias said to his father, "These are my friends, Peter and Mary." Turning to them, he continued, "Here are my father and my mother."

Mzimande shook hands with the guests and murmured, "Peter and Mary. Peter and Mary . . . I have heard these names before from the *umfundisi*.* They are beautiful names. Are you going to help us to build our church?"

Peter looked at Elias, who explained his father's question.

"No, oh no!" exclaimed Peter. "We have just come with your son, who is our friend. We want to help him—"

Elias interrupted, and simply asked everybody, "Shouldn't we go inside? We will talk later."

Peter understood his friend. He kept quiet and obeyed. Mary followed. All four sat down on neatly arranged stools. From the look of things inside the hut, Elias could see that his

---

* *umfundisi* (Zulu): clergyman, priest (any denomination); vocative case, *Mfundisi*

parents had had prior notice of the visit and had made preparations. Now that he was at his own home, there was no hurry to bring out the boxes and suitcases from the car. There would be time enough for that.

For Peter and Mary it was getting late. The horizon blazed orange behind the darkening hills. From the neighbouring huts came shouts and shrieks of joy. The women had their men at home. They had come by bus from Durban for the weekend. Many of these men had been away from their homes for months on end. They, like Elias, had changed in many ways. They too had shed a lot of what they once had, and now carried a lot that once they did not have. Some of them had corns on their toes for they had begun to wear shoes. Almost all had callouses on their palms from the picks and shovels and wheelbarrows they worked with. Some who had left their wives in Umzinyathi had, with the compulsion of their hungry, sensual bodies, slept with women of easy virtue while they were away from home. These women, not legally qualified to be in the city, survived there by plying one of the few trades open to them. What the consequences might be, for them or for their clients, meant nothing to them. All that mattered was the number of men they slept with and the amount of cash they could get out of them. Now the women of Umzinyathi thought only of being with their men.

At the Mzimande hut the lady of the house had excused herself and gone outdoors to prepare the meal. Elias could see her through the open doorway. Meticulously, she picked up pieces of firewood. She made a heap of these. A three-legged pot, round and fat-bellied and containing chunks of meat, was placed over the wood on three small, flat stones. With her tough fingers she struck a match. The glow from the flickering flame lit her face. She placed the burning match among the pieces of dry wood, went down on her knees and stirred the fire with deep and regular mouthsful of air. The wood burned. Apparently satisfied, she repeated the whole process to boil a pot of water in which she was going to make her mealie pap. Rising from the fire, she dusted her knees and rubbed her eyes, stinging from the gusts of smoke. She turned to leave her kitchen. At that moment, Mzimande got up and went out to speak to his wife. Elias overheard his parents' low voices.

"I am going to ask our guests to stay the night with us. It is dark and they may get lost on their way back."

"I would be disappointed if you did not ask them to stay."

"Then see to it that there is enough to eat."

Thandi Mzimande nodded dutifully. Her husband tilted her chin up a little and whispered, "They are our son's friends. Can you believe it? By God! They are our son's friends! And they are here, in our own home. From here our son has moved into their world. Oh, my woman, aren't you proud of our son? He has such friends. They will make a better man of our son."

Elias's mother said nothing; she caressed her husband's weather-beaten, hairless chest. Mzimande went back to his son and his guests.

Before long Peter and Mary were persuaded to spend the night with the Mzimandes. Huge plates of meat and pap were offered in honour of the guests. The khamba, full of home-brewed beer, was passed around. While all the men and Mary sat eating, Thandi was busy preparing her best hut for the two guests. She sprinkled cold water on the dung floor to keep the place cool. Then she covered the damp circular floor with two grass mats, and arranged the woolly sheepskins and the colourful blankets neatly for her guests' comfort. She placed in the hut an earthen bowl of water and a homemade lamp that flickered unevenly. After dusting the opening that was the window, she stood back at the entrance and glanced around the room in satisfaction. This was her best room and her son's friends were going to have the best she had, for as long as they were there.

CHAPTER 6

The eating and drinking were over and the men were in serious discussion about Elias's marriage. It was agreed that the wedding would take place, if Nomsa's people agreed, within the week, and that old man Mzimande, with senior members of his family, would call formally on the bride's family the following day.

Elias, whose presence was not required in the discussions, showed Peter and Mary to their room. They had brought overnight bags with them, as white people do when they may be away from home, even for one night.

As they walked across the courtyard from Mzimande's hut to the newly cleaned best room, Elias asked in the darkness of the night, "Peter, are you used to sleeping on the floor?"

"Oh, we will manage."

Elias apologised. "Our best is worse than what you discard . . . and I am upset for having caused you both this inconvenience."

"You don't have to worry, Elias."

They reached the door to the hut and Elias pointed, "Here, this is your room for tonight. I hope you two sleep well, and as you say, 'Good night.'"

Inside the room, the kerosene-fed wick flickered in a bottle.

Peter held Mary's hand and they entered softly and carefully, crouching forward to get through the door without hitting their heads on the frame. It was cool and quiet inside.

Peter removed his jacket, rather awkwardly, and hung it on one of the wattle beams that held the thatch in its symmetrical form. He put his tie in his coat pocket. Mary stood still in the half-lit, half-dark hut and watched her husband.

Peter went to the "window" and bent to look through it. Lighting all the darkness around stood the beaming, teasing moon. Entranced by what he saw he called out, "Mary! Come here."

She walked slowly to the window. Sensing that she was just a breath away from him, he urged, "Look at what I'm seeing."

Peter drew Mary closer and ran his fingers through her hair. He caressed her neck. Wanting to continue his caress right down her back, he came upon the zip of her dress. He held the head of the zip firmly between his fingers and drew her dress open, down to her buttocks. They stood facing each other. Mary sought Peter's eyes in the half-lit night.

Peter woke first, at dawn, with an urgent need to leave the hut. Crouched behind a bush, in a mobile shelter built over a shallow trench, he wondered about his wife, whether she would be able to use this contraption.

It was early on Sunday afternoon. Rows of neatly dressed country folk were walking towards the distant church. A makeshift structure with no steeple, it was situated on a high hill and appeared to be looking down on the recently washed but already sweating parishioners. Mary and Peter had not brought their Sunday best with them, but what they had was better than the best the parishioners had. They dressed, like their hosts, for church.

Elias's father looked satisfied with his new, heavy overcoat. The day was not cold enough to require the coat, but old man Mzimande was not going to miss the opportunity of wearing it among his equals who had not been endowed with sons who had friends like Elias's friends. Or, so far, they had not. What the future held for his equals was not his concern.

He and his family delegation had visited Gumede that morning, and agreement had been reached on the date of their children's wedding. Mzimande had returned home without delay, in order to proceed to the church with the Evenmores by car. There would be none of the dust and sweat that covered the others who were trudging up the hill. He and his party were going to arrive clean and neat at the church, the privilege of very few. It would be pleasant to meet the future in-laws with such signs of distinction.

The priest was waiting. And His people arrived, though not in droves. Those who came loved the ceremony. It was particular and it was different. Adorned in their best they entered and were led in prayer. Then outside the church, they laughed together and talked. Elias Mzimande, his father, Nomsa's father, Peter and Mary got together and, as if they all knew what should be done, approached the priest. The two elders led the way and the rest followed. Old man Mzimande confronted the priest.

"Father, Gumede and I want our children to be married."

"That is very good but do you seek my permission?"

The priest turned to Elias with a wide grin on his face.

"So you are a big man now. You have come by car, I believe, and are about to discuss your marriage. Looking at you I see you have become part of the city. And now you are going to be part of yet another world."

He patted Elias on the shoulder. His long black robe gave him a look of aloofness, a distance. He too had adopted many of the white man's ways. The white collar that was stiff around his neck seemed to be suffocating him. "I shall be pleased to bless you and Nomsa now, but—"

Peter, who had been listening, butted in, "I shall be glad to witness the marriage."

"That won't be necessary. The elders of the couple are here and I feel sure they will want to do that." He turned to Elias and said, "I see your friends from Durban are just as impatient as you are."

Then addressing himself to the respective fathers he asked, "I trust you will make all the arrangements for lobolo?"

"Yes, Father," replied Mzimande.

"How soon do you want to have your children married?"

The two future in-laws looked at each other and then they both looked at Elias. Elias's expression said "right now." But he looked aside and pretended he had not heard the question.

"Will it be possible to have the wedding within the week, Father?" asked Peter.

By now the priest regarded him as a thoroughly interfering stranger. But he answered politely, "Yes."

"But Mfundisi, what about my people, my wife and family? What about Nomsa's mother, her sisters and her own family . . . our two families? How will they participate in the wedding?"

"Do all that you have to do, that is, if you want to. And here, here in our church we will have a different kind of ceremony, short and simple."

Alien to Umzinyathi, Peter did not know that there was more to this wedding than he imagined. He turned and faced Mary. With his back to the other four in the room, he pondered a moment and then went over to where she was standing slightly apart from the others.

"Peter, what now?"

"I don't know. It seems a quick church ceremony now, and the traditional wedding later in the week, as we had hoped, are out of the question. How I wish I had known what was involved, then we could have sent Elias on ahead to get things going."

Elias joined them.

"I don't know what's happening either. I guess my father

and Nomsa's father know best. But with this priest and his ways even my father is confused. Peter, I am sorry for all this."

"You needn't be, Elias. It's not your fault. I'm sorry but it's not possible for Mary and me to remain here for days on end. We would have loved to stay for your wedding but I have to be at work tomorrow. You have a week's leave. I haven't. And we'd be in the way. Mary and I will leave for Durban this afternoon, and we will come back next weekend to fetch you and Nomsa. That is, if you are married by then."

"Oh, of course, by next Sunday they will be married," interjected the priest. "I foresee no problem. The church ceremony will be this coming Saturday at eleven in the morning, after tradition has been observed."

The fathers of Elias and Nomsa rose, and, with satisfaction and relief, made an obeisance and thanked their agent of God. Until the arrival of the Church it had been their ancestors who represented God, Love and All.

Elias stood apart, with Peter and Mary.

"Won't you join me for tea?" enquired the priest of Peter and Mary. They looked at their new friends.

The priest added quickly, "Yes, please join me for tea, all of you."

Peter and Mary relaxed. With smiles they accepted the invitation. All six went into an adjoining room, apparently a sitting room for the Reverend Father. There was good, neat, fairly expensive furniture. Looking at Peter and Mary, the priest said, "Please sit down and make yourselves comfortable." After a slight pause he continued, "And, of course, you too . . . do sit down." Notwithstanding the distance that had developed with the introduction of certain new ideas, the three blackmen sat down. The priest left his guests sitting there and went out to order tea for six.

The walls were fresh with the smell of whitewash. The concrete slabbed floor was newly laid and cool. There were four steel-framed windows with perpendicular steel bars to keep out burglars. With new things around anything might happen, and it would be silly to take chances. On the wall opposite Mary and Peter hung a beautiful picture of Jesus Christ nailed to the cross, blood stains and all. On a sort of shelf just beneath the picture, incense was burning. The streaks of smoke rose unevenly in front of the picture, giving it a hazy look. And from the wall behind them jutted two glassy-eyed stuffed heads of the local buck. Judging from the size of the horns and the width of the necks, they must have been the pride of the hunter's pickings. Between them was displayed a shield with an assegai across it. Below that stood, impressively, a large earthen vase, without any flowers in it. All five kept silent in this room.

Without any warning the door was flung open and the priest came in, followed by his Sunday school assistant, a lad, who carried a tray laden with cups and saucers, a pot of tea, sugar, milk, spoons and a strainer. The lad placed the tray on a highish table and left the room. The priest took over.

"How many sugars for you, Mrs Evenmore?"

"Two please."

"And you, Mr Evenmore?"

"Two, please."

The priest poured their tea, added the required sugar with care and handed the cups, one by one. He returned to the table. Without any questions, he poured more tea into the other cups, added sugar and brought the cups to the two elders. They rose to accept them, and sat down again. Elias took his own tea and remained standing. Peter and Mary were a little surprised at the gradations in politeness shown by their host, but for the others there were some things new and most things old. After tea Peter, Mary and Elias headed for Elias's home to drop off his belongings, which were still in the car.

About an hour later the two elders bade farewell to their

priest. They walked in silence, relishing their new interreliance and togetherness, now that their families were to be joined in marriage. Then they talked, and their deep resonant laughter was happy. The birds in the trees, in the low unkempt grass, in the shrubs and bushes, rose in their uncountable numbers and flew all around them. Their chirps, as they scattered, became noises of protest for being disturbed. They flew far and wide, seemingly without destination, but somehow they came back twirling, diving, flying.

Mzimande and Gumede walked on towards their homes. Then Mzimande said with authority, "You know, Gumede, let us be frank about our children. They have known each other for some time now."

"Yes, Mzimande, they have. And I think they love each other very deeply. There seems to be no doubt about that."

"Oh yes, don't you see the restlessness in my son?"

"In my Nomsa too. I think their relationship is too far gone for us to say anything."

"You have been lax with your daughter, haven't you? But never mind, I like Nomsa. I will be pleased when she becomes a daughter in my house. And I think since they have known each other so intimately there will be no need for a formal betrothal. Don't you agree? After all, we are all of us churchgoers."

"Yes, I agree with you. I am almost certain they have already made love with each other."

They stared at each other. With compassion and understanding Gumede tried to explain: "Nomsa is my daughter. And I did not have the courage to stop her from seeing your son and making love with him."

"I don't think either of us could. In any case, if we did, it would have been against what we are taught in church. After all, in terms of their law, children over a certain age can do what they wish to do. Am I not right?"

"Yes, you are. But we have our own laws too, don't we?"

"Of course we have, but they are bending to fit in with the wider world," said Mzimande.

"Then how do you propose to settle the whole affair?"

"I don't think there is any real problem. You are here. I am here. And we are talking. Whatever is to be discussed and finalised we can deal with together. After all, the priest is ready to marry them and the ceremony will not be delayed. Such marriages in the church will be good for the church. People, others who are not yet convinced, will come and join us there. Our congregation will increase in numbers."

"How do you propose to do it? What about the village folk? What about our families and friends? Aren't they going to participate in the wedding? Aren't they going to be with us like old times?"

"Of course they will."

"But how?" Gumede kept quiet for a moment or two and then proceeded with his dilemma. "The girls of my household will want to be part of the whole affair. Nomsa has been very close to them."

"Oh, Gumede, that's the past now. Come on, we have a church. And there is going to be a shop here very soon. I am told they are going to build a bridge across the Umzinyathi. And after that another one across the Umgeni."

Gumede and Mzimande went into another spell of silence. They adjusted their rubber sandals securely as they neared the river's edge. Slowly they entered the clean waters. They waded across, stumbling occasionally. On the other side of the river, they clambered over a few rocks, then held onto the river weeds to pull themselves out of the water. Standing securely on the riverbank, they shook their limbs vigorously and shed some of the water off themselves. Down their black limbs ran miniature streams. In hollows and crevices where the water collected they brushed it off with their hardened peasants' palms. Gumede wiped his forehead with the back of his hand and said, "Let us slaughter beasts and exchange presents. And, oh yes, what about lobolo?"

"Yes, Gumede. You have raised Nomsa. You are entitled to have lobolo from my son. This you will have, I assure you. Even if we cannot settle it with cattle we will do so with cash. Elias has good connections now. He has already brought many presents and clothes for Nomsa."

"I know. They nearly left them at my place."

"What?"

"Yes. Yesterday, Elias in his fervour, I think, forgot."

"Well, well. It doesn't matter. They are for your daughter in any case."

"I thought so. But I sent him back to you so that you should not feel slighted by his forgetfulness."

"That was very nice of you. And very proper too. I tell you what, Gumede. About the beasts and the presents. Let us agree to exchange them after the wedding ceremony. The ceremony in church will not take long and we will be able to spend almost the whole day feasting. I will announce the lobolo at the feast. Our guests will witness it."

"It sounds good to me."

"Then it is settled."

"What is?"

"The marriage, the beasts, the gifts and the lobolo."

"What about the lobolo?"

"Oh, I see. About that." He meditated and, looking at Gumede out of the corner of his eye, he asked, "Will five head of cattle or fifty pounds do?"

Gumede did not answer.

"Will ten head of cattle or one hundred pounds do?"

Gumede looked at his new relation and nodded.

"Then I will announce it at the wedding and just to keep you at peace I will make the formal arrangements among our families. Is it agreed?"

The two stopped suddenly at the top of the hill. They embraced. They had to part here to go their different ways home. Another meeting of their families was arranged for the morning of the following day, at Gumede's house. It was agreed between them that all the formalities would be settled then. Elias was to accompany his father, his mother and the other elders of the clan with the presents and part, at least, of the lobolo.

On the day of the wedding, the church bells rang. Down the aisle, on her father's arm, walked Nomsa. She felt awkward. They reached the altar. Elias was waiting with his usual impatience in the front pew. He smiled at Nomsa and moved forward towards the priest.

Some things were said and some things were done. In response to a question from the priest Nomsa said, rather inaudibly, "I DO."

CHAPTER 7

The mouth of the Umgeni was wide open. Durban's northward spread had long crossed the river, and streets and buildings lined its banks. Peter and Mary had parked their car at a point overlooking the estuary. They sat in the car watching the murky river waters spread their brown stain in a wide band along the coast. The waves flung themselves onto huge rocks and stone breakwaters that had been built out into the sea. Spray sprang high and settled in a salty mist on the windscreen and windows. The rocks and stone blocks stood firm in the loose shifting sand, solid buttresses against the conflicting flows of water.

Fishermen standing on the rocks looked aghast at the speed of the surging river waters. In its higher reaches, the Umgeni is fed by the Umzinyathi and other tributaries, and there had been heavy rains inland. The river was draining into the sea at enormous speed. A heavy wind had blown up, heralding a storm, and the fishermen left the rocks; those who had cars ran to them for shelter. The river water pouring down and the threatening storm had ruined their anglers' hopes. Those who had no car disappeared rapidly on foot. Men and women, barefoot and in shorts, made for cover across the beach; the

sand, whipped up by the wind, stung their legs as they ran. Crabs took refuge in crevices between the rocks.

"We must be moving, Mary. Elias should be married by now. I am sure he will be waiting for us to rush him back to Durban."

Peter turned the car away from the sea and took the winding road among banana plants and thick subtropical bushes as far as the Connaught Bridge that spanned the Umgeni. They crossed the swirling, swollen river and headed north towards Umzinyathi. As long as they were on the tarred road Peter could determine and hold his speed. The dirt road he took later was bumpy, stony and unkempt. Here the car and he were at the mercy of the gravel, the stones, the pebbles, the holes and ruts. But Umzinyathi was not far off. In a short while he would be back on this road, with Nomsa and Elias on their way to Durban.

The rain had begun as they left Durban, but here it was dry and dusty. Only the wind had accompanied them. It blew the dust all around and laid a yellowish-brown film over the car. Every now and then they had to open a window a little to let some air into the hot car, and the dust collected in their nostrils.

As they approached Elias's village, they saw from a distance a black woman shutting the door of one of the huts. Then she ran frantically from hut to hut, closing each one's door. She grabbed a bucket and flung something into it. Bucket in hand, she ran into one of the huts. Other people, coming seemingly from nowhere, joined her. Their togetherness, it seemed, was their security, even against the hazards of nature. Some elderly men—few of the younger ones had not been lured to the city —drove their chickens into pens, while others secured the goats and cows. All of them, men and animals, seemed frightened. The sudden activity, the surge of self-reliance and self-protection, indicated imminent danger; in many ways things were normally left to the care and discretion of the ancestors.

Swarms of small swift black birds, with long tapered wings and forked tails, migrants to Umzinyathi, were gathering. During the season of sowing, these creatures heralded rain and good reward. Now their departure cast fear and doubt in the minds of the people. Perhaps the ancestors were beginning to get angry.

Peter stopped his car. There were smiles and greetings all round. Elias was waiting. He had been waiting since the early morning of that fateful Sunday. For hours before his friends' arrival he had been dressed and looking out anxiously. He had instructed Nomsa to get dressed. Their things were packed in one suitcase and a cardboard box, and precious items were wrapped in a colourful blanket. They were ready to be taken to their new destination, to their new world.

In the excitement of seeing Peter and Mary Elias forgot all his native hospitality. He simply blurted out, "Peter, can I get my things into the car? I think we will have to leave quickly before this horrible wind brings in the storm and the rain."

"You're right."

Elias started to run to the hut, suddenly remembered something and shouted back, "Peter, why don't you and Mary come in away from the dust?"

Nomsa had not appeared. He called, "Nomsa! Nomsa, where are you?" He looked around.

Nomsa, in a new dress, a gift from Mary and Peter, hurried up to the car and signalled to her guests to follow her into the hut. The fierceness of the wind was so great by then that if Elias and Nomsa had not been there to invite them in, it would simply have thrust them into the nearest hut. As it was, they were ushered into the family's best day quarters.

Elias, emerging with a bag and the blanket-wrapped treasures, almost collided with them. The hut was clean inside, and smelt of the fresh dung with which the floor had been newly smoothed. Nomsa pulled up two homemade wooden chairs and beckoned to Mary and Peter. In her own tongue, which

Peter now spoke fairly well, she enquired about their well-being.

"We are well, thank you. But we wish to congratulate you and Elias—"

"What about Elias?" interposed that person, who had run back to fetch the cardboard box.

"Nothing. We were just congratulating you two on your marriage."

"What's congratulations?"

"Blessings and all . . . "

"Oh! Thank you. We want children. We want money. We want to be rich and be like you. Yes, that's what we want, don't we, Nomsa?"

Nomsa stood baffled; not understanding what her husband said she did not reply. Coming up close to her, Elias tilted her chin with his fingers and said very lovingly, "You will understand, my woman. We are just married. We are married to each other. From this day on we shall be married to another world. In that world there is plenty."

"But Elias, I don't want plenty. I only want you, our children and our love. I want our home. Like here in our little village . . . we play here, we laugh here, we sing here and we are happy here. I don't want plenty. Elias, I don't want plenty."

"Oh Nomsa if you only knew, like I do. Peter and Mary know, and so do thousands of others who have left places like this Umzinyathi and gone to Durban. Nomsa my darling, now that you will be with me in Durban there will be no need for us to come back here. From today all these things here, for you and for me, must be yesterday."

He turned round and asked, "Isn't it so, Peter?" Then looking Peter straight in the eye, he continued, "Look at them, Nomsa. They have come thousands of miles, from across the sea, to our country, to Durban."

"Have they left their people and come away?"

"Yes, they have."

"I don't like it."

"Why don't you like it?"

"Do you like it, Elias?"

"Who cares if we do or we don't. They are here, aren't they?"

"I can see they are here. But why have they left behind all that was theirs . . . their people, their father and their mother?"

At this stage Peter had to come to his own defence: "We came here so that we could make a better life for ourselves."

"What was wrong with your life at home?" asked Nomsa, struggling against tears.

"Nothing very much. Only, there is more money here. And it is a young country."

"So you came for more money," said Nomsa, almost inaudibly. She turned to Elias. "Elias, are you sure you know what you are doing? Are you sure I will not be destroyed? Are you sure I will not lose my mother, my father, my sisters and my brothers? Are you sure they will not lose me?"

While Elias was trying to reassure his wife, Peter, the architect of many designs, Peter, the alien who had come to make a better life for himself and Mary, was jolted into the realities of sociology: of architecture, town planning, the migrant labour system, compound life, the fast-developing ghettos for the thousands of black men coming to work in the towns. He suddenly wondered whether this simple little girl Nomsa was not justified in her fears. But he reminded himself that her fears were not as strong as her love and desire for her man.

Elias said to Nomsa in a reassuring, appealing voice, "Now come, come smile, my woman. Be brave. I am with you and will always be with you. Come my Nomsa, today we leave, for tomorrow is waiting."

They all walked out of the hut into the vicious wind, dust and dirt. A small crowd of sad-looking relatives and neigh-

bours had gathered to bid the newlywed couple farewell. In some ways it seemed as if they were wishing them a pleasant honeymoon. But the unspoken fear of the elders was that from that moment on Nomsa would forever be another Nomsa. Her parents, her brothers and sisters and the girls of her neighbourhood had come to see her off. It seemed that the girls had come to remind her that they too would marry some day, and that she should not forget them. Nomsa went with tear-stained cheeks and reddened eyes to her parents. She fell into her mother's arms and sobbed aloud. Between her sobs she blurted, "Mother, oh my mother, I am frightened. I don't know where I am going. You will not know my new place. Oh my mother, will you come to see me?"

Gumede came close enough to caress his daughter's back and in his own way he consoled her.

"Don't worry, my girl. You will be happy, I am sure of that. In your marriage you are not only leaving your home, to go to another's, you are also going to another world. There, according to Elias, is great hope and a wider horizon. Stand with Elias and be part of his life. Your happiness with him will, in turn, be our happiness."

Elias came over and joined his wife and her parents. Gumede looked at him and said, "And be happy too, Elias. I will pray to our ancestors for both of you. But always remember, my son, if ever I discover that you have ill-treated my daughter, I will not only tear her away from you, but I will also tear you to pieces—no matter how much you once loved her."

"Yes, Father, but I will never need to remember that," replied Elias.

"That's my son. Nomsa, we all think you are a lucky girl."

Now everybody who was anybody in their respective households came up to the couple with ululations and warnings, blessings or blunt teasing. The gusts of wind blew stronger and the huge gum trees, which grew all over the

Umzinyathi valley, swayed and hissed. The tall ones, majestic and deep-rooted, and the very young ones, supple and close to the ground, withstood the storm; but many that were not so young or not so firmly anchored in the soil were uprooted and fell to the ground. Their branches would be used at once for firewood, and the trunks as timber in the city of Durban.

Streaks of lightning brightened the dull sky. Peals of thunder frightened the young children and they ran into the huts. The parting had to be quick. The people gathered to say goodbye ululated one last time, loud and clear and together. The men's faces were solemn. Nomsa stood still beside the car, whose door was already open for her, and gave a long loud cry from the depths of her being. The wailing wind swallowed the sound of her grief at leaving her people and their little world. The cries of those who were being left behind merged with hers; the music of her departure from Umzinyathi was the whining and sighing of the wind in the trees, the weeping of her home-folk and her own mournful cry—it could have been a requiem mass.

Elias shut the car door, battling against the wind. Peter drove slowly away. Nomsa pressed her forehead against the window to try to catch a last glimpse of those she loved. Through her tears, she smiled at Elias, as if to say, "I will always be with you. You were, you are and you always will be my love. And from today you are also going to be my law and my God."

Standing in the dust, and beaten by the angry wind, the kinsfolk were full of pain and misgivings. They prayed, they waved and they cried their farewells. The men, too, sobbed unashamedly. They were the pillars and protectors of their people. Their numbers in the home villages were decreasing as more and more able-bodied men were taken or lured to the city. Their Nomsas were the lifeblood and guarantee for the future. Many of them were also being taken away. This was a Sunday for dirges, not hymns of joy.

By now the car was well away from the huts. It swayed in the loose sand, it bumped over stones and it heaved over the undulating surfaces, moving steadily away from the Umzinya-thi of Nomsa's innocence. She kept quiet, trying to comfort herself. Elias, who had been married to his Nomsa for barely a day, was thrilled at the prospect of his future, with his own wife, his love. He had Nomsa with him at last.

Miles away from Mzimande's village they crossed the Um-zinyathi River by a ford. When the river was in flood the ford was submerged, cutting Umzinyathi off from access by this route. On the Durban side of the river, the roads were better kept, for they had to bear a lot more traffic, including the buses that carried commuters from the remoter areas. The bumps and lurches were less frequent. Overtaking an ox-cart, Peter cautiously changed into low gear, for they were at the foot of a hill and he felt the car might slip on the loose surface. With an intuition that this might be her last chance, Nomsa looked back from the crest of the hill on the open fields, the gum trees, the fields of maize, the undulating hills, small and big, thou-sands of hills—the whole panorama with its sparsely dotted huts was the background of her childhood and youth. She heaved a deep sigh. In a moment the car was over the top of the hill and the picture was gone. Only the reddish-brown soil of the road and its verges remained of what she knew. She was holding it all tightly in her memory, for all time.

On either side of the road there were houses now. They were not grouped. They were built of wood and iron. To Nomsa's eyes the wood was all right, but she was shocked to see the hideous roofs of iron. She only knew thatch. She saw more and more of these houses. They seemed to have no unity among themselves, nor any of the attributes of a home. Some of the houses had walls of iron instead of good dear mud. She noticed that the children playing around these ugly houses were black. They were not laughing or singing. She wondered how people, especially children, who for her were joy incarnate, could spend their lives in such ugliness and dirt. They were passing the squatter camps of Inanda. Farther on, she saw a brick building with a flag fluttering over it. The men standing outside were dressed identically in stiff clothes with heavy belts, holsters, and caps. So this was where the policemen she had occasionally seen at home had come from.

"Why are there so many policemen?" asked Nomsa.

"Oh, they keep peace and order," said Peter. "You will see a lot more in Durban."

"Why a lot? Is there so little peace and order there?"

"What's that?" asked Elias.

"I asked, is there so little peace and order there?"

"Oh, I see what you mean. You see, Nomsa, there are a lot of people and a lot of different kinds of people living in Durban and therefore they require lots more of these policemen."

To Peter it appeared that Elias had already assumed the role of interpreter of new norms and new ideas to Nomsa. It made it easier for him. It is said that converts are more fanatical than those born into a faith.

Elias pointed out a large building. "You see there, Nomsa, that's the place where your father and my father buy their goods. You know, things like paraffin, candles, clothes and matches. They also sell blankets and beads."

"I see," replied Nomsa.

They were on the tarred road. Peter accelerated and the car purred smoothly over the hard black surface. Nomsa sat uncomfortably. The increase in speed caused an empty sensation in her stomach, and the vibrations of the motor shook her to the core. She belched, and suddenly knew she was going to be sick. She patted Elias's arm and made a sign to him. Quickly she placed her left hand over her mouth. Elias shouted, "Peter, stop the car."

"What's the matter?"

"Just stop the car. Quickly!"

Peter did. Elias jumped out. He held Nomsa with one hand and beseeched her, "Come, come quickly now."

She was only half out of the car when her control gave way and she spewed out all she had eaten in Umzinyathi. Elias helped her to clean herself. Peter drove on. Looking despondent, with dirt on his shoes, little traces of yellow and brown, and a damp smudge next to him on the seat of the car, Elias took tissues from Mary and tried to clean up. Somehow the stains remained, and this annoyed him. Holding a tissue against her mouth, Nomsa tried to say how sorry she was for making such a mess. Afraid of becoming dizzy and nauseous again, she cupped her face in her hands, closed her eyes and leaned back in her seat. This way she could not feel the speed of the car so acutely, nor could she see everything in front running away behind her.

They drove on for another half-hour. The wind had abated but the rain was falling steadily and hard. Rainwater had swept away the dirt from the tarmac and was splashing into clean puddles in the road. Elias had begun to extol the virtues of tarred roads and was comparing them with the trails and tracks of Umzinyathi. The water falling on the windscreen looked like icicles, because the wipers could not keep pace with it. The glass was frosting inside.

Peter drove as best he could, and his passengers in the back seat—Nomsa had taken her hands away from her face—tried to look out. Nomsa gazed at the strange new sights: the box-like structures, their uniformity, their sharp edges, the few sparse trees. She could not see well through the misty windows. Ochre-coloured lights came on, on top of tall poles along the streets, and in the houses. Nomsa was fascinated with all these lights. She saw their reflections in the shiny black surface of the roads. As they entered the city she heard the shrill and gruff sounds of a railway engine and saw a train. These little brown homes on wheels were moving faster than the car in which she was travelling.

"Here, my woman, we will spend the rest of our days. Here in Durban. How I have waited for this day! With you beside me, I shall overcome anything from this day on." And now Elias found the courage to tell her: "Nomsa, until we find accommodation for us to be together, I will be staying at the compound and you will be living with the good baases here."

Nomsa was dumbfounded. She kept silent, more in fright than in submission. But although she was frightened of being apart from Elias, she tried to understand his predicament, his inability to find a home for both of them, despite his great desire to do so. She also knew he wanted her to be near him, to stand by him, to love him in the city and not from far away in Umzinyathi. Above all she knew she needed him, wanted him and loved him. She asked, "Will this arrangement help you, Elias?"

"Yes, my woman."

"Then you must do what is best. I will stay wherever you say. But when and how will you come to me?" She took his hands in hers and gently caressed them.

"Tell Nomsa," Mary said to Peter, "that here in the city there is no fear of diseases that come from unclean water. Tell her about electricity, to cook with and to warm and light our homes with. I know her life will be different here. But we are going forward, the whole world is going forward and these are great achievements by man for man."

She wanted to say more but feared she might only confuse Nomsa. Elias had not been pushed; he had simply seen and learned. He was going to be the best teacher for his wife. Peter translated briefly and Elias elaborated. Nomsa nodded and sat quietly. It was getting late. Elias had to report for work early the next morning, Monday. He had to be in his compound by eight that evening. As Peter ran back into the car after opening the iron gates to his property, he asked, "Elias, are you sure Nomsa will get used to things? I hope for her sake she will soon learn."

Somehow Nomsa sensed the significance of what had been said. She smiled. Whether she smiled at the newness of things around her, at their strangeness, at Peter's strong, dominating manner or at Elias who had taken her for granted, who could say? She did not mind being taken for granted by her husband, but the man to whom she had given her love was not the same man as this husband who sat beside her.

Behind the Evenmores' house stood the servants' quarters: a room with a narrow bathroom and toilet next door. The structure had a low roof of neat tiles. The red tiles blended with the cream-painted walls. The door of the room was ajar and a little of the heavy rain had seeped in and lay like puddles of oil on the red-polished cement floor. Inside were two beds, one of them raised on bricks, an upright chair, an old wardrobe and beside it a two-plate cooker on a low table. The remaining floor space, in the centre, was covered with a piece of green carpet, about two feet by four. This was the khaya, which Nomsa would share with Lucy. Elias carried the suitcase, the cardboard box and the blanket bundle into the khaya.

Peter looked at his watch. "We'd better be quick . . . that is, if you want to be in time at the compound."

"Peter, I don't feel like going to work at all, now that Nomsa is here."

Nomsa looked up at Elias and was surprised at what she thought she had understood. She took a chance and admonished, "No, no, Elias. You must go to work. You must never stay away from work for my sake. I will be all right here."

Mary was satisfied with the arrangements, and now attended to her own prime concerns. Lucy was hovering at the kitchen door. She called her over.

"Was the baby all right today?"

"Yes ma'am." Lucy spoke English well. Her fluency had developed in many white madams' kitchens in Durban.

"Did you give her her bath?"

"Yes ma'am."

"Is she asleep now?"

"Yes ma'am."

"When did she go to sleep?"

"A little while ago."

"Did she cry a lot?"

"No ma'am."

"Have you got all her things ready for tonight?"

"Yes ma'am." Lucy was staring at Nomsa. She was the no-nonsense type. She continued to address her madam while looking at Nomsa. "Pam has had her food. The boiled water is in the flask. Her nappies are in the drawer with her clothes."

As Mary was going into her house by the back door she asked, "Lucy, have you had your supper yet?"

"No ma'am."

"Then can you organise supper for an extra one?"

"Is it for her, ma'am?" She scrutinised Nomsa more closely. "I can, ma'am. But who is she?" She rolled her eyes in Nomsa's direction.

Mary turned back and faced Lucy.

"Don't worry, Lucy. You are very good. We have brought Nomsa, that's her name, from Umzinyathi. Her husband is Elias. Nomsa is going to be a great help to us all, especially you. Won't that be nice for you?"

"Oh yes, ma'am."

Mary and Lucy went into the house. Lucy busied herself in the kitchen while her madam went through to the bedroom where the little Evenmore was fast asleep. The room was lit only by the soft glow of a bedside lamp with a delicate pink silk shade. The baby was warmly wrapped, a tiny bundle under her blanket. She had not needed to be lullabied. Piggybacked on Lucy, she had become tired waiting for her mother. With the first sucks at her bottle she had fallen asleep. Mary stood over the pretty white cot and looked through the mosquito net at her own flesh and blood. Her cheeks, pink in the lamplight, flushed redder as she watched her baby sleeping. Softly she undid the corners of the rectangular net and removed it. She bent over and attempted a gentle kiss. She could not reach her baby's face. Helplessly she caressed her child, patted her and ran her fingers through her hair. The baby twitched a little, opened her eyes a moment and fell asleep again.

The ceiling light snapped on.

"I'm taking Elias to his compound now," said Peter. "They have tight controls there—he mustn't be late."

"Then what about Nomsa?"

"Yes, what about her?"

"Peter darling . . . they've just been married. We can't leave her in the khaya, without Elias."

"Is there an alternative?"

"Can't we keep her in here with us?"

"And Elias? He has to go to the compound."

"Can't they both stay one night here, with us?"

"What? Here, in the house with us? No no, Mary. I do know how you feel. I feel the same. But you see, before long the neighbours will be talking. And what about Lucy? We can't possibly keep her out and Nomsa in. It's not fair to her. She might become envious."

"But Peter, Nomsa is Elias's wife. Lucy just dropped in to sell her labour. We have brought Nomsa here."

"Come Mary, let's leave the arrangements as they are. Let's not get too involved in their lives."

"Would a bit of a hand for their first night in Durban be too much, Peter?"

"Yes, I think so."

Peter stood a few paces away from Mary, and said, "I am going now. Elias should be waiting."

Mary did not answer. She merely looked at everything and at nothing and recalled Nomsa's own clusters of clean huts, the hut with the soft air and cosy feel that she and Peter had had for their comfort just a few nights before. She lay on the bed and flung her head into the softness of the pillow. Her head reeled with the heaviness that was, in a true sense, her heart.

Outside at the khaya, Elias was giving Nomsa the last of the day's lessons about their new life in Durban. Her fears and her doubts were somewhat allayed with the knowledge that she would be safe at the Evenmores'. Lucy would be there. Nomsa, with Lucy, walked with Elias and Peter to the car. Lucy, as senior domestic hand, was gaining her first impressions in a situation where she would, in a way, take charge. Elias looked young and strong to her. Nomsa was innocent, and obviously needed help. At the car, Elias said to his wife, "You must not worry about me. I will see you often now. If I don't come every day to you, I will come for sure on Saturdays and Sundays. We will be together then."

"Yes Elias."

Elias put his arms around her shoulders and whispered into her ear, "I will miss you."

"I will be waiting for you, Elias, and please look after yourself. You must eat well from now on. And sleep well too."

Peter smiled at them, and Elias got into the car. At the end of the driveway Peter looked into the rear-view mirror and noticed that the light in the bedroom was still burning bright. He hoped it had not disturbed his baby. He did not know that his wife had joined the baby in sleep. He drove out into the street. Nomsa stood watching the car drive away with her Elias. She walked back to the khaya and asked Lucy in her native tongue, "Have you been in Durban long?"

"Yes, about ten years."

"Where did you come from?"

"Where exactly, I do not know. But my people once lived near the Umzimkulu."

"Yes?"

"Do you know where that is?"

"No."

"I thought not."

With laughter in her voice Lucy admonished, "You will learn, my dear. The ways of this new world will make you learn. You will learn so much that when you are thirsty for water you will want to drink Coca Cola."

The light from Mary's bedroom shone onto the pathway outside. There, right in front of Lucy and Nomsa, on the pathway, lay a small, wet bird's nest. It had been washed down by the heavy rain. The half-naked young, feathered just a little here and there, were nestling up to each other. But the wet blades of grass were too soggy to provide them with shelter any more. Nomsa picked up the nest. Holding it gently in her hands, she protected the birds from the rain. Lucy felt Nomsa to be as innocent as the little ones in the wet nest. Nomsa began to walk briskly and left Lucy a few paces behind. By now both women were wet. Inside the khaya Nomsa very gently removed the protesting young from the nest and placed them on the floor. Knowing what to do next, she picked one up and dabbed it dry with a piece of cloth. She picked up another, and then realised that their loud protests had faded to simple signs of surrender. One died, a little later another, and the third, trying to get near the others, died too. All these deaths, on her first day in Durban . . . Nomsa shook her head. Without a second thought she picked up the three dead ones and all that remained of the soggy nest. She went out of the khaya and, in the first patch of soil she saw, dug a little hole, placed the three little ones in it, and covered them with wet, loose soil. She placed the remains of the nest on top of this grave. When she came back to the khaya she found Lucy busy with plates and spoons and ready to dish up their supper.

"I hope you won't start crying now because I will not know for whom you are crying, your husband or those three little things," said Lucy, without turning round.

"Are there different kinds of crying?"

"Oh, I don't know. Here you forget to cry. So how should I know about the different kinds? The last time I remember crying was when I was a little girl, crying for my mother and father. I never saw them again. Come, let us eat. You have your whole life ahead of you to learn and to know about the city."

Long after Lucy was asleep, Nomsa lay awake.

CHAPTER 8

The rain had stopped. Now not the chirping birds, the clucking chickens, the cackling geese and the crowing cockerels awoke Nomsa but the jingling of milk bottles, the piercing sounds of car engines and hooters and the sirens of factories changing from night to day shift. Nomsa opened her eyes in the semi-darkness of the khaya. Across on the other bed lay Lucy, breathing heavily, fast asleep.

Nomsa pushed her blanket to the foot of her bed and without even thinking she made for the door. She undid the bolts and softly pulled it open. The cool breeze after the wet night caught her full in the face. She stretched her arms and took a deep breath of air. In the yard she saw a wash basin with a concrete wash stone. Not knowing that on this stone she was going to rub the coming months of her life, she sat securely upon it. She dangled her feet as she was accustomed to doing from a rock perch above her native river, and sang her love song. Her soft voice was audible only to herself.

Drops of water were falling from the rim of a tap. They fell, one after another, with regularity. Standing up, Nomsa went closer and held her palm beneath the tap. A small puddle gathered in the hollow of her hand. She raised it to her face. The icy water tickled her. Enjoying the effect, she turned the tap, as if she had done this all her life. She collected two palmsful of water and splashed it against her face. She did this over and over. The more she turned the tap, the more water poured out. She was enjoying this. She was, she discovered, able to control the amount of water coming out of the pipe. This was so different from the Umzinyathi, where the river and the streams, governed by the rains, dictated how much water would flow. She remembered that when the Umzinyathi was in flood the people's drinking water was murky. Here the water from the tap was clean and cold and it tasted so good. In Umzinyathi they had to carry the water on their heads. Here there was no carrying, and with almost no effort from her, the water poured out of the tap. In silent wonder she thought, even a child could get water whenever it needed it. Oh my ancestors, these people here in Durban are so different and so clever. Why don't you . . . ? Why are you not so kind to us in Umzinyathi? Why don't you make us have these things too? Why can't you make our people do these things for us?

She stopped to think for a while and realised that if Elias or anyone else had told her about this kind of water before she came to Durban, she would not have believed them. It would be so nice for my mother, she thought.

Satisfied with her cleansing in this clean, cold water she walked towards a bushy section of the Evenmores' garden, snapped off a little twig and removed the rough edges and the small leaves. She put the twig between her teeth and slowly started to chew it soft. Manipulating the twig across and between her teeth she cleaned them to a slippery white.

When she came back into the khaya Lucy was awake.

"I was wondering where you were."

"Oh, I woke up early and I was sitting outside."

"It looks as if you didn't sleep well."

Nomsa merely smiled and began to put on her dress.

"Did you have a bad night, Nomsa?"

"In a way. Outside it is cool and open. We had the windows closed last night. You know at home, we often sleep outside."

"Yes I know, but this is Durban. A beautiful girl like you cannot sleep outside. You mustn't, my girl. These chaps chase after me. I don't know what they will do to you."

Looking deep into Nomsa's eyes Lucy saw her own reflection in the half-light. She began to think of her own youth and innocence when she first came to Durban. She had been, she felt, another Nomsa. But she had come without an Elias, without a Peter or a Mary. She came to Durban, she remembered, with the assistance of a distant relative, to live, to survive. But in the process of surviving, she lost herself. Abruptly she turned away and said, "Come. The morning is going to pass very quickly. We have work to do. Let us not worry about ourselves. We have got to worry about them inside, and she will be wanting us very soon."

The rain seemed to have washed away all the dirt from the city's surfaces. It was a bright, clean morning. The clouds had dispersed, but pockets of morning mist still lingered over the little vales of the town. It seemed as if even the smog that clouded the city every day had had to give way to the cleansing rain. The air was light. Palm trees, planted with care but not too regularly along the streets, swayed in the breeze. The freshness would not last.

Inside the Evenmores' house, Mary too had risen with the dawn. She removed the bucket containing her baby's soiled napkins to the bathroom, and came back to pull the curtains, admitting the morning light full onto Peter, who was still asleep, sprawled across their double bed. He grimaced, turned over and fell deeper into his pillows. That the light should not disturb him again he grabbed another pillow and covered his closed eyes with it. Mary looked at the wall clock, and consoled herself with the thought that it was still too early for Peter to get up.

Taking a dressing gown from her closet, Mary shook her head and threw back her hair, ruffled during the night. With one foot, she dragged her slippers out from under the bed and slid her feet into them. The light silk gown was draped around her slender body.

Quietly she went through the kitchen to the back door. She unbolted it, and opened it hesitantly. She stood in the doorway and looked out.

"Good morning ma'am," said Lucy.

"Oh, good morning, Lucy."

"Good morning," said Nomsa in her native tongue, and added, "ma'am."

Mary came down to the path where Nomsa was standing. With a wide smile she said, "Good morning, Nomsa. Did you sleep well?"

Nomsa, half-understanding, nodded and smiled at Mary.

"Lucy, I don't think Nomsa slept well. She looks as if she's been awake the whole night. Tell her she mustn't do that, it's bad for her health. And if your health is not good, your work will suffer." Mary came nearer to Nomsa. "She will have to learn to live with us here, in this big city. This city requires us to live together." Mary put her arm around Nomsa's shoulders and led her into the house.

In the kitchen she moved from place to place to show Nomsa where the things were kept. Mary pointed out the sink, the hot and cold water taps, and various utensils; without any warning she flung open the fridge. Drops of water were dripping from the ice around the freezer. Mary ran her palm along the thick ice and quickly placed it on Nomsa's warm cheek. Nomsa gave a little shriek and Mary laughed.

Peter awoke and rubbed his eyes. He wondered what was going on in the house. Mary's laugh reassured him. Still laughing, Mary went from window to window and threw them open. At the third window she turned and looked at Nomsa.

Her eyes shone and in a quivering, unsure voice she said, "Well Nomsa, today we start another day, but we start it together."

Lucy's arrival rescued Nomsa, who was trying to understand what Mary had just said. Lucy interpreted, "Nomsa, the missus says that all of us are going to work together and that we are going to start today."

"Oh!" responded Nomsa.

"Come here, Nomsa." Mary beckoned Nomsa to follow her to the bathroom. Lucy followed too, knowing she would be needed again.

"Ask Nomsa if she knows how to wash. Tell her it would be nice if she washed these clothes and hung them up to dry. And when she's finished you can show her how to use the iron and how she should iron the dry clothes. She need not worry too much, I know that these things are new to her. From time to time you will show her, won't you Lucy, and once you get used to them, they become a matter of habit. And, as you will soon discover, Nomsa, these things are very good. Isn't it so, Lucy?"

"Oh yes ma'am. Nomsa will soon get used to all these things, and I am sure she will like them too."

She held Nomsa's hand and said encouragingly, "Of course I will give you a hand whenever you need it. You can count on me. I will help you all the way. I will help you to become one of us."

This was said in Nomsa's native tongue, and with so much encouragement and support she felt she was ready to start the day's work. She collected all the soiled clothes from the bathroom. Mary took two cakes of Sunlight soap out of a cupboard and handed them to her. Washing clothes was not going to present any problems for Nomsa. It was a job she knew well. Soap and an empty bucket in one hand, and a bucket full of soiled clothes in the other, she walked out of the bathroom and with a fixed expression made for the wash stone at the back of the house.

This was the stone where she had sat and dangled her feet and sung her love songs. She separated the coloured clothes from the white ones and dumped them into separate buckets. She opened the tap and filled each bucket. Then one by one she rubbed the dirty clothes against the surface of the hard stone. She had to squeeze the dirt out of some of the garments. With her full peasant strength she rinsed and wrung them. In neat rolls she placed the clean clothes to be hung later in the morning of this first working day. For the work she had just done she did not require any lessons. This work was in many ways like her tears. In the night she had sobbed, without her Elias, and way back in Umzinyathi too, she had sobbed without him.

About five in the afternoon the sirens of many factories sounded. The simultaneous, discordant wailing attracted Nomsa's attention. She came out of the kitchen and looked around, searching for the source of the sounds. Lucy explained that it was time in the bigger factories for the workers to down tools, so that the next shift might pick them up.

"In the city," Lucy said, "there are some machines that have to work all the time without stopping. The machines must keep going and the workers must always be there, at all sorts of times of the day and night. Such is the power of the machines and their owners. You know, Nomsa, how funny all this is? When the machines fail and stop working, the people have to stop too; they call it short time, and they don't get paid. When the machines start up again the workers have to start too. But here in the houses it is not quite the same. When the floor polisher breaks down, we have to go on our knees and polish the floors by hand. Agh, come Nomsa, you will learn faster than I did. And you should stop ironing now. You know the missus said we could both knock off early this evening."

"But I haven't finished what I started."

"I see you haven't. She won't mind if do the rest tomorrow."

"Then what . . . ?"

"Come on, Nomsa. I am going to wash and change."

Lucy went into the khaya, and shouted from inside, "The evening looks quite pleasant. I am going out to meet my man. He is very handsome and you know, he actually drives a car."

"He must be very rich."

"In a way."

"Why in a way? Isn't he rich? Doesn't he drive a car?"

"Oh yes he does."

"Then?"

"Well you see, it isn't his own car. He drives it all day for his baas, and then about this time each day he parks it in the garage and comes to me by bus."

"Oh I see. Then your man drives for his baas?"

"Yes. Nomsa, come pull up this zip on my dress. I cannot reach it."

Nomsa came in and stood behind her. "How?" she asked.

Lucy laughed and showed her in an understanding way. Then she sat down on a small wooden stool. She pulled up the hem of her dress, caressed her thighs and calves, and began to pull on her stockings. Fastening the tops to her suspenders, she advised Nomsa about the elegance and protection of suspenders and stockings.

"When you go out with a new man you must be careful . . . "

"Oh Lucy, you are so clever. You know everything about everything."

"Come quickly now. He should be waiting for me at the gate."

"Why at the gate? Isn't he coming here?"

"No Nomsa. Not yet."

"But why?"

"Oh dear, you don't seem to understand." After a short pause she added, half-smiling, "I said not yet. But he will, sometime later."

"Oh, then I will go and finish my work."

"Don't you want to meet him?" Lucy stood up and half commanded, "Come. And I will introduce you to him."

Standing on the pavement outside the gate was Lucy's man. He wore a white cap and a white coat, and beamed a broad, happy smile. He looked over Lucy's shoulder and noticed Nomsa's lithe, supple body as she approached.

"Lucy, I see you have a new friend?"

"Oh yes. Come Nomsa. Nomsa is my fellow worker; she shares my room. Marumo meet Nomsa. Nomsa, this is Marumo."

"Nomusa! Oh, mother of kindness! I am so pleased to meet you."

Nomsa smiled. Lucy, a little uneasy, interrupted.

"Come, Marumo. We must be going. Nomsa's husband should be coming any time now, today, tomorrow, maybe." Lucy had made her point but as usual she was not satisfied, and had to go on, "In any case she has got to go back to the house."

Marumo, fascinated with Nomsa, wanted to know more about her.

"What did you say? Her husband! How did that happen to her?"

Nomsa had stood there listening to them discussing her.

"Well I guess we must leave now," Lucy insisted, in an insecure way.

"Yes, yes," Marumo agreed, still staring at Nomsa. "Yes, let's go now." Then to Nomsa he remarked, "I hope I'll have the pleasure of meeting you again, Nomsa."

"Oh yes, by all means. I am sure you will be coming often to see Lucy. I think I will be here for some time."

Marumo took Lucy by the arm and led her away. Nomsa walked back to the house.

"You have quite good company, Lucy. And beautiful too," said Marumo.

As if she were indifferent to this remark Lucy said, "Yes, Nomsa seems to be all right."

"I envy you in some ways."

"I'm sure."

"You are an understanding girl, you know."

And they kept walking, towards a destination they had not yet chosen. The evening was theirs.

As they walked off down the street, talking, laughing, joking, Peter was driving home. His car lights were on and he was looking forward to his evening. Relaxation at home was what he had yearned for during the hours of the working day. His pipe, his whisky and soda, his roast or grill, and later, just before bed, a warm shower and a nightcap, a small brandy perhaps. And now in the garden, at dusk, his Mary would be waiting.

Elias's day had come to an end too. He went back to the compound. Nomsa did not know where the compound was. This was as well for her. She waited, but in vain.

From the gate Peter announced his arrival home with the sharp sound of his horn. Mary ran out of the house to meet her man in the garden. She threw herself into his arms. Full of desire they kissed hard, and for some time they were oblivious to the world around them.

Nomsa was in the garden removing the last of the day's washing from the line and putting it in a bin. She stood watching them in the half-light, and felt happy for these two young lovers. Silently she prayed, and a certain vibration shook her. She had not seen Elias for a whole day, and the coming night was the third since their marriage. She prayed, Oh my ancestors, these two lovers are young and good, they are lovely and they are loving. Please, my dear fathers, look after them and guide them.

Quickly, not wanting to be seen, she moved behind a shrub and then walked very fast into the khaya. Once within its privacy she threw herself on her bed and sobbed silently. She pressed herself down on the bed and yearned for her Elias. She imagined he was there and with this imagination as her only company and her only access to what she desired she dropped into sleep. She had not eaten that evening.

Learning all the time in her new calling, Nomsa lived through the rest of the week.

On the Saturday morning Nomsa was the first to rise. Not knowing what to do with herself she just paced the room. When she was tired of this she opened the door quietly and stepped outside. She turned the tap and splashed her face with cold water. She turned it on full and held her face underneath it. She hoped the dawn would break soon.

The sounds of running water had crept into the main house. Peter woke up. Although it was not a working day for him, he got up. He put on his dressing gown and slippers, muttering, "What is the matter outside? I hope it's not a burst pipe." His wife and baby slept on, the baby in her cot. He went out, leaving the bedroom door and the back door ajar. A slight breeze came in, but mother and baby remained tranquil in sleep.

Peter stood on the *stoep*, about three feet above ground level. He saw Nomsa sitting by the tap with the water running on her legs. He stepped down into the garden and called, "Nomsa!"

"Oh, good morning, baas."

"Good morning. What are you doing so early in the morning? Actually it is not quite morning yet. I can hardly see you."

"Oh!"

"Well, what are you doing here, with the water running, so early?"

"I don't know, baas. I thought I was alone. And I didn't mean to disturb you."

"But what are you doing with the water?"

"Oh this? I was just having a wash."

"But you were merely sitting there."

She turned off the tap.

"Yes, I know."

Peter came closer to Nomsa. From where he now stood he could see her agitated face. He remembered that it was the end of the week and tried an explanation: "Nomsa, I am sorry I haven't seen you during the course of the week. You know, that reminds me, I haven't even seen Elias this week either."

"I thought you saw each other every day?"

"No." With guilt in his voice he continued, "I think he was taken to work on some other site, and I remained at the place where I worked last week."

"Then you don't know if he is well? You don't know whether he will be coming here today, or not?"

"Oh, I am sure if he is not working today he will come. But they do sometimes work overtime."

"What is overtime?"

"That is if they work extra hours, for more money."

"But, don't they get tired doing that?"

"They could. But if you want to get on and make more money, then you have to work overtime."

"What does Elias want with more money?"

"He is now married and you are his wife; he has to provide more now."

"Do you work overtime, baas?"

"Not always."

"Elias doesn't have to. I am content with what I have."

"Here in the city you will have to have a lot more than what you have now."

"Why? Isn't he happy with what he already has?"

"I don't know. But what I do know is that once you are happy with what you have, you remain where you are."

"You mean Elias is working hard so that one day he can give me a house like yours?"

"Maybe."

"You mean we can have a house like yours here in Durban?"

"Well, not in Durban. But somewhere in your own area."

"Where is that?"

"In the location, in the township for your people."

"Does Elias want to take me there?"

"He must know best."

"Hasn't he told you yet? I thought you were friends."

"Hasn't he told *you*? You are his wife."

"No, we have never discussed that. I was just happy being with him and I never cared to ask him about his work, his time or his money."

"You had better ask him now." Moving a few steps away Peter continued, "I do hope for the two of you that he will come here today."

"Yes, I am waiting for him."

"Is that why you were up so early?"

"Yes baas. I am waiting."

Peter stopped his pacing and looked away in silence. With his back to the house he saw, between tall trees and red tiled roofs, the streaks of light in the East where the sun would soon come up out of the sea. The sky had grown brighter. He walked away into his scented garden. Plucking petals here and there he put them to his nostrils and inhaled their fragrance. Preoccupied, he took a cigarette from his pocket and placed it between his lips. The glow of the struck match brightened his face. He sat down on a raised concrete slab, which served as a garden stool and as a buttress to contain a mud bank.

The colourful slate tiles were neatly placed and cemented. They were all still wet with the morning mist. A butterfly sucked the nectar of a new bloom. Peter was watching absent-mindedly. With his face cupped in one hand and the cigarette burning in the other, he sat deep in thought. How long he sat there he did not know, but the burned-out cigarette was firmly held in his fingers at the filter, and a lump of ash lay near his feet.

Very quietly Mary made her way out into the garden. By then the sun was out and everywhere the mist was drying. She saw her husband sitting on the stone, and went slowly towards him. Afraid that she might interrupt his thoughts she stood still awhile, only a breath away from him. Then mustering some courage she put out her hand and very lovingly tried to take the cigarette stub from between his fingers.

"Why were you up so early?" she asked.

"The sounds of running water woke me; the tap was open and Nomsa was there. She didn't care about all that water just flowing away."

"Nomsa? She may have been washing."

"So she said. But at 4:30 in the morning?"

He looked in the direction of the tap to see whether Nomsa was still there, and continued, "In the chilly air, she was there, dangling her legs in the cold water. And with no thought for her health or the waste of water. I think she is anxious about Elias."

CHAPTER 9

Meanwhile Elias, too, had risen. Somehow the grey walls of the compound were bright in the morning sun. There was a kind of reflection in their sullen colour. It could not absorb all the sunlight, and had to throw some off. In his enthusiasm to be ready quickly Elias jumped over the rows of bodies lying there in their tired sleep. He was at the wash basin long before the queues started forming there.

By now Elias had become accustomed to looking at himself in a mirror. His first experience of this had been in the windows of the landrovers that came to Umzinyathi. In the city he peered into the plate glass windows of the shops. In these glass cases he saw the many wares displayed to attract customers—they attracted him too—and he also saw himself in there and felt he was part of the goods displayed. This pleased him, and then he bought a small mirror, which he kept locked in his suitcase. On this Saturday morning he took particular delight in placing it on a windowsill, where the vertical iron bars between the timber horizontals supported it. The compound windows were about waist to chest height, and he bent down to look into his mirror. The angle was wrong and he couldn't see himself properly. He knelt on the floor and stared into the mirror for some time. There was no doubt, he liked what he

saw. Gently, he patted his woolly hair and ran his palm across his face. He stood up, wiped his mirror and put it back in his suitcase.

He put on his trousers, blue flannels that had been well used before he bought them, and pulled the overall in which he had slept over his head. He tied a piece of thickish cloth around his waist to keep his pants up. Satisfied with his makeshift belt he put his hands in his pockets and spread his knees apart. Fairly comfortable, he thought. Then he grabbed a shirt and put it on. He did not tuck the shirt in, and its black and white diagonal stripes hung in unblending contrast with his pants. His broad chest was bare—he left all the shirt buttons unfastened. He did not have a pair of socks, so he wore his boots over bare feet. From under his pillow of hessian and feathers, he took his week's pay packet. He separated the paper notes from the coins and walked out of the compound. The coins jingled in his pocket with each step he took. He liked the sound of these coins. Elias was on his way to Nomsa.

Outside the Evenmores' house, he stood for a while. He was amazed that he was already there. Then hurriedly he opened the gate and ran up the driveway. Peter and Mary had seen him and were tempted to call out, but they didn't. They looked out of their window at the impatient Elias, and smiled at each other.

Nomsa had heard Elias's voice calling out to her. She came towards him. In sheer joy, she stood still and stared at her smartly dressed man. She was searching for something in him. Dabbing away the sweat from his forehead and his chest with a small piece of cloth, she smiled.

"My woman, I have missed you so! Come let us go in. I want you."

"Go in? Where?"

"Into your room."

"Lucy is in there. She is still sleeping."

"Never mind."

"No, Elias. We can't go in with her there. I would not be happy with her around."

"I have waited all this week, just to be with you."

"No Elias. Let us sit here in the yard. Soon I will make some coffee for you and I have some bread left over from last night. I am sure you haven't eaten this morning."

"I forgot. Let me help you make the coffee."

"Oh no you don't! It's going to be our first breakfast alone and it's going to be made by me."

From inside the khaya Lucy enquired loudly, "Nomsa, who are you talking to? Is my man already here? Or is it your man?"

"It is Elias, my husband."

Turning to her husband, she chided, "You see, she was awake."

Nomsa went into the khaya and Elias sat down on a low brick wall. Picking up little dry leaves, he kept crushing them in his palm. And when they were reduced to powder he threw them away. Some of the powder stuck on his clothes, but he didn't notice. The brooding Elias was suddenly awakened by a friendly drawl. Peter Evenmore had come out of his house.

"You here, Elias?"

"Oh, good morning, baas Peter."

"Happy to be here?"

"What's that, baas?"

"I asked, are you glad to be here?"

"Oh, yes."

"I see you are thinking a lot this morning. Haven't you seen Nomsa?"

"Yes, I have. She has gone inside to get us something to eat."

"Oh I see."

"This will be our first breakfast together."

Coming closer, Peter asked, "Do you miss Umzinyathi, Elias?"

Elias gathered the hem of his black and white shirt and, gripping it tightly, creased the already creased garment in his fist. With a lostness in his voice and eyes, he answered, "In a way."

"Aren't you happy here?"

"I don't know."

Peter sat down beside him. He had put a few loose cigarettes in his dressing gown pocket and some of them were already half-crumpled. He took one out and with long straight fingers he tried to roll it back to its original shape. He failed, but shrugged and lit it. With the cigarette in his mouth he observed very gently, "Elias, I know how you feel and I have observed Nomsa these past few days." He lied. He hadn't seen Nomsa until the early hours of that same morning. Considering his lie, he continued, "Here in Durban things are different."

"Yes they are, Peter."

"It is very different. You are wanted here."

"It is a little less than that, Peter. I am needed here."

"Of course you are. Everything we want to build here would be just a dream without you and your people."

Elias looked at Peter in disbelief. With his eyes half-closed he saw the twitches in Peter's cheeks. Elias felt sorry for him. He held Peter's hand in his own and said nothing. Then Peter, slightly hesitant, went on, "Yes Elias, I am serious. You are not only important. Your people are indispensable to the city's growth."

Elias was aware of Peter's continuing uneasiness.

"Why didn't I see you last week?" Elias asked. "I kept a lookout for you but I didn't see you. I couldn't leave my gang."

"Were you working at another site? I stayed where I had been the week before. I did ask your supervisor where you and your gang were working. He did not know and I left it at that."

"Yes, I was taken away, and we always got back after dark. It was a tough, rough week."

"You must have made good overtime this last week."

"Yes, but I got too tired. They wanted all of us to work today and tomorrow. But luckily there was no baas to supervise us. He had to attend to some personal business, so all the work had to stop." With a slight chuckle he added, "Baas no come, gang no work . . . simple as that."

"You were lucky."

"Not exactly."

"Why not?"

"The others, twenty of them in the gang, were keen to go on working. In any case they had nothing else to do. I had Nomsa to come to and they had no Nomsa to go to. They wanted the money."

"I see."

Elias had risen and was standing in front of Peter.

"Baas Peter, look, here comes my Nomsa."

With an uncomfortable jerk Peter got up and stood aside.

"Are we ready, Nomsa?"

"Yes, we are. Lucy is going in to make the baases' breakfast in a minute or two. As soon as she goes you will have yours."

Inside the Evenmores' house Mary had already brushed her teeth and was in the kitchen when Lucy announced herself. In her usual manner she asked, "Shall I fix the bacon and eggs, ma'am?"

"Yes Lucy," Mary answered without thinking, and left the kitchen.

With deft, trained hands Lucy got the breakfast. Quickly, she had everything ready: bacon and eggs, a stack of thin brown toast, fresh orange juice and a pot of tea, all neatly laid out on the table for two.

In the khaya, Nomsa had her own breakfast ready for Elias and herself. Their first breakfast alone as man and wife. They walked in excitedly, Nomsa in front. Elias closed the door behind him. As soon as the lock clicked, he grabbed Nomsa's arm and pulled her to him. He licked her face, throat and arms, something he had never done in Umzinyathi. Nomsa, overwhelmed, could not even wince. She loved her Elias, whatever he might do. They had forgotten Lucy had just left the khaya. Nomsa clung to Elias, gasping as her womb contracted. The faster her breathing became, the tighter she held Elias. She dug her fingers into him through his shirt, and he dug his into her through her blouse. He dug his fingers into the sides of her buttocks, into her waist, into her shoulders. Elias tightened his grip on her and bit deeper. Standing, he pounded, he thrust at her. She responded with matching throbs and thrusts. Suddenly, he came, along his own strong thigh. The dripping warmth ran down and met his trousers. Panting, he gathered Nomsa into his arms. She was still clasping him around the waist but she let go a little so that she could be properly gathered. She looked up into his face and wiped the sweat from his brow.

He pulled off his pants and flung them onto a chair. Standing there face to face with his wife, in his long, coarse black and white shirt, he said, "Now we will have breakfast together in bed."

"What, again?"

He swung her round, carried her to her bed and painstakingly undid the buttons of her blouse.

Half an hour later, Nomsa brought down a large white enamelled mug from the shelf and poured lots of sweet black coffee into it. From a parcel wrapped in newspaper she took a few slices of unevenly cut brown bread and placed them on a plate. With coffee in one hand and bread in the other, Nomsa, the young wife, walked towards her husband and held them out to him.

She smiled and sat beside him and they shared the coffee from the common mug and the bread from the one plate.

Time for Nomsa and Elias was running out fast. Her free time was going to be curtailed by Lucy's afternoon off. And

Lucy had her own plans. The Evenmores had left soon after breakfast for the city. After they left, Lucy ate the remains of the bacon and eggs and toast. She had the last of the tea from the pot.

Peter particularly wanted to see the production that evening of *Othello*. The adoptive country had not yet matured enough to fill his cultural vacuum. It depended a good deal on Britain to furnish art and especially theatre. This English production was being presented in Durban for the first time ever. Tickets had to be secured. They had told Lucy they would be back for lunch.

For the Evenmores, Lucy set the table. The dumplings and the roast leg of mutton were in the oven. The cooked rice was draining in the colander. The salad was made, and keeping crisp in the fridge. The gravy was already boiling. Lucy ran her palm down her skirt from the waist and murmured to herself, "I think everything is almost ready. The baby should be fed about three in the afternoon. I will remind Nomsa about that."

As she went out through the back door, Nomsa came in. Peter and Mary had arrived.

"Hey Nomsa, I have everything ready. Will you remember to feed the baby?"

"Yes."

"Do you know how to feed her?"

"Yes, I do."

"You won't forget to burp her?"

Nomsa smiled at Lucy and reassured her. "Now don't worry. Go and have a good time and relax. If I don't know what to do I'll ask the missus."

Lucy nodded and walked happily away to the khaya. Elias was dusting his boots as she came in.

"You look quite comfortable here."

"What?"

"Don't worry about me, make yourself comfortable. I will be leaving in a few moments!"

Waiting to Live

She untied her apron strings and pulled the apron off. Adjusting her belt she asked, "You love Nomsa a lot, don't you?"

"Yes, of course."

"She is a lucky girl."

"I am lucky too."

Lucy looked him squarely in the face and pleaded with him, "Please don't teach her my ways. Even if you have already learned some of my ways in the city, don't you ever teach them to her."

Without apologies, or another word, she slammed the door behind her and ran down the driveway to meet her man.

Outside on the pavement, Lucy met him. This time, it was another man. He was tall, broad-shouldered, urbane, a man of this new world. He knew his way about the city, a real man about town. Lucy grabbed his hand and together they ran on, away from the beautiful houses with their equally beautiful gardens full of sweet fragrances and vibrant colours, leaving behind them the geraniums and zinnias, arum lilies, poinsettias and roses. They gasped for breath, but did not stop running until they reached the bridge.

There they halted and gazed down on the Umgeni. Soap suds, detergent foam, chemicals, though they were all white, marred the clarity of the water. Along the banks were heaps of dirt disgorged by a nearby factory. A stench was in the air. It came from the "pure cane spirit" distillery about half a mile upstream. The distillery ran twenty-four hours a day, seven days a week. The people had to have their intoxicant, the tangy spirit that turned many a Lucy, and many others like her man, into what they were. The waste from the pure cane juice dripped incessantly into the Umgeni; slowly, it oozed. Not only did it sully the waters—its stench tickled the nostrils.

"That smell excites me, man. If only there was a shebeen around this cultured place."

"That, there might not be." Unfastening the buttons he opened his jacket. "But I always take care of important matters."

He revealed the half-bottle of spirit. She gave a cry of joy and clung to him.

"How understanding and helpful you are!"

"You really think so?"

"Oh yes, I do."

"Then kiss me to tell me how much."

"After a swig from the bottle," said Lucy, laughing.

"No, not here. Let us go farther down the river. There, where we can't be seen."

They stood still, and the man added, "This I brought for our joy. But you know as well as I do that it is not legal for us to buy the stuff. If it is found on us it will get us into gaol. And as it is the weekend, who wants to be in gaol till Monday? There's no admission of guilt for this offence. The blighters would want to know the source, the supplier—"

"Oh, you always know all these things."

They walked along the bank. Months, years of pollution had left their dark black stains on the trees beside the river. The dumping of refuse was allowed in this area by the local authorities. Indiscriminate loads of almost anything were dumped almost anywhere. Between these dumps Lucy and her man wove their way towards the shelter and privacy beneath the bridge that spanned the Umgeni. The steel and concrete props stood firm in their deep greyness, and the ceiling provided by the underside of the bridge was rough and rugged and showed its age.

Sitting on the rough stones and pebbles, they sipped, then took deeper draughts, straight from the bottle. The spirit burned Lucy's lips and throat and heated her from within.

"If only we could drink this stuff properly," she murmured. "You know, with food, in our khayas or in their hotels. If only we were able to buy their liquor freely from their bottle stores, or drink it in their bars."

"You wish for too much, little girl. Just you remember, if only your auntie had a certain thing, she would be your uncle."

They laughed.

"Aah! Let's forget about what we wish and what we want. We're here and let's enjoy being here."

Suddenly she wanted to sing and shout, but her man grabbed her by the shoulders, turned her towards him and sealed her mouth with his. He forced her to the ground. The pebbles on the bank, rough and pointed, blunt and flat, all hurt her naked buttocks. But inside her body, aroused and gratified, she found solace and pleasure, and forgot the external pains. The spirits helped.

After that, she wanted more. Lying there prostrate, helpless as if in prayer, bottle and crumpled panties in her hands, she gazed along the riverbank into the cluster of steeples. Their bells were ringing. From another direction came the piercing sound of the muezzin's call to prayer. People had to pray. The sun was setting. Lucy had no desire to be reminded that the day was ending; neither was she inspired by the jingling of bells or the calls to prayer.

In the khaya at the back of the Evenmores' house lay Elias, recuperating from his morning's exertions, full of joy and contentment. Here in their love, Nomsa and Elias had given notice of a new life. With Elias lying restfully, blissfully in the khaya, Nomsa went gingerly about her chores in the house. Sometimes she felt she was floating in the thought of what this new bond meant to her. Now, she had love in her belly. Way back in Umzinyathi she had not understood, she had only felt and wanted; in her innocence she had not cared. Now, in knowledge, she understood and sustained care, care for her coming flesh and blood.

CHAPTER 10

In the evening Peter and Mary were ready to leave for an early supper in town and the theatre. While he dressed in front of the long mirror, Peter looked again at a memorandum that had been left on his drawing table the day before. When he had first read it, he had sworn in disbelief at its contents. Now he told himself he would not allow this document to spoil his evening out with Mary. But as he closed the front door he mumbled indistinctly to himself. And as he opened the car door for his wife he mumbled again.

"Did you say something, dear?" asked Mary.

"No, no."

After a brief silence, Peter explained: "The municipality can't get a sufficient labour force to begin the new project I planned for them. They say, under the present circumstances we can't start work. According to these fools the labour was to have come from Bizana."

"Where is that?"

"Ask me another. But according to their map it's about ninety-five miles from here by road, somewhere in Pondoland. The damn bureaucrats say that the papers for these workers are not in order or not complete or something. They have to have papers, papers—the bloody pass," he jeered bitterly.

"Why don't they get their labour from some place nearer?"

"I don't know." After a short pause he continued, "But they say the workers must be drawn equally from different places and different tribes. Why, I cannot understand. What does it matter where they come from and who they are as long as they fill the need?"

"Maybe the city fathers want to play one group against another."

"It seems their needs are different from those of architecture or economics; the city fathers seem to have their own unpublicised needs. If only they would go out to Umzinyathi, I am sure they could recruit more men, and quickly, too."

"But if only . . . "

With the allusion to Elias's home, Mary's words tailed off and she pondered, gazing fixedly at the haze on the windscreen. "Peter, did you see Elias before we left?"

"No. Why?"

"I didn't either."

"Why? Should I have seen him?"

"Don't you think so?"

Peter did not answer.

"You didn't see him the whole week and he only came to the house today."

"I know." With some measure of guilt he admitted, "I saw him sitting waiting for his breakfast this morning. This memorandum made me forget everything else. I know Elias's dilemma. I also feel for him. But what in hell can I do? He is here. I didn't go out and bring him to this city. He came. He was brought here by the others. I didn't even know what the likes of him were, before we got to this country."

Sharply, he swerved left and into a parking space. "Here *we* are and let us not allow Elias's shadow to mar our evening. I am sure he will be all right."

Peter opened Mary's door with a certain firmness. He waited for her to get out and closed it equally firmly. He had to lock the car because he had a few possessions in it. Together they walked into the hotel, which was lit up with loud neon signs. From inside came the blare of a saxophone. Looking at his watch in the flickering light of the signs, he said, "Well, we have just an hour for dinner. The play begins at eight. We had better be quick."

Nomsa was sitting in the dining room when they got home. She said the baby had slept all evening. She retired to the khaya.

Sunday morning came into the Evenmores' bedroom through the coarsely woven curtain and the open window. The morning breeze gently embraced the rolling curtains. Mary and Peter awoke to the soft, cool draught and rose for a quick breakfast and church. As usual the morning meal was ready and waiting for them. This Sunday morning Nomsa was primly dressed in her best, a white dress now partly protected by an apron.

"Is Elias still around, Nomsa?" Peter asked.

"Yes, baas."

"I hope he was comfortable?"

"Yes, baas."

"Did Lucy come back last night?"

"No, baas."

"I do hope you and Elias spent the evening together while you minded our baby?"

"Well, baas . . . "

At the thought of what she and Elias had done on the bathroom floor the previous evening, she blushed.

"Is Elias still sleeping?"

"Yes, baas."

"Do you think the two of you can join us today? We want to take the baby out for a drive. You could both come, and you could keep an eye on her."

"I think so, baas." A few seconds later she said, "I will ask Elias."

"Lucy is off for the whole day, isn't she?"

"Yes baas."

"Then you can come with us."

"All right, baas."

Whether heaven was or was not on this earth Sunday service had to go on, and it had to be attended. Belief in God and his son was not enough. There had to be the ritual. The Evenmores with their daughter, Pam, and Nomsa with her husband drove off to church. Outside the church, Sunday best was much in evidence. Even the bells had a certain bestness about them. Female parishioners were arrayed in beautiful frocks with matching hats. Women, like their men, had to engage in the rituals. They had to dress up and cover their heads, but the style of their clothes and the shape of their hats were governed by the changing whims and fancies of manufacturers, milliners and couturiers. Within minutes of their arrival Mary was an integral part of the scene. Peter was at her side.

The church had a sharp, pointed, symmetrical steeple. They entered through the wide doors. Inside the Lord's house, consecrated by man for man's worship, the children sang, and with a little encouragement from their choirmaster, praised God in the words of George Herbert:

Let all the world in ev'ry corner sing,
My God, my King!
The Church with psalms must shout,
No door can keep them out;
But above all the heart
Must bear the longest part.
Let all the world in ev'ry corner sing,
My God, my King!

The organ resounded in glorious melody and harmony. It was housed in lovingly carved and polished wood. The organist touched the array of black and white keys; the sounds vibrated and echoed in the ears of the congregation. Mary was visibly possessed by the music and the words that accompanied it. The hymn came to an end, and the voice from the pulpit cut into the lingering echo. Everyone listened, Mary especially.

"For I am persuaded, that neither death, nor life, nor angels, nor principalities, nor powers, nor things present, nor things to come, Nor height nor depth, nor any other creature, shall be able to separate us from the love of God, which is in Christ Jesus our Lord."

Outside, the beautiful trees abounded with buds and blooms. The Pams and the Nomsas and the Eliases had their shelter beneath them, while the others were inside the church in prayer, in communion and in the hope of being with God. Those outside, among the flowers, bees and beetles, on the grass in the shade of the trees or in the warm sunshine, were waiting, for they could not go into the church. The Pams, and there were many of them, were too small for prayer or comprehension. The Nomsas and Eliases were too black.

Inside the church Mary silently asked herself, Doesn't Elias wear a pendant cross? Didn't we go to the priest to arrange his wedding?

She had an empty feeling inside her, and stared heavily at her feet. Her eyes began to glisten and she didn't stir. No part of her could be seen to move, not her head, nor her hands, nor her legs, nor her shoulders. But her heart stormed within her: Lord, Paul forgot to say, to include in the rhapsody, "nor colour, nor colour"!

Mary was no longer listening to the sermon, and her heart went out beyond the walls to her Pams and her Nomsas and her Nomsas' Eliases, beyond, into the shade of the trees, into the breeze among the blossoms and blooms where all those who were not permitted to enter the house of God were waiting. With her mind and her heart outside in the church garden, she wondered whether she herself, alone if need be, should not say or cry a little prayer in honour of Him who was being dishonoured in this church—in honour of those outside, who were being dishonoured. She searched her bible and found the passage from Isaiah that she wanted. Silently she read: "But he was wounded for our transgressions, he was bruised for our iniquities: the chastisement of our peace was upon him; and with his stripes we are healed. All we like sheep have gone astray; we have turned every one to his own way; and the Lord hath laid on him the iniquity of us all. He was oppressed, and he was afflicted, yet he opened not his mouth: he is brought as a lamb to the slaughter, and as a sheep before her shearers is dumb, so he openeth not his mouth."

Mary's hands shook and she gently closed the book and kept it between her folded hands.

All that was to be done on Sunday—prayers, confessions, penitence, candle-lighting, incense-burning—all the rituals were fulfilled.

The rituals that were to begin again the next morning were waiting. Monday, like all Mondays, heralded the arrival of another week. Those who had been to church on Sunday and those who had not been to church were obliged, on Mondays, to respond to the demands of drawing boards, industrial boards, boards of directors, commercial boards, legal boards, blackboards, agricultural boards and a host of other boards, and then they had to abide by the decisions of all these boards. Only the Nomsas and the Eliases and the Lucys were spared the perils of the decision-making processes, but they knew, all of them knew, that while they were saved from these perils, the boards' decisions were going to be their ultimate lot.

CHAPTER 11

Months passed, and Nomsa and Lucy worked harmoniously together. Nomsa noticed that Lucy's belly was growing like her own.

Lucy laughed. "You see, I'm pregnant too. I didn't tell you."

Innocently, Nomsa asked, "Is your husband in Durban?"

"I don't know who the father is."

Their shared condition created a bond between the two young women.

Then it all happened. As if it were all planned, as if it were destined to happen. As Lucy complained about the weight in her belly being heavier and just that bit more uncomfortable, Nomsa instinctively put her hands on her own protruding stomach. She caressed her rounded belly and with a sigh she asked, "What's happening to you, Lucy?"

"Why? I think the thing wants to come."

"How do you know?"

"I am getting sharp pains."

"I have a pain, too, since early this morning. It wasn't bad. But this afternoon it is a little worse."

"But it's too soon for you, Nomsa! You're not even eight months yet!"

"Oh Lucy! Elias is not here and I don't know what to do. You must help me. My mother is so far away. How I wish she was with me. My aunts and my mother would have known and they would have looked after me. I do not know what to do. Lucy, promise you won't leave me. You will be with me all the time? No matter what happens to me you will never leave me? I need my mother more than ever. You must stay with me, Lucy."

"Of course, Nomsa. Anyway my baby is going to come, too. Cheer up. I will go and tell the missus that the time has come."

As she left the khaya she said, "Nomsa, you sure you can't wait a few days?" She burst into laughter. "I was just wondering who's going to do the work for the missus when both of us are gone to the hospital. But don't worry, I'll see if I can get her to contact Elias for you."

From the house, Mary shouted, "Where is Nomsa? Nomsa, are you all right?" She didn't wait for an answer. "Don't panic," she said to Lucy, "I'll get a taxi quickly, and I'll try to get Elias too."

Mary found the number of a taxi bureau, dialled frantically, and asked for a car to be sent urgently to her address. The man said she could count on them, and it wouldn't be long.

"Thank you. Do you have the address right?"

"Yes madam. Don't worry."

By now Nomsa had joined them.

"Now I will try to get Peter and ask him to find Elias at his work place and tell him what's happening," Mary added. "Don't worry. You will not mind the pain. You will forget the pain when your baby suckles you."

Lucy got up with difficulty. "I'll just go and open the gate, ma'am. Otherwise we might not hear the taxi arrive."

"Good idea." Mary dialled her husband's telephone number at work. Abruptly she looked away and blurted the news into the mouthpiece. Lucy came back as she replaced the receiver. Mary was by then in a frenzy. She asked Nomsa whether she had all she would need in the hospital, for herself and for her baby. Lucy answered: "Yes ma'am. I have a few things packed in a carrier bag. Nomsa can share them with me."

The taxi came up the drive, and the driver hooted softly. Mary ran out and greeted him. He smiled.

"You in a hurry, lady? They said it sounded urgent."

"One moment, it's not me."

"Well where's my passenger then?"

"They are inside my house."

"Oh, two people?"

"Yes, take both my maids to the non-European hospital, please."

"Your maids?" The driver's smile had vanished. "You mean black girls."

"They are both Africans."

"Sorry ma'am, you'll have to call for one of *their* taxis, or a non-European ambulance. We're not allowed to carry them. We can carry only Europeans."

"But they are in labour."

"That's not the point: the hospital is not far. The point is, this is a white taxi. You'll have to make other arrangements. I am not here for your kaffir girls!"

Mary clutched at the man's sleeve and begged, "Would you want your own wife or your sister or your daughter to be left like this? In pain and at risk? Tell me, would you?"

"Sorry lady, but rules are rules."

"Can't you be a little merciful? Can't you brave the rules and be yourself? What are you made of? You can't spend your life at the mercy of the rules?"

The driver said suddenly, "Oh well, if you put it like that . . . where are they?"

"Thank you, thank you," were the only words that Mary could blurt out.

She hurried into the house and came back with the two

women. As they were getting into the car, the driver said to Mary, "You know, I could lose my licence for this."

"And at the same time you will know this was a normal, Christian act of mercy."

"Yeah, I know. But what can I do? I don't make the rules."

Mary thrust two pound notes through the window into Lucy's hand. The two passengers smiled wanly and waved, and with anxious well-wishing Mary stepped back. The taxi backed out into the street.

The driver glared ahead without uttering a word. In less than ten minutes, they were approaching the hospital gates. A board said "Maternity," with an arrow. Lucy looked for the building, and realised it was a long walk from the gate. Cars were driving in. But the taxi stopped there, and the driver said, "Out! Quick!"

His passengers didn't argue. Lucy put the two pounds in his hand, and they bundled out, Lucy clutching the carrier. They had hardly shut their doors when the taxi moved off at speed, and disappeared into the traffic.

Nomsa and Lucy trudged up the long road to maternity admissions. There, the patients were asked their names, their addresses, their place of work, their husbands' names. Lucy hesitated a moment, and said, "No husband."

A nurse appeared, and took them to curtained cubicles for a cursory examination. Yes, they were in labour, Nomsa apparently prematurely. Admission was justified. Then they were trollied away to a side room that was a makeshift labour ward. There they were washed and shaved. Urine specimens were taken, and a little blood. Blood pressure was also taken: the sister raised her eyebrows when she read Nomsa's. All these procedures baffled Nomsa.

A white doctor came. He examined them in turn. He said to each of them that it would still take a while, gave the ward sister some instructions, smiled at the patients, and left the ward.

They lay beside each other, within touching distance. Nomsa looked at Lucy.

"What are you looking at?" asked Lucy.

"You," answered Nomsa.

"And what is there to look at? Today, I look just like you."

"I know that. But I was wondering."

"About what?"

"You know Elias is not here yet."

"I forgot about him. True, he is not here."

"I wonder if he knows that I am here."

"What's the difference?"

"Oh Lucy, he is my husband."

"They are all alike."

"He is different."

"Yes, I know. Once I also thought that all the men in my life, those with whom I had slept, were different from one another. Sis, they are all the same, with the same things. Babies! They are ever willing to give them to you for the asking."

The ward sister appeared and took Nomsa's blood pressure again. "You are angry with your man, aren't you, Lucy?"

"I am angry with them all. I just don't know whom to hold responsible for the condition I am in. Not one of them will admit he's the father."

The ward door squeaked a little and a cleaner poked her head into the room. She asked in a loud, matriarchal voice, "Is anyone here expecting to see her husband? I have a man outside who says his wife is in here."

Lucy and the other women looked at each other, but before anybody could say a word there was a quick movement in Nomsa's bed. She jumped up off it like a frightened cat, and without bothering about her half-naked body she ran to the door. She grabbed the round handle and pulled hard. With joy in her face and anxiety in her eyes, she yanked the handle, and the door flew open and bumped with a hard thud on her protruding stomach. She winced and gave a shriek of pain. Automatically she pressed her hurt stomach. The pain was not in any way comparable with the joy of seeing Elias. She ran into his arms and began to sob like a baby.

"Oh Elias, I am so frightened. I want you to be here. Please, Elias, don't go."

"Come my woman. We are going to have our first baby. Our first child."

He held her closer, as close as a protruding stomach would allow. He whispered, "I am here now. I am sorry you had to come here without me. I had to be at work, and this is the city . . . sometimes you and I have to do things alone and without each other."

Elias's eyes welled. From the direction of the ward a nurse approached Nomsa, and encouraged her in the language of Umzinyathi, "Come now, my girl, you will be all right. There is nothing to worry about. We deliver babies here and we know our work. This is a hospital. It is here to help you. You will be very calm and contented, quite soon. You will be in no pain; you will feel very serene after everything is over."

Holding Nomsa by the elbow, the nurse walked her away from Elias, and as she helped her into bed, she advised, very tenderly, "You must not get upset like this. It is bad for both you and your baby."

Tears rolled down Nomsa's cheeks and she sobbed out to Lucy, "Are you sure you will look after me and my baby?"

"Yes, Nomsa, I will."

"A promise in the name of our ancestors?"

"Yes, a promise in the name of our ancestors," answered Lucy.

The sister in charge of the ward came in and approached Nomsa with a pleasant look on her face. "You must rest now. Come, Nomsa, I must examine you again. Let's see how things are with you. The excitement with your husband outside was not good."

She drew the curtains around the bed. Again she took Nomsa's blood pressure. This time there was no mistaking her alarm. Without examining Nomsa, she hurried to the duty room to page the doctor. She ran back to the ward to wheel Nomsa away to the delivery room.

Swiftly she made everything ready, and with more than her usual concern strapped Nomsa's legs into position. The young doctor who had smiled arrived. He was serious now.

"Have the resuscitation table brought."

"It's here. I thought—" The doctor could not hear the rest. Nomsa was screaming in pain and crying out for help and begging Elias to come to her.

"Come, my girl. Now take it easy. Just do as I tell you and all this will soon be over. Come, take a deep breath. It will be a little painful but after that you will rest. Now take a deeper breath . . . yes, that's good, push as hard as you can. Come now, do that. Your baby and you need that. Push harder. Take another deep breath and push hard." Nomsa did as she was told.

"Keep a watch on her pressure."

The sister alerted him to the reading.

"Forceps. We'll have to rush it now."

Nomsa was passive as the doctor worked.

"Oh thank God, here we are."

The baby slithered out of Nomsa's womb. Her child was born: a small but perfectly formed boy. As he emerged from her, suddenly she gasped and jerked, and began frothing at the mouth. The doctor was attending to the baby, but he noticed at once.

"Oh my God, she's fitting. Quick sister . . . "

Nomsa did not know what was happening. She had not seen her baby boy.

The team worked desperately, but they knew it was hopeless. Nomsa fell into a coma, and nothing would bring her out of it.

"Massive brain haemorrhage," said the doctor.

She was dead. Her body was still warm. She died, but she left Elias a son in his own image and of her own flesh.

Far from the delivery room, down in an untidy waiting room in the yard of the hospital Elias anxiously awaited news. Suddenly he rushed out of the room, and stopped on the pathway that led to the maternity wards. He grabbed hold of a cold iron rail and leaned against it. The rail was straight and strong, and painted a meticulous white, but it was dirtied with constant handling by all kinds of people with all kinds of hands. He clung to this piece of iron as if his life depended on it. Had he not held on, he would have fallen on the cement floor. He tried to stand up firmly, but his anxiety for Nomsa and his baby overwhelmed him.

He collected himself and began to walk towards the labour ward. The smell of detergents was strong; that of floor polish was fresh; clean linen was being taken into the different wards. From a two-bedded ward came music from a portable radio. The soft sounds of the guitar mixed with the doubtful thumpings of his own heart. With his cap in his hand, with his eyes wide open, with streaks of sweat across his temples and beads of the same smelly sweat on his forehead Elias ran towards the labour ward where he had left his wife. There was no hospital staff around at the time to stop him. He opened the door gently and peeped in. He saw that Nomsa was not on her bed. He pushed the door wide and shouted, "Where is Nomsa?"

A nurse in a soiled uniform, with her cap a little askew on her head, entered the ward. She took Elias by the elbow and said, "Come with me please." She avoided looking him in the eyes and continued, "Your baby is being washed. He is very small, but a handsome boy."

"Where is Nomsa?"

"Come with me, please. The white man wants to talk to you."

"Where is Nomsa?"

By then the nurse had quietly opened the door to the doctor's room. Sitting with his head cupped in one of his large hands and a smouldering cigarette in the other, the doctor looked up at the opening door.

"This is the husband of the last case, Doctor."

"Oh!" He sprang up and offered Elias the chair opposite him. He made an effort to speak in Zulu.

"Come and sit down. Do you smoke?"

"No. Thank you."

"Are you Nomsa's husband?"

"Yes."

"Were you married for long?"

"Less than a year." Elias rose and demanded, "Where is Nomsa? I can answer all these questions later. Now tell me, where is Nomsa?"

"She was a brave girl. Tell him, nurse."

"It happened just as the baby was born," the nurse began.

"Nomsa is dead!" shrieked Elias.

After a while the doctor left the room, signing to the nurse to follow him. Elias stared at the blank white wall. He stood motionless. He stood like that a long while: he had lost his sense of time. Eventually the doctor and the nurse came back to the room where they had left Elias alone with his loss and his agony. As soon as they appeared, Elias grabbed the doctor by the shoulders. In shock, he stood still. Elias tightened his grip and then howled, "You killed her. The nurse killed her. This hospital killed her."

The doctor tried his utmost to console him, but Elias kept sobbing, and through his sobs he repeated, "She wanted me to be with her. She wanted our baby. She was so young. Why?

Didn't you know? She wanted *our* baby. You didn't care and you don't care—"

"Please be calm. It is our duty to save lives. We don't kill people here. We save, we try to save their lives."

"Then why didn't you save my Nomsa? Why did she have to die? She was well such a short time before. Why didn't you save her?"

"We don't know for sure why she died. We will know in a few days. We will do a postmortem, and then we'll know exactly why."

The joy of his son's arrival was annulled by the agony of his wife's death. As Elias walked out of the doctor's room, his mind went back to his early days with Nomsa. His days with her in the fields of corn, in the wilds among the trees and birds, streams and rocks, all came back vividly to him. He remembered how, together, they had planted beans. As children they had tried to find out the fate of a bean. What happened to it? How did it sprout? They had tried to find out together. He remembered how they had laughed and marvelled at the simple wonders of nature in the bowels of the earth. They had carefully dug out a bean some ten days after his mother had sown it, and both of them had held it gently between their fingers. The seed had already sprouted. The stem that was pushing itself up towards the light was already strong enough to bear their human handling. The root, too, in its search for sustenance had pierced itself deep in the soil, and great care had to be taken not to injure it.

At the door, he looked back, his eyes still glistening with tears, and asked the doctor, "Where is Nomsa's body now?"

"It is still in the side ward, and soon it will be moved to the mortuary. While you are still here, it would be wise for you to identify her."

"I would like to see her before you take her away."

"Of course. I will come with you."

Silently the two men walked down the corridor to the side ward. When they were both inside the room, the doctor pulled aside a curtain and gestured to Elias to come closer. Elias was quivering, and mechanically he moved over to the bed. He stretched out his hand towards the shrouded corpse. Gently and hesitantly, he drew the shroud from the still face. Suddenly he burst into tears and, half-lying across the bed, he gathered the body into his arms. Tears rolled down his cheeks and onto Nomsa's cold face. Perhaps he believed that his cries and his agony might rouse her, at least to say goodbye to him. He cried and tried to talk to his dead Nomsa. The doctor realised that Elias was losing himself completely in grief, and put his arm firmly around the black man's shoulders. He pulled him up gently, saying, "You cannot go on like this. You will have to be brave. You have a son to care for and for the sake of your beloved wife you have to give her child strength and love. You must go to see him now. I am sure that will help you."

Elias stood up. He stood straight. Unblinkingly, though with tear-stained eyes, he stared at Nomsa's lifeless body, and looked as if he wanted to say, "You deserted me!"

Respectfully, the doctor drew the shroud across Nomsa's face and said to Elias, "Come with me."

Elias walked away with him, looking back over his shoulder. Within seconds they were in the nursery, where they found the son who had just lost his mother. Elias tried to feel the baby's cheek with the tips of his rough fingers. The child moved.

"My son. Our son. If only your mother could share you with me!"

CHAPTER 12

Mary and Peter Evenmore drove into the hospital grounds and parked in the area reserved for hospital staff. They were not questioned: they had come in by car, and they were not black. They walked across the tar and nodded to hospital orderlies who stood almost to attention to greet them. Perhaps the jingling of coins was audible to them. But they got none. Following the arrows, husband and wife made their way towards the maternity section. Lucy's child had been stillborn. They had come to visit her, and to see Nomsa's baby. They half expected Elias to be there. They had last seen him on the day Nomsa died.

They followed the covered walkways past the children's ward. It looked like the compound where Elias lived. From inside stared and howled disease's helpless harvest. These were black children, in a black hospital. Mary instinctively grabbed her husband's arm as they saw through the open doors the endless rows of sick children, most of them mere bones and skin with discoloured hair, though some looked bloated. All these little patients suffered from kwashiorkor. Then they passed another ward where the children were yellow with jaundice. Some parents were hovering around them. All Mary saw was disease and pain. Peter just walked on. It was only when his wife stopped suddenly that he observed the hollow, blank stare in her eyes, reflecting the hollow, blank, pathetic stares of the children.

Mary wondered aloud, "How many of these children will survive?"

Without answering, Peter urged, "Come on."

They found Lucy quite easily in the mothers' ward. Elias was standing beside her bed. At her breast a baby was suckling. Mother's milk, pure and white, was dripping down the baby's chin. Lucy's breasts hung naked, full of milk. Lucy knew the pain of childbirth and the agony of losing her baby. Now she was experiencing the joyful, prickling sensations of breast-feeding a child. She was marvelling at the dependence of another life on her own. She turned a little and adjusted the position of the contented child.

"Hallo, Lucy!" Mary said in an embarrassed tone.

"Good morning, ma'am. Good morning, baas," she answered. She looked pale, sad, run-down, but in her eyes there was a certain glow.

"We are sorry. We heard." said Mary from a distance.

Elias and Lucy had their eyes fixed on the child.

"Nomsa was a very good girl." With these words Peter went up to Elias and in a comforting way embraced his late maid's husband. In the meantime Mary had approached Lucy, who had begun to cry. Mary stood motionless. "Be brave, be brave, Lucy."

Lucy wiped her tears and said indistinctly, "I will try to, ma'am. I will try to."

"Is this Nomsa's baby at your breast?"

"Yes, ma'am."

Mary turned to Elias. "You must be very proud of your son?"

"Yes ma'am," was all that Elias could venture.

"He looks so much like you," commented Mary.

"And like Nomsa, too," Elias said.

"Yes, of course, he does have Nomsa's lips and her nose. Don't you think so, Peter?"

Peter nodded in the full knowledge that he had not noticed Nomsa's lips or her nose. Luckily for him, there was an interruption: a hospital orderly, accompanied by a staff nurse, approached Lucy's bed and addressed himself to Elias:

"You are wanted by the boss in his office."

"Who?" asked Peter Evenmore.

"Mr Elias Mzimande," said the nurse.

"Oh."

Looking at Peter with frightened eyes, Elias asked, "Will you come with me, baas? They will be careful in what they say to me if you are there, won't they baas?"

"Sit down Elias," said the white-coated, cigar-smoking, elderly superintendent.

Looking up, he noticed Peter. "May I ask who you are?"

"My name is Peter Evenmore." Peter stretched out his right hand.

"I am Dr Blake."

They shook hands.

"Please sit down."

Peter began, "Elias wanted me to accompany him here. I hope you do not mind."

"No no, you're welcome." Dr Blake looked at Elias, and squarely he put his points: "Elias, I want you to know that we are very sorry for what has happened to you. It is two days now since your wife died."

Aside to Peter, the doctor said, "Eclampsia. It happens. Occasionally, there is nothing anyone can do."

The doctor spoke again to Elias: "I was wondering whether you wish to have her body removed from the hospital for burial, or you could, if you agree, have her left here. We are a teaching hospital and her body could be used for research purposes. This would release you from a great deal of expense and . . . bother."

"I will take my wife with me, Doctor."

"Please sit down, Elias. I didn't mean to hurt you."

Elias ignored the doctor's apologies and turned his face away. He didn't speak. He looked at Peter in anger and help-lessness. Peter responded: "Don't worry. It's all right, Elias. We will take Nomsa."

"Where to, baas?"

"Wherever you want to take her."

"To Umzinyathi, to Umzinyathi."

They rose together. Before they could reach the door Dr Blake came round rapidly from behind his desk and barred their way.

"How are you involved in this case, Mr Evenmore?"

"Just like the rest of us, Doctor. Only this time with a little difference."

"What do you mean?"

"Just that, Doctor. Like the rest of us in this country. Don't we need these people? I needed Nomsa's services during her lifetime—she worked for me. All of us depend on them, don't we, Doctor?"

"I see what you mean."

"I am glad for you. Please have the formalities completed as soon as you can, so that we can remove Nomsa's body to a funeral parlour."

"Can the husband afford that?"

"Please have the formalities completed," Peter commanded coldly, and he walked away with Elias to the ward where Lucy and Nomsa's child were huddled together. Mary was standing there, watching.

Visiting time was over, and an electric bell rang all over the hospital. This was the polite signal to visitors to leave. Elias looked around him in anguish and doubt. He gave Lucy a long, parting look, thankful for her full breasts, at one of which his own flesh and blood was sucking. He started to walk away. When Lucy called his name he stopped abruptly, and slowly turned back towards her.

"Please come here," she asked quietly.

He went nearer, and she continued, "I am sorry for you and for your baby. But please be brave and face this world courageously. What's happened has happened. We cannot undo it, can we?"

Elias nodded and before his lips could begin to lose their sombre expression in violent quivering, Lucy patted his hands and comforted him with the words: "Nomsa loved you very much and she loved you well."

Lucy watched Elias's hunched back disappear into the corridor as the door swung closed, and she heaved slightly.

Mary and Peter had been waiting for Elias outside, and the three of them walked in silence towards the car. For a long time they were quiet, and then Peter asked in a matter-of-fact tone, "Elias, have you notified your people about Nomsa?"

"They should know by now. Yesterday I sent a message with a distant relative of Nomsa's."

"Good. I think you should leave for Umzinyathi immediately."

"But what about my baby and Nomsa?"

"Oh, I will take care of things. A permit will be required to take Nomsa from here to Umzinyathi. I have connections here. I will do what is required."

In subdued silence they drove away from the hospital. They had been on the road for some five minutes when Elias asked, "Where are we going?"

"To the undertakers', the people who carry and bury the dead," answered Peter. "There we will have to make all the arrangements to have Nomsa's body fetched, and instruct them when to take her to Umzinyathi. You will have to sign the forms. Will your parents and Nomsa's parents agree with our arrangements?"

"They must know about all this. In fact they must decide."

"I know that. But will they agree with our arrangements?"

"They must be asked."

"Of course they should be asked. But we are here and they are in Umzinyathi."

"Do you think we can make all the arrangements now, without them?" Elias sounded unsure.

"Will it be all right with your people if the funeral takes place on Saturday? It gives us all enough time."

"I think so."

"Then let us go in and instruct these people here to bring Nomsa's body from the hospital mortuary. This is the first thing. After keeping her here they will take her to Umzinyathi on the agreed day and at a fixed time. Will that be all right?"

Elias nodded.

Elias and Peter got out of the car and walked up the steps to the undertakers' offices. The scent of fresh flowers, mingled with the perfume worn by the receptionist and the typists in the clean, airy room, caught the two men in the face as they came in through the swivel door. At the desk stood a smiling young girl who ignored Elias and enquired of Peter, "Can I help you, sir?"

CHAPTER 13

The squeaking brakes of the heavily laden diesel-powered bus announced a halt. Passengers began to alight. Some of them had parcels in their hands, while others had suitcases or other baggage on their heads. Elias, the last to get out, was empty-handed. The bus moved on. He stood there alone. Long after all the other passengers had walked away, he was still standing there. It was not long since he had been the first to set off from the bus stop, and then not walking, but running. He took a few deep breaths as if he consciously needed them, and forced himself to move. He felt himself breathing. He swallowed his saliva, which was choking him. His drooping head felt heavy, and it was an effort to look around. In this dejection he saw the setting sun moving farther and farther away from him. He kicked a little pebble here, and a stone there. He realised that the shadow of the distant hill was already long. Instinctively he increased his pace to a half-run. But this time, it was not a real run; this time he was not breathless with anticipation; this time he did not gasp in greedy passion, and he did not sing songs to herald his arrival.

He came to the top of the little hill from where he could see in the distance the scattered groups of huts. In a way, for him, this was a homecoming, but he bit his right thumb in the left corner of his mouth, wrapped his left arm across his chest and pressed it hard against himself. His vision had blurred: his eyes were full of tears. From near and far he heard the moans of the wind. The lamentations of cattle from the nearby villages echoed around him as the animals were taken in for the night. Elias mourned his own fate. His sorrow was shared with no one.

Painfully, he walked down the hill, oblivious to all things around him. Even though it was growing darker, he did not quicken his pace. He was in no hurry. He passed, but did not see, the blooming yellows of the sunflowers that stood in the midst of the leaf-shedding, yellowish syringas. He passed them all but he saw none. Then abruptly, as if he had just woken up, he stood, all alive, on the bank of the flowing Umzinyathi. It was almost dark. But Elias looked around him as if he were seeking something or someone. He rolled his pants up to the knees and slipped out of his shoes. Holding them in one hand, he plunged into the water. In midstream, he stopped. The chilly, biting water did not disturb him. He flung his shoes onto the opposite bank and there, in the semi-darkness, he stood.

All of a sudden, he started to take up handsful of the Umzinyathi to his face. He licked the water and kissed it at the same time. He splashed his face with it. He grabbed handful after handful, and began to sprinkle the water all over himself, as if it were a holy gift from God, with a sacred message and a sacred, secret hope. He thought of Nomsa's wet, innocent body that was bathed in this very Umzinyathi. He remembered her joyful laughs; in this life-giving water she had first given him her body.

Little lights were already burning in and around the villages of Umzinyathi. He came out of the river and continued his journey home. On the distant hill he saw a little twinkle. Then he turned back to look at the river through the darkness. In that moment he remembered Nomsa's eyes; he remembered her holding herself up against his chest for protection and love; he remembered her trembling in fear and in ecstasy, and how she had surrendered herself to love and passion. Reluctantly, he moved away from the river.

"Yes, my son! Come! We have been waiting for you." His father's words came from the dark courtyard. Elias saw his mother and his father through the darkness.

"Mother, I am finished," he cried.

"Be brave, my son," she consoled.

In moments all the household had come out into the dark yard. Simultaneously, they began to ululate. The grief that had been contained in the family suddenly found its way out in the cries of all. Elias stood motionless, but his heart was bursting with the pain of Nomsa's death. Then his father came to him and, holding him around the shoulders, led him away.

Elias and his father and mother and his brothers and sisters and uncles and aunts and cousins and nephews, all gathered this time in common grief, sat together deep into the night. In their customary way, they discussed what they were going to do next. But Nomsa's people were not present, and they agreed to make no decisions until their arrival in the morning.

The morning came. In his exhaustion Elias awoke later than the others in the family. When he did wake from his short sleep he heard murmurs outside his hut. The neighbours had gathered there. Slowly he rose and walked out to meet them. They embraced him in turn and said very little. What they had to say was expressed by their sombre, lost looks. The local black priest, the umfundisi, had also come. He was in serious discussion with Elias when Nomsa's father and her mother arrived. Then the wailing started again. It was the first time death had joined these two households together. Elias, his head bent, went up to his father-in-law and in a broken voice he whispered, "Father, I am guilty."

"No, my son. This is not your fault. It is the will of our ancestors. She loved you dearly and now she has joined our ancestors. They will look after her."

Father-in-law and son-in-law held each other close, and in this embrace, Gumede asked, "How is your son?"

"He looks so much like Nomsa."

"Is he well?"

"Yes, Father."

Mzimande had joined them. Gumede continued, "Is your friend, the white man, with you in your plight?"

"Yes, Father."

"Is the baby with him and his wife?"

"No, the baby is still in the hospital."

"I see. Now we must discuss the funeral."

"Yes, Father. You see, you see . . . I hope it is all right with everybody in the family. Peter will be coming with Nomsa's body on Saturday at about ten in the morning. We have decided to have the funeral on Saturday. Is it all right with all of you?"

The two elders looked at each other in astonishment. These things were not done like this. But they knew that many things, in fact all things, had changed and were continuing to change in their daily lives.

"I think so, my son," was his father-in-law's answer. Then, turning to Mzimande, Gumede asked, "Is there any objection from your side, my brother?"

"No, I don't see anything wrong with the arrangement. It leaves us enough time to make our own preparations here."

"Yes, my brother. You will now have to arrange Nomsa's funeral as we once arranged her marriage. It is strange. The ways of this world are strange, aren't they?"

After a little pause and a gulp of saliva he said, "Today we are with death in our house. Together we have to bid farewell and together we will welcome the son in our house. Come, my brother, let us go."

Waiting to Live

. . .

As usual in such circumstances, neighbours and relatives and friends from distant places volunteered to dig the grave. They walked to the chosen spot in silence, carrying their picks and shovels. These had been introduced to Umzinyathi long ago and were valued tools there. Other members of the community were buried in that place. There were no agreements, no undertakings among the people for the creation of this graveyard. Their common need had led them to a common practice, and they buried their dead with all dignity, in unity and interdependence. Nomsa would naturally be buried there. Nobody asked questions and nobody was in any doubt. Crosses on little mounds of stones and sand, with patches of grass here and there, showed clearly that this was the garden of the dead. In the serenity of the dead, quietness reigned in the graveyard.

Up on the hill stood the gravediggers with their common purpose. After a while Elias arrived, alone. Quietly the others turned and looked at him. Elias came closer. The pick he was carrying swayed alongside his tired legs. He walked into the group and said, unexpectedly, "I had planned a home for my wife and me. Now my friends and I have come here to dig a grave for her . . ."

As he spoke a sudden flash of lightning and a peal of thunder shook them all. They stood still. Elias, leaning on the tip of the handle of the pick, looked into the space, the empty space, in front of him. In the silence all around him, the thunder and the lightning had passed. His mind's ears heard the thunderous song of love he had once shared with Nomsa. The song was mixed with the pain of the gravedigging. He heard it and he wept.

His face was dripping with sweat and tears. His hands were clammy. He lifted his head and turned to his fellow gravediggers. He whispered through a sad smile, "Come, let us dig."

. . .

On the Saturday morning, with all the necessary arrangements attended to by Peter Evenmore, Nomsa was on her way,
home-coming. The corpse arrived at last. With all their native
ceremony and tenderness the people of this South African
village drew Nomsa's coffin out of the hearse and placed it on
a pedestal. She lay there, in death, and her own Elias wept at
her cold, outstretched feet. The incantations of the priest had
begun. Elias, his father, his in-laws and many others of their
two families had robed themselves in black. Those who could
not afford the full black apparel had little bands of black on
their sleeves. They wore their sorrow and showed it. In the
presence of death they were solemn, but the sadness of losing
their Nomsa, black bands or no bands, robes or no robes, was
assuaged because they had lost her to their ancestors. Seated
around the raised coffin, some prayed. Others just looked about
them, not believing that Nomsa, of all of them, had had to die.

Some of the elders in the community had already begun the
task of preparing the food. Earlier in the morning two goats
and an ox were led into the yard of the Mzimande household.
They were there to be slaughtered. The bowels of the animals
were needed for the customary funeral ritual. And then the
people who had come from near and far would have to be fed.
Huge three-legged pots were filled with crushed mealies.
These were boiling from the early hours of the morning. It
took a lot of time and a lot of water to make this maize dish
edible. Those who were not utterly grief-stricken were busy
making dumplings to be served with the meat. Elias, wrapped
in a warm blanket over his black clothes, sat silent between the
dead body of his Nomsa and the makeshift kitchen.

The umfundisi had suggested in his imperious way that
because the church building was not in a convenient and easily
accessible place, the funeral service should be held at the Mzimande home. The yard was big and the people were already
there. Having obtained agreement, he suddenly gave forth a

command, and Elias's attention was jolted back to the proceedings. "Let us pray!" said the priest.

Everybody rose. Nomsa was surrounded by mourners. The priest opened the Zulu translation of the Bible and, passing his lips over it in a light kiss, said, "What shall we say then?"

He looked about him. "Shall we continue in sin? Shall we continue to sin so that grace may abound? God forbid! We who died to sin, how shall we any longer live therein? Or, are ye ignorant that all we who were baptised into Christ Jesus, were baptised into his death? We were buried, therefore, with him through baptism into death: that as Christ was raised from the dead through the glory of the Father, so we also might walk in newness of life."

Over by the fires, where the crushed mealies were boiling, four young girls removed from their heads the round earthenware vessels they had filled at the river. One by one they handed them to the older women in charge, who added water to the pots, stirring in salt from a cloth bag.

"For if we have become united with him by the likeness of his death, so shall we be also by the likeness of his resurrection; knowing this, that we were crucified with him, that the body of sin might be done away with, so we should no longer be in bondage to sin; for he that hath died is justified from sin."

A delicious aroma wafted over the congregation from the fat-bellied pots in which the dumplings were rising to the surface.

"Even so reckon ye also yourselves to be dead unto sin, but alive unto God in Jesus Christ—"

Peter and Mary, who were seated together, looked uncomfortably at each other. They turned to Elias, but he did not catch their gaze. The priest in the meantime had uttered many words of praise to the Lord; he was about to start the hymn "Nearer, my God, to Thee, nearer to Thee" when there was a shuffle of feet at the back of the crowd. Mr Mzimande was being called away by some of the village folk to check on the quantity of goats' intestines necessary for the washing of the gravediggers' hands. The umfundisi had begun the hymn and was leading it loudly in his baritone voice. The chorus of voices joined in. Solemnity reigned in the front yard, but at the back where the cooking was being done all was bustle and activity. Mzimande walked into clouds of smoke. An elder who was supervising the preparations approached him.

"We are about ready with the food for the feast."

"That's good."

"We think you should hurry the funeral. The weather looks very threatening."

"All right, then. I will go and tell the umfundisi."

"Yes, I think you should do that. They still do not understand our ways."

Mzimande returned to the hymn-singing.

As soon as that hymn was over, Mzimande rose from his seat and approached the priest. He whispered to him, "Everything is ready at the back and I am asked to proceed with the burial."

Wondering whether the priest would feel his authority had been usurped, he yet ventured to say, "We are ready."

The priest listened, and then, without answering Mzimande, he pronounced, "We will now proceed with the last rites of our dear Nomsa. Please come up and let's do ourselves honour by shouldering, for the last time, one so dear to us."

Elias had stood lost all the while, but the priest's words shocked him into the realisation that these were going to be the last moments left to him with his wife. He walked up first to the coffin. Standing beside it and leaning shakily over Nomsa's body, he appeared as weak as a child. Slowly he lifted his right arm; he hesitated a moment, then he tenderly caressed Nomsa's lifeless, innocent face. Tears ran down his rough cheeks and splashed onto Nomsa's face. Gently, he wiped them from her face with his bare hands, and in his quiet way placed a little flower on her forehead. With equal gentleness, but with great reluctance, he lifted the lid of the coffin from a stool next to the box, and placed it in position.

When he had closed the coffin he stood there quietly for a few seconds and then he looked around. He saw that everybody was watching him. Softly he walked to the front of the coffin. There he waited for his friends and relatives. Eight men, including Elias, lifted the coffin onto their shoulders and began to walk towards the newly dug grave. The graveyard was not far away. Yet the folk of Umzinyathi took turns at carrying the coffin. Peter too had his opportunity.

They lowered the coffin into the grave. Elias came forward. Holding a spade in his hand, he collected the first mound of earth and slowly dropped it into the grave. He did not have the courage to drop it on the coffin. Just as these last rites were being performed for Nomsa, it started to rain. And it rained as if it were never going to stop.

Everything was wet and the ground was muddy. The trees swayed in the strong wind, and the swallows dived to and fro. Everywhere, life asserted itself. The plants and the grass sucked in the rain for their own life and regeneration.

It was raining in Durban too. And in the hospital it had suddenly grown cold. The sick were being tucked in and made more comfortable. For the babies, the newly born, it was feeding time. Warmly wrapped, Nomsa's son arrived in the ward in the arms of a nurse, who hesitated a moment at the door, then walked over to Lucy and handed her the baby. Lucy took him and brought his face to her lips. As she kissed him, the nurse said, "It's Nomsa's funeral today."

Lucy lifted her head and looked enquiringly at the nurse, who went on, "I think the ceremony should be over by now."

Lucy stared at her and said nothing. Her mind went back to the days she and Nomsa had spent together. Her reverie was interrupted by a small cry from the hungry child. Lucy raised him to her breast. She looked at Nomsa's baby through glistening eyes. He wriggled a little. Then for no apparent reason he started howling and screaming. Lucy was baffled. He kept on screaming. What he sensed and why he cried and cried, she could not guess. Lucy tried, gently and patiently, to comfort the boy. He has just lost his mother, she kept telling herself. Somehow he knows. As soon as his cries showed signs of subsiding, she put him back to her breast and led the nipple into his mouth. The baby began to suck.

In Umzinyathi, after the burial, the people had returned to Elias's home. Here, some of them washed their hands with the intestines of the slaughtered animals. All of them, friends, relatives and neighbours, were eating chunks of meat with dumplings and samp. Though there was sadness and solemnity still hovering in the atmosphere, and the air was heavy with rain and cold, the food that had been prepared had to be eaten, and everyone ate. The people left after they had eaten to follow their different paths home in the mud and rain. Some of the men covered their heads with their coats, and the women protected theirs with their shawls. But most, unprepared for this weather, just walked away into the rain and the slippery mud. Peter and Mary drove off to Durban.

A week passed. Supported by his people, Elias in some small way had worked himself out of his pain and begun to help with the domestic chores. All of them in that household still wore the signs of mourning. One late afternoon, just before dusk, the Mzimande family were sitting around a dying fire in their front yard, talking. Pieces of forest wood, which until recently had been live and identifiable, smouldered and darkened in the fire. Much of it had already burned to cinders and turned to ashes. Elias took a half-burnt stick of wood and stoked the fire, which with that small provocation burst into little flames. Those nearest the fire felt the heat of the flames and withdrew a short distance. Old man Mzimande asked, "Elias, what about your son?"

"Yes, Father."

"He is the son of this house, you know."

"I know, Father."

"When are you going to bring him to us?"

"I don't know, Father."

The older man raised his authoritarian voice. "He is almost two weeks old. Go and bring him here. We'll want the son of our house with us."

Elias looked into his father's eyes, in the light of the half-dead fire, and wondered whether the old man was going to lose his temper.

"You see," Elias hesitated a moment, but mustered the courage to say, "he has to be looked after and fed. There is nobody here who would be able to do that. At the hospital they have all the modern foods and modern methods of feeding. They are good."

"Who do you think looked after you and fed you? The hospital didn't do that. Or do you think you didn't need looking after and feeding?"

"No, it's not that, Father."

"Then what is it?"

"You see the child is still in hospital."

"Well, go and get him out of there and bring him here."

"I think it better for him to get stronger there."

"How long will that take? Why can't he get stronger here? Is he sick? Is there something wrong with him?"

"No, but these doctors and nurses, and their food and their medicines, are not only different: they are better than what we have. When the time is right, my son will be immunised against many diseases that our children here suffer from."

"What food are you talking about? What does your boy eat there that we cannot provide here?"

"I have just told you, Father. They are different, and they are good. They save lives."

"If they are so good, why didn't they save your wife's life?"

Elias sulked; he was shocked by the question. His father didn't want to hurt him but he hadn't hesitated to make his point. Mzimande continued, "We do have our troubles here, but you must not deceive yourself and imagine they do not have troubles in the city."

"I know, Father, but I want my son to grow up in Durban. I think of the schools he can go to, the clothes he can wear, the new man he can become. I don't want him to grow up like I did. Father, I don't want to hurt you, but he must never be like me. Let us allow him to grow up there, in Durban, and let us give him a chance to be a man of this world and not merely a man from—and only for—Umzinyathi. There, in Durban, is the key to our growth. Don't feel hurt. Please, please don't feel hurt; let us not allow him to be like you and me."

"You don't want to bring him here?"

"No, Father. Try to understand."

"Understand what? That you don't have a home in Durban and you want to keep with you a little child? Understand that he cannot live with us, his people? Understand that you yourself do not know what is going to become of him? Understand that you have a world full of dreams for your son, even when he is just a baby?"

"It is not like that. I have just pleaded that we give him a chance in life that neither you nor I had."

"How are you going to do that when he is still a child?"

Mzimande rose. His full height and his full weight, emphasised by his clothes, appeared overwhelming to the seated Elias. Standing over his son old man Mzimande said, "He is still a baby. I as father of this house and your mother as mother of this house should know better than to allow you to make a fool of yourself. Your baby needs to be cared for; he needs a mother more than he needs Durban. He needs us now more than he will ever need us again. Don't you know that? Now, you go to Durban and bring your child to us, do you understand?"

"Yes, Father."

The old man walked away to his hut. He knew from his own experience and the experience of his ancestors that one did not have to go far afield in search of the past. It was all there in abundance in their small world of Umzinyathi. But with the adoption of new ideas and new faiths, the Mzimandes were demonstrating that they could not live in isolation: that would mean, for his society, backwardness and decay. Mzimande knew that he and his kind would have to play a part in the development of the new interdependence. But he was not willing to tear everything down in Umzinyathi. He was willing to seek and learn, but not to abandon his own roots and his own distinct anchorage. Old man Mzimande did not want to be an interloper: he wanted to be an equal and a comrade in the creation of the new.

Elias got up and stood over the burnt-out fire. He kicked a few embers to check whether there was any life left in them. He saw none, and began walking away to his hut. His mind was in turmoil.

If I bring my son here, he thought, I may not be able to control his life. Everything and everybody in Umzinyathi will control it. But my father is right. Where the hell will I keep him? Where the devil will I get the time to care for him? Here, there are my people. Here, they have not only the time to care for him—they have all the affection to give to him. Here, my child would have not only my people but also Nomsa's people. My child belongs to both these families.

In the darkness he entered his hut. In the darkness his mind reached out to his father and his mother, the bonds of blood and flesh from which he was trying so hard to tear himself away. He felt sorry for himself, because those to whom he was tied did not feel the way he felt. In the dark shadows of the night he already felt his distance from his people. Suddenly he stopped, in the middle of the hut. With very little concentration he could hear, coming from the distant hills, the weird, melancholy, tremulous beauty of the Umzinyathi chants. The voices mingled with the soft strings of a guitar, sometimes drowned, sometimes deepened by the sweet, sonorous sounds of a trombone. The country people had learned to play these foreign instruments. He felt more and more separate from his people as the music became more distinct. Then he ceased to listen, and merely thought, I will wait and see.

He lay down and fell asleep.

CHAPTER 14

The bus from Umzinyathi had reached Durban in the early hours of the morning. It was not yet dawn. The clouds hung low and it was threatening to rain. Mist was everywhere. Smoke from the billowing chimneys of the factories in and around Durban merged with the mist. In many places the smoke appeared to form its own dark clouds, which hung heavily in the still air.

Elias Mzimande walked with long strides towards the Evenmores' house. It was not very far from where he had got off the bus. He wanted to go to the hospital, but chose to go first to the Evenmores'. He remembered the ease with which he had gained entry to the hospital when he went with a white man. He did not have to wait until visiting hours and he avoided the long queues. In any case it was too early in the morning for him to appear at the hospital. He walked faster, and before the sun had risen he was standing in front of the Evenmores' gate. He wondered what to do. Only a few weeks before, he had not had to think for a second about what he would do. This time, he did not go round by the back yard where the khaya was, but instead entered the garden, which was in full bloom. He walked up the tarred pathway. All round the house there was silence. Suddenly, with pressure on the doorbell, he disturbed the peace. The piercing ring inside the house woke everyone. Peter Evenmore came rushing to the door in his pyjamas. Without hesitation he unlocked it and flung it open.

"Elias!"

"Yes baas."

"When did you come back?"

"This morning."

"Don't just stand there. Come in. Mary, Elias is back!"

Gladness radiated from Mary's face, too. She had put on a dressing gown and come into the lounge.

"Oh Elias, I am so glad to see you," she said softly.

Elias just smiled and looked away. Sensing his discomfort, Mary said, "Now listen. You two sit here while I make breakfast with Lucy."

Elias was shocked at the sound of Lucy's name. He wondered about his son, about his feeding and where he was.

Peter went to have a quick wash and get dressed.

Left alone, Elias crossed the room to the window, drew back the curtains and looked out into the morning. He almost choked: the garden tap was running, filling a bucket. Lucy walked up to the tap and turned it off. He saw her lift the bucket and walk away. I should help her, he thought. A thousand and one other thoughts rushed into his mind. He went out of the house by the front door, through the side garden to the khaya. There he stood and for many moments he did not stir. From outside he could see the few belongings that he recognized as Nomsa's. Elias swallowed hard. His mouth was dry. He wanted to cry.

From behind him Lucy said, "Elias."

"Yes, Lucy."

"They didn't allow me to bring the baby."

"I see."

"I fought with them. But they said I couldn't."

"Oh!"

"Elias, you are all right, aren't you?"

"I am, Lucy. But how are you feeling?"

"I am fine. But I miss your baby. I have got so used to breast-feeding him. And I've still got lots of milk. I have to keep pressing it out."

"Was he well when you left the hospital?"

"Yes, he was. He is a fine strong little fellow. I wonder if you were as greedy as he is. You know what I mean, when you were his size?"

"I don't know. You must ask my mother."

"Elias, look at me!"

He turned and looked her full in the face. A face smitten with pain and sorrow at the loss of her own child, and of her friend Nomsa; a face reflecting a kind of tenderness.

Quietly but firmly, she said, "Elias, I want to take care of your baby as if he were my own."

"But it is not fair to you—"

"What is not fair? To let me give a baby what I can and want to give, is that not fair?"

"It's not that, you see . . . your life . . . "

"I know I am not a woman like your Nomsa. I am openly a whore, aren't I? Isn't it that, Elias? I am cheap in your eyes? I am so cheap I cannot be a mother? I am vulgar and I am available to any man who is willing to pay for a few hours of fun. Isn't that so?"

"Don't be so hard on yourself, Lucy. You are—"

"All right, Elias, I know I don't deserve such pleasures in life. I am wrong to want such pleasure. It is the preserve of all those who don't live like I have lived. But Elias, I have been happiest when I was feeding Nomsa's child, your child."

She walked away, and was about to go into the house when she retraced her steps and came back to him with the words, "But you must do what is best for you and best for your son."

She hurried across to the Evenmores' kitchen, where Mary was busy with the breakfast preparations. She closed the door

145

behind her and leaned against it, wondering whether she would be given the opportunity she yearned for.

With the load of Lucy's suggestion resting heavily on his mind, Elias walked back from the khaya to the house. Mary and Peter were already at the breakfast table. As soon as Elias appeared, Peter called, "Elias, come and join us."

"No, thank you. I will just have some coffee."

He was standing beside the table where the Evenmores were sitting. Mary gave him a cup of coffee. Still standing, he sipped the coffee and with every sip he thought of Lucy's offer. The coffee went down with difficulty, but he finished it, and as he put the cup down he asked, "Baas, may I ask you for another favour? You have done so many favours for Nomsa and me already that I feel very guilty asking you for more."

"What is it, Elias?"

"I would very much like to go to the hospital to see my son."

"That is no problem. We will go together."

"Can we go this morning? Can we go *now?*"

"Yes, as soon as I have finished breakfast."

As they were leaving, Mary ran after them with a carrier in her hand. "Wait," she called, "here are a shawl and some little things that are too small for Pam. When you take your baby home, he'll need them."

All formalities, including security, were waived at the hospital. Elias was in the company of a white man. Together they entered the building. Peter Evenmore explained that he had to be at work in an hour, and that matters should be expedited to enable him and his friend Elias to fetch Elias's baby. The black clerk at the reception desk said, "Yes sir!" Shuffling his files, he assured Peter, "That will be no problem." He wrote something on a piece of paper and handed it to him. "Here, sir, take this note and tell the staff nurse on duty that you and your friend are allowed in."

It was not hospital visiting time. A minute or two later, the staff nurse in the nursery received the two privileged visitors. Elias approached the cot in which his son was sleeping. He stood gazing at his child for a moment, and then he bent to pick him up. The child squirmed a little but he had begun to like the touch of human hands. Elias brought his son closer to his face and kissed him tenderly. He tickled the baby's nose with his own. He was talking silently to his child: I will look after you my love. You are a gift to me from my Nomsa. He held his son close to his face.

Peter was watching Elias. His heart bled with sorrow and pity for the young man and the little baby. Elias returned to the thought of what Lucy had said that morning. Her pleadings, and her self-contempt, reverberated in his ears.

He turned to Peter and asked, "Baas, can we take my baby away?"

"Yes. But where to?"

"I think I know where to."

"Back to Umzinyathi, I hope."

"No sir, not there."

"Then where to?"

"This morning Lucy offered to be mother to my son."

Peter gasped.

"Madam and you won't mind if Lucy has my son with her? At least, with him so near, I will be able to see him often."

"I see no problem. But can Lucy manage?"

"She begged me this morning."

Peter was at a loss for words. He wondered whether Elias had understood the ramifications of such an arrangement. He was unaware of the exchange Elias had had with his own father concerning the baby. Here in Durban there was no fatherly authority over Elias. Here there was just a decision being made by a father on the destiny of his son. Having tasted the fruits of imitation, Elias in his enthusiasm for the new world was ready to hurt his aging father by ignoring the traditions that had held for generations. On alien foundations he was ready and willing to build his own home. With foreign products he was going to garnish its shelves.

Elias thought: Here is the opportunity I wanted for my son. If my ancestors and my own Nomsa didn't will it, why would Lucy have offered mother-love to my child? I will not go back to Umzinyathi. I will do what Lucy did years ago. I will remain here in this city, and give to my son all that I did not have for myself. I will not allow my son to be dragged back to Umzinyathi.

Peter paid Nomsa's hospital bill. The baby was changed into his hand-me-down clothes and bundled into a little parcel by one of the nurses. She handed Elias his son, and while still hovering over the child's face, she said: "I hope God will look after him and I wish you both the best in the world."

"Thank you."

Elias held his son in his arms. He looked into the baby's face and smiled at him. Peter was back from the accounts department and had joined them in the nursery. Elias cuddled the child to his chest.

They made for the car. Elias held his son like an experienced father. In his free hand were items the hospital had provided: a filled feeding bottle and some disposable nappies.

Peter drove into his driveway. He was not sure he had been right in doing what Elias wished. Mary and Lucy were in the house. The two men got out of the car, Elias carrying his son. Peter went to the front door, and Elias towards the khaya. As he passed the kitchen window he called to Lucy, who came running out of the house. Mary was amazed, but before she could make a move Peter beckoned to her.

Together they walked out of the house through the back door. They stood on the stoep and watched, and from there Peter heard: "I accept your offer."

"Oh, Elias, I am so happy for myself and for the boy. I will always be grateful to you."

"Lucy," he extended his arms, "take my son, Themba, and from this day on care for him and love him as if he were your own. I will never tell him who his real mother was. You are going to be his mother. I will see to it that you and he will never be in want of anything. To provide will be my pleasure and my responsibility."

"Themba!" Lucy opened her arms. The name meant trust and hope. Suddenly she was holding the little child so tightly that she forgot all else about her. She kissed him and caressed his tender face; she kissed his eyes and snuggled his face against her own. For those moments, she had forgotten that Elias was there, and that Mary and Peter were watching.

"What was he telling her?" Mary whispered. Peter translated from the Zulu.

CHAPTER 15

Some six or seven months after his son's birth, Elias came to the Evenmores' late one Saturday afternoon. He came regularly, every weekend he was free. He paid for his son's keep. He had not learned what he should buy for his baby, but he knew he had to provide for his needs. He was by then accustomed to leaving this intricate task to female hands. He also knew that he wanted to visit his son as regularly as possible. This he did. This Saturday afternoon was somehow different. He felt it in the air. He was very anxious and in a way he was frightened. He knocked at Lucy's door. Inside the khaya Lucy was seated with little Themba on her lap. She was singing to him and he was listening happily. Disturbed by the knock, she called out, "Who's there?"

"Me, Elias."

"Come in."

Elias opened the door and stood on the threshold. He looked at the child, his child, on Lucy's lap. There was joy on his face and there was joy on the little child's face. Elias stood gazing at his son. Then his eyes moved on to Lucy. She was looking contented, even happy. He wondered whether she was still visited by her boyfriends. She had not mentioned this and he had not dared to ask. Why he was afraid to ask he did not know. He had taken Lucy for granted the moment he had handed her his baby. Today he stopped in the doorway and was full of thought. Lucy glanced at him.

"And what so preoccupies Elias this afternoon?"

"Eh?" Elias tried to say something but he could find no words. When he was a little more composed, he asked, "And how is my precious little boy today?"

The child seemed to recognise his father's voice. He made gestures of joy and opened his mouth, still wet with Lucy's milk. Deftly, Lucy wiped the wetness away and handed the baby to his father. Elias came forward to take his son. He bent his head and stretched out his arms. As he received his child from Lucy, Elias's arm fell against hers. For a few moments their arms were touching. The warmth of one warmed the other. They searched each other's eyes. With the baby still between them Elias leaned closer to Lucy and kissed her gently on the lips. Lucy did not mind. She kissed him back. She did not resist, and she ran the fingers of her left hand over his woolly hair. His hair was damp and a little untidy.

There was a sweet, soapy scent in the khaya. Elias asked, "Are you wearing a perfume? It smells so good."

"No, Elias, it is not a perfume that I am wearing."

"The place smells nice."

"I have just given this little brat of yours a bath. The missus spared him some of her own shampoo. And she gave me some baby oil. It is so smooth and it makes his skin so soft. These things are so good—but I think they are very expensive."

"If you say these things are good for the baby then I will make sure that you have them. You can ask the missus to buy them and I will be able to pay her at the end of the week when I get my wages."

"Well, I have already given her the money to buy some, and she said she would get them for me on Monday."

"Lucy, you shouldn't have done that. This boy is my responsibility."

"From today on, he is our responsibility."
Elias looked at Lucy, understanding.

After that fateful Saturday Lucy and Elias spent as much time together as they could, caring for little Themba and caring for each other. Elias had become an integral part of Lucy's life, and she of his. Though not husband and wife on paper, they were closer to each other than many couples who had a certificate to flaunt. They learned to love each other and they quietly began to respect each other. Their affection did not require the stamp of marriage. They did not mind what was said about them. Months passed, a year, and they grew closer and closer. They began to think of getting their own home. A new township was being built. A large part was already finished, though the whole township would take years to complete. Its creators, who lurked in the city's bureaucracy, and in the capital of the country, had agreed among themselves, before the township was born, to christen it Kwa Mashu.

Elias's name was placed on the waiting list. He had expected certain problems over his contract with the railways, for the endorsement in his pass book read that he was a compound-dweller. He would need permission from the local authority to change his place of residence. But his friend Peter helped, and with power such as the colour of the Evenmore skin behind him, Elias encountered no hitch. Although he was not qualified to be the city's tenant in Kwa Mashu, at least he was employed in Durban, his migration had been approved by the authorities, and his income was adequate in proportion to the rent. Under the umbrella of rent were included fees and charges for whatever amenities or facilities might be there in the future. At the time, there weren't many. Elias had been used to living communally in Umzinyathi. He did not own land there and therefore he could not own his home. Among his people, traditionally, individuals had only the use of the land. The concept of private property, in relation to land, was entirely foreign to them. So, to have just the use of a two-roomed brick dwelling with an asbestos roof in Kwa Mashu, at a rent set down by the Durban city fathers, was not strange for him. Once he had said to Lucy, "At least in Kwa Mashu you will not have to walk two or three miles to fetch your water as some of our women have to do at home. We may not have a tap inside the house, but there will be one out in the yard. There will be electric lighting in the streets, and a bus service. There will be schools and shops. I think we will be quite settled and happy in such a place."

"Do you think so?"

"Yes, I do."

With the blessings of the Evenmores, Elias and Lucy, with little Themba, moved into their "home" at number 303 E Section, Kwa Mashu. They had not only arrived physically; they had become, so to speak, householders. They were going to furnish their house. And if they did not have the cash to buy furniture, then because they had now begun to enjoy the status of privileged township dwellers, who qualified to enter into hire purchase agreements in the white men's stores, they would buy what they needed on credit. The sellers ran little risk, for if they were not paid, repossession of the goods was made easy by the customers' being ghettoed together in black townships such as Kwa Mashu.

To this segregated township came Elias, his son, Themba, and his beloved common-law wife, Lucy, to build for themselves a new world. From Kwa Mashu Elias travelled daily to his place of work. From there Lucy too, with little Themba piggyback, took the train to work. Her fares were subsidized by the Evenmores. She was an accomplished maid and the Evenmores relied on her. Their comfort was assured after Lucy vacated their khaya, for they engaged an additional domestic who was willing to sleep in. She was needed for evenings when they entertained at home, and for babysitting when they went out at night. The arrangement suited everyone concerned.

Months passed. After almost a year the home that Elias and Lucy had put together was far from luxurious, but it was home. They spent most of their spare time inside the asbestos-roofed house. They had collected various possessions, and had made sacrifices to make the place comfortable. Some of the furniture was secondhand, but most of it was new. Much of the equipment in the kitchen was old and used. But all these things were theirs and they had begun to attach themselves to them. One day, they hoped, they would replace the older things with new pieces, but for now, they cherished them. They were happy, if not exactly ecstatic, in their new environment. They did not have children big enough to roam the streets or run the risk of being killed by the speeding cars or noisy buses. They only had Themba, and he was not big enough to be left alone.

One Thursday, Elias's gang had been sent home early—their supervisor was in deadlock with the city engineer over responsibility for a burst pipe that had flooded the site. It was also Lucy's day off. Late in the afternoon, they went for a walk in the streets of Kwa Mashu. With little Themba holding his father's hand they strolled along. They marvelled at the number of their brethren who were already housed in this suburban outpost. These others were just like them. They had come to sell their labour, and they had to live somewhere. They could not be integrated into a common society in the city of Durban. So said the city fathers and the country's political architects.

A truck went by, with three tanks on trailers hitched to it. The mechanical horse was pulling its trailers slowly into the township. Elias asked Lucy whether she knew what was in the tanks.

"Don't you know? *Juba*, the beer the municipality makes for us. It's being brought in to be sold over the weekend. They have to start transporting it on Thursdays so that it's all here for Friday evening and Saturday. That's when our people need it most, after payday. And when they have money, they must drink."

"I wonder why they encourage people to waste money on liquor."

"According to the People's Congress, there is a design to get our people drunk over the weekends. In their free time, instead of doing those things that would help to build a community, our people, men and women, are either drunk and sleeping at home, or they are drunk and watching soccer—where in their enthusiastic support for their chosen teams, and in their drunkenness, they axe each other. And the profits from the sale of juba in the beer halls are used to run this township, don't you know that?"

"They use the rent we pay, surely?"

"That too, but it's not enough. They don't pay us enough to pay higher rents."

"If they want us drunk, why do they forbid us to brew our own beer?"

"The city wants the profits. They want us to spend our money in their beer halls, not in the shebeens. The People's Congress says profits are the mainstay and the chief motivation for all the injustices we blacks suffer today."

"But no one forces us to buy juba."

"No. But have you noticed how many beer halls we have here? Do we have other places of entertainment? Yes, a soccer field, and I told you about that. If they wanted us to be sober, would they build all these beer halls? Would they bring in all this juba?"

"Lucy, you have a complicated way of thinking. I know I'm not an educated man, but I think it's simpler. I think they bring us juba because we want it. If we didn't, it wouldn't be sold."

"Elias, you don't drink. I don't know why not. But you have me and Themba at home, and we love each other. You are not quite the same as the others, most of them. You haven't been here alone, or with someone you don't much like, on a Friday night with nothing to do."

"That's my good luck, I suppose." He smiled at her.

"Well, imagine: you've done a hard day's work; your woman has not cooked for you; she is lazy, or sick, or she is not even at home when you come. Perhaps you are new here. What do you do?"

"Well, I suppose I would go out and try to meet people, make friends—"

"Yes. Where?"

"I think the People's Congress does too much thinking."

"Too much for the liking of the whites. They are terrified of them. One day the Congress of our people is going to rule over all of this country. The whites took it from us with the force of their guns and they will not share it with us, and what is taken by force, what is maintained by force, will be got back only by force."

"Lucy, I'm just a simple man, but I know that's not the answer. People can be killed, or maimed. It is wrong."

"There is no other way."

Elias spoke slowly, weighing his words. "I don't believe that. We can talk to them. We can negotiate."

"That has been tried. We *can* talk to them, but they won't talk to us. Actually, they won't listen to us either."

"Perhaps we have not found the right arguments. Perhaps we have not tried hard enough. And what about mass meetings? Peaceful demonstrations? They often talk about that in the tea break at work."

"Where have they got us?"

"So far, not far, I admit. But this Congress talk is not our way. We are a patient people, Lucy, we can wait."

"Nice, good, soft methods have failed. We won't live forever. We will pass on this mess to our children. We will have done nothing to make things better for them."

"Well, I think we need to learn more. Face it, Lucy, they

are very clever, the white baases. They do know more than we do. They can do so many things we never even thought of."

"They want to stay on top, and they will, until we wake up. I tell you, our people have pleaded in vain. According to the People's Congress we have delayed our own liberation by adopting methods that were taught us by the enemy himself."

"Wait a bit, Lucy. You have just told me that the whites took what they took by force. Now you tell me we should use force. And at the same time we must not borrow their methods!"

Lucy stood still, and made rings in the dust with the toe of her shoe.

"Let's not fight about it. We both know we're not getting a fair deal. We work so hard, and it seems we can never do more than just survive."

"It's true," said Elias. "We give a lot, and we get very little. When I see all the things the white men make, Peter's beautiful house, and his car, and that hi-fi set, and their clever ways of making life easier, and more agreeable . . . I thought we were going to work hard, and learn more, and then earn more, so that we could have our share."

"They will not share."

"But if we tried to use force, if we fought them, all of us would lose. All that knowledge: how to build a great warehouse, how to buy goods from over the sea and have them sent here in ships; the hospitals, the schools—it would all be destroyed."

"But the country was ours, and they have taken it. They'll never share the best of it with us, unless we force them to. Right now we get their leftovers, if we are lucky."

"They will share some, and then more and more. Even you and I have things of theirs that we would not like to lose."

"And they have land of ours, which we would like to get back. Oh, Elias, they decide everything! How can we let them do that? They decide where we may live, what work we may do, how much we'll be paid, even what cattle we may have on the land they have let us keep. And—remember?—what we may drink."

"And they give us work, and money for working, and a chance to leave those old ways of ours behind and take part in their achievements."

"They are destroying us. The only answer is to destroy them, while we still have the strength."

Elias took a deep breath and said quietly, but very steadily, "No. We do not want that. We don't want to destroy them, or their cities or their inventions. We want a bigger share in them, yes. I want this boy here to be educated, so that he can move up in the world. I think the whites have a big start on us, that's all. While our children tend cattle and herd goats and listen to the elders, their children are at school. It's always been like that. We must learn to be more like the white men, and live more like them."

"And let them decide what is good for us?"

"When we know more, and can talk to them as equals because we are equals in achievement, we will also decide."

"The People's Congress says that is how they have caught us. There are too many of us who want to be like them."

"Where is the People's Congress?"

"Everywhere, everywhere, Elias. Wherever our people are suffering. It is in the hearts of all of us who suffer, but cannot do anything about it. We have waited so long."

"If your Congress had its way, innocent people would suffer."

"All of us are suffering now. The People's Congress is clear about one thing: they do not want to attack innocent people. They want to regain our lost power. If they used force, it would be against the powerful, not the innocent."

"Lucy, we are not so very far apart—at least, I hope we are not. We agree that our people are suffering; perhaps we don't agree about how much, or why. But the solution you see is not the only one."

"I cannot see any other."

"Where did you learn all this? Did you read it all, or have you heard members of the People's Congress talking?"

"I have read some of it, and it made sense to me. And I have felt some of it in my heart. And you know I used to meet many . . . men. Some of them told me things."

Themba was starting to whine. Lucy had an apple in her pocket, and gave it to him.

She went on, "I was at school, as you know, until my aunt refused to pay my fees. We had history classes. I have not forgotten them. Our rulers went to war once, for themselves. The whites know what they did to us, and they realise what we can do. That is why they do everything they can to keep us down. That is why they are dividing us."

"Lucy, I am glad that *we* are together. Our rulers can't separate us! It will be good for our Themba to learn from you: you do have more education than me; and I will tell him the other side, ordinary common sense that needs no education. Perhaps he will find a new answer, better than yours or mine?" With authority Elias added, "I don't want Themba growing up with these ideas. Don't push him, Lucy. I don't want him becoming a part of the People's Congress if they can't find other solutions."

"But we are already part of it, Elias. We are part of it just by being where we are and being who we are—being black."

Themba was getting tired, and Elias carried him the rest of the way home. They were about twenty-five yards from their doorstep when they heard the screams of children and women, coupled with shouts and curses from about a dozen teenagers. The shouts and screams and curses, all of them, came from one direction: their own front gate. Elias and Lucy were horrified at what was happening.

"You bastard son of a whore, I'll kill you!" shouted one of the teenagers, who was barefoot and scruffily dressed.

"What? Did you call me a son of a whore, you bastard? I will push this steel into your belly and tear you upwards," yelled another teenager, who was being restrained by a pretty young girl.

There, right in front of his house, Elias saw for the first time what violence in words and deeds meant among those who had opted for the city and the new life in the township.

"You goner dog, I'll push lead into you."

"You devil! You think only you can do that. You see here?" The young thug drew out a revolver from his pants pocket and aimed it at his opponent's head.

"Stop it!" shouted Elias.

"Who's he?" asked a member of one of the two gangs.

"God knows," answered his mate.

"I know who I am and I will tell you," Elias shouted for all to hear.

Lucy held him back and pleaded, "Please, Elias, don't interfere. These chaps are dangerous. You see the knives and the gun. They will harm you. Please leave them alone."

"No Lucy, I will not." He put Themba in her arms and walked a few paces closer to the warring youths. "I am Elias Mzimande. I live in this house."

"We are in the street," teased one of the teenagers.

"That I can see. But you're in my way."

"Then find another way," howled the gun-toting youth.

Elias stood his ground. "Why should I? Why don't you go and find another place to kill each other?"

"It's our business where we fight and where we kill them. The front of your house is as good as any other place."

"Then go to any other place and leave me and my family in peace."

"He wants peace. And we want their blood and we want revenge," howled the one with the gun to his mates. He beckoned them and continued, "Come, let's get them. These bastards from this section are all the same. We'll kill all of them!"

"You just try and you'll see what we do to your gang, you bastard," challenged his opponent.

Elias stood motionless; bullets exploded, and found the belly of the youth who had uttered the last challenge. The bullet-ridden body slumped, bent forward, and fell onto its side. There in front of Elias's home lay a young man who, a minute before, had been full of life, full of challenge, full of bravado —now full of bullets from the gun of another youth who was living and growing in this same township, Kwa Mashu. Kwa Mashu, where Elias and Lucy had chosen to rear little Themba; where together they dreamt of making their future.

The dead boy's mates tried to show some bravery, but they were overwhelmed by the power of the gun. Their knives and their knuckle-dusters were poor alternatives. The shots had attracted people, and someone had gone to alert the police. Leaving the body lying there, the killer and his cronies fled. But the dead boy's gang stayed to establish among themselves where their dead mate had come from and where his parents lived. Then they too fled, leaving the onlookers, those who had nothing to do with the warfare, to sort out the mess.

All the mess, the dead body and all, lay right in front of Elias's home. His horror turned to anger and he swore at the cowards who had fled the scene of the fighting. Some old newspapers were placed over the corpse. There was blood all around. Elias gathered handsful of soil from his garden and sprinkled it on the blood.

The police arrived two hours later. They were usually astute enough to give the warring gangs time to disappear. They were not going to risk their lives at the hands of these youthful killers. From the door of his house Elias watched them go through the motions. Their lackadaisical manner irritated him. He wondered why the police didn't try harder to wipe out this gang-fighting. He wondered what they did and why they were only available after such events had occurred, and a good while after at that. Meanwhile, they had picked up the corpse and dumped it in the back of their van. It was an accepted thing in the townships that such bodies were not accorded the dignity of an ambulance or a van from the mortuary, where the corpses were taken for numbering and identification. Loving families would call at the mortuary to collect their dead kin for proper burial, but in many cases the parents of those who met their death in gang warfare had adopted the attitude of the police: "good riddance to bad rubbish."

Such was life in the township, where "like" lived cheek-by-jowl with "like," and yet all likeness, rooted in common origin, common hope, common suffering and alienation, failed to cement a sense of community. The planners of such townships were busy housing the labour force. It was not their intention that a natural community should develop and grow.

Some of the inhabitants of the new township were beginning to feel that what posed as the benevolent provision of proper housing was in fact eyewash and humbuggery, and that the uprooting of men from settled communities and their resettling in ghettos was not benevolent at all. A place for the work force to live and adequate control of that place were the twin aims of the rulers. There was only one entrance, which also served as exit, to the township whose population already numbered tens of thousands. How easy it would be with just one plane to bomb these thousands of men, women and children if ever a rebellion occurred.

Elias was standing with Lucy at the door of his house. One of the policemen, smelling of the deadly home-brewed liquor *gavini*, approached him and asked, "Is this your home?"

"Yes."

"Then you saw all that happened?"

"No, I didn't," was Elias's instinctive reply. He was learning fast, the fast ways of the township.

"Didn't you see all that in front of your house?"

"No, I did not." Lucy winked at Elias as if to say, That's my man . . . don't get involved.

"You are lying," shouted the policeman.

"Why should I lie?" asked Elias.

The policeman turned to his mate and shouted, "This fellow says he didn't see what happened."

"Does he know who this dead kid is?" his mate shouted back from the van.

"No, I don't know," replied Elias.

"Hell, this is going to be one hell of a problem. Here is one dead kid and nobody knows who he is and nobody knows what happened."

"Well, that is correct for me. I don't know if the neighbours know."

"You mean you didn't even hear gunshots?"

"That I did."

"Then who were the fellows who shot this kid?"

"I don't know."

"How many of them were there?"

"I don't know—there were many people out there."

"Were there two gangs of kids fighting each other?"

"I don't know."

"Don't you even know what they looked like or who they were?"

"There were too many people and I didn't know who was who."

"Would you be able to recognise some of them if we showed you pictures of them?"

"I don't know. But in any case why do you ask me all these questions? I don't want to be part of all that rubbish."

"What rubbish?" asked the policeman.

"That in front of my house."

"So help us find the kid or the kids who did that."

"I am sorry. I can't help you. I don't know what happened and I don't know who the people were."

The policemen left. A murder docket would be opened. More often than not these dockets remained dockets and the murderers remained murderers, enjoying a kind of freedom to murder more of their fellow men.

Elias stood there and watched the empty street. He wondered what his people were doing to each other. Lucy's words lingered in his mind and he thought to himself, *Now I see what we are doing to ourselves. I see why my father wanted me to bring my child home to where we were once a people. We must get back what we have lost. But we have to get it without destroying everything, without destroying people.*

He said quietly to Lucy, "God, what a waste. What a waste of energy."

He lifted his little son in his arms and started to talk to him: "I will see to it that you never get involved in that kind of thing. I will make sure that you won't be like them. You will be well educated and you will lead these people away from all this; I will see to it."

"OK, OK, leave my son alone. You will see to a lot more in the morning on an empty stomach. Now come here and rest awhile."

Elias obeyed and sat down beside her. Themba was still in his arms. Holding his son closer, he asked Lucy, "Why have we come into this hell?"

Lucy went into the kitchen and came back with two mugs of tea. "We chose to come," she said.

"Did we have any choice?"

"Elias, the moment we say, first to ourselves and then to those who rule over us, 'Enough is enough, we will not take any more of what you dish out to us,' at that moment we will have made our first choice, and all the other choices will follow from it. We won't starve."

"Is that what the People's Congress is saying?"

"They have said it for a long, long time. They say the power to withhold our labour is our greatest strength."

"Then why don't we use it?"

"Because now we cannot do without the white man and his products—though it would be just as true to say that he cannot do without us: the labour we provide for him on the one hand, and the consumers we are and always will be on the other."

"I must confess you are muddling me."

"In some ways it's just as well if you don't understand."

"Why do you say that? I want to know and I want to learn."

"But do you know that with knowledge there has to come responsibility, and the courage to act, or else the knowledge is worthless? Many people do have knowledge, and they are like me, cowards, because like me, they lack the courage to do something with what they know."

"What do you think they should do?"

"I only know that if we put our heads together, and if our hearts come together in anger at what is happening to us—what has happened, what is going to happen—only then will we know what is to be done. Until then, each person and each group will be doing things their own way—and failing."

CHAPTER 16

Several months later, far away to the north at Sharpeville, a "location" just like Kwa Mashu, the tragedy occurred. A state of emergency was declared, and various organizations were banned. Towards the end of that year the emergency order was lifted, but the resistance groups remained banned. Elias and Lucy followed events as best they could, and Elias revelled in the fact that Lucy could read the Zulu newspapers to him. He felt he was gaining some understanding of what was happening, and why. But he knew in his heart that the conflict between the two sides—the rulers, and those who favoured active protest—would lead to losses, and more losses, for all, before freedom came. He was torn by fear and doubts. One winter evening in the middle of the following year, after supper and his usual play and cuddle with his son, he asked Lucy, "Did you actually join the People's Congress?"

"You know I have a pass," she answered, her face full of self-mockery. "I went with the madam to get it, not long after the government said we women must carry them too."

"Why did you do it? I remember many leaders said don't."

"The inspectors came twice. I couldn't afford to lose my job, or my place to sleep."

"I asked you if you ever joined the People's Congress."

"I didn't go to an office to sign up, if that's what you mean. I didn't go to meetings. But I belong, Elias, as we all do, whether it is banned or not."

"You won't do anything silly, Lucy, promise me?"

"Of course not. Though I know I should be braver. I have too much to lose, now. And I told you, I am a coward, like so many of us. I know I should be acting, not talking. It's not enough to say 'Mayibuye!' "

"Mayibuye, i-Afrika," said Elias thoughtfully. " 'Come back Africa.' Oh my dear Lucy, Africa is here already. We are here, we have living communities where we came from. And we have families, jobs, dealings with the white man, goods invented by the white man. We are all linked. Our people's way is to help each other, care for each other. We look after our old people, our sick, our handicapped. It is not our way to break things up."

"But I say we are used by the white man: the Evenmores need me to do the heavy work in their house, the railways need you for your strength."

Themba had fallen asleep. Lucy and Elias were growing tired and lay down in each other's arms. Although their minds were agitated about what was happening around them, they were at peace with themselves and each other. Each found the strength of the other.

They stretched their arms and loosened their muscles and joints. They felt nimble and light with the coming of the morning. They looked at each other, and with unbrushed teeth they exchanged a quick kiss on the lips. They smiled and were happy. Themba was still asleep. They tiptoed around the house, and before long both had dressed and prepared their early morning meal, a combination of breakfast and lunch. They had to economise; Elias could not afford the luxury of an outside lunch, so a good solid breakfast at about five in the morning had to do until his return between six and seven in the evening. In between, there was plenty of water to sustain him. Lucy was lucky enough to be working in a household where she was provided with lunch, and she had acquired the habit, recently, of keeping some of it aside to share with her man and his child. These titbits saved her own household a good deal, especially when she made too much pot roast or pastry or stew or mutton curry. How much of this excess she made on purpose, only Lucy could tell.

Lucy woke Themba, and dressed and fed him. They tidied their home hurriedly, locked it and made for the station to catch their early morning train. Many of their fellows were already milling around on the platform. All of them had one thing in common: they were going to work. The sea of workers filling the station was a daily sight, but this morning Elias, for the first time, stood aside and really noticed. Then he heard the excited hum of his fellow black men's talk. Some who had had the advantage of formal schooling in the English language were poring over the morning paper. The headlines read:

MAIN LINE SABOTAGED
PEOPLE'S CONGRESS CLAIMS RESPONSIBILITY

Elias moved closer to the group where the report was being discussed. Lucy picked little Themba up and, carrying him piggyback, followed Elias through the crowd.

"What is the excitement about?" Elias asked.

"We have hit another railway line. The main line from Johannesburg to Durban. The bloody government has been hit hard. It says here that it will take the better part of two days to put the line back in working condition. All passenger and goods movements will be disrupted."

"Who has done that?"

"The Congress."

Elias was silent, his thoughts agitated. *So this is how the brave should act: blowing things up! This goes against our whole way of life!*

Then he heard, from somewhere in the crowd, "MAYI-BUYE!"

Near him a woman's voice responded instantly, "i-AFRIKA!"

A neatly dressed black man, in suit and tie and shining shoes, began to stare in his direction. A cold silence held those who a few seconds before had been jubilant at the news of the railway line's being sabotaged. There was glee among the same group a little later when someone read out from the paper that the night train from Johannesburg had been derailed.

"What's that to us?" someone on the edge of the crowd asked.

"Luckily," said another, "there was no life lost."

All were silent but as soon as the train pulled into the platform there was again a spontaneous cry, "AFRIKA! MAYIBUYE!"

The well-dressed black man, who was also on his way to work—at the offices of the security police—merely cursed to himself, "Those bastards don't know what's good for them."

The train left the station. These masses of people, black people, were on their way to work, to build what their brethren were destroying. Some said the saboteurs were wasting their time—the power of the rulers was too great. Some were thoughtful, and said nothing. Others rejoiced in the news, proof that the spirit of protest was alive. They laughed and exchanged jokes about the sabotage. None seemed to care a damn for what they were going to do that morning. None besides the well-dressed black man, and others who were not identifiable, who were in sympathy with him. People like these were increasing in number every day. These black men were going to assist those in power to catch, arrest and destroy any of their brethren who opposed the rulers. Their sense of national duty differed from that of those who were laughing and enjoying themselves as they welcomed the news.

Elias arrived at the depot where his workmates had gathered to begin the new day. They were clustered together, being harangued. Usually, the day's instructions took a few moments. But this was totally different. The foreman's tone was commanding, impersonal; there were streaks of fear in the orders barked out:

"Now is that clear?

"Now do you understand?

"Now you will remember that there must be absolute silence about what you see there.

"Now you will take orders from us from time to time, and you will not do anything on your own.

"Now get your equipment and line up.

"Now there is going to be danger, and I cannot give you any undertaking that there will be no danger for you.

"Now I cannot give you this undertaking because these communist bastards don't care who gets hurt.

"Now for everybody's safety steel helmets will be provided, and there will be first-aid teams on hand.

"Now we have to proceed to the scene of the sabotage and do our utmost, our damnedest to restore the services to normal."

There was a shuffle at the back of the crowd, and murmurs came from there.

"Agh, what has that got to do with us?"

"Serves them right!"

"Pity the whole train was not blown up."

"What was that? Did I hear that from my boys?"

The foreman was anguished. No one in the crowd volunteered an answer. The foreman was chasing a rainbow if he thought anyone in the crowd would give himself up. Even the spies could not make a move for fear of being identified. There was no answer.

"All right then. . . . Don't forget we have our own ways of

finding out, and when we do find out which of you are sympa-
thisers with the communist bastards, then we will fix you up."

"Before that we will fix you up," came the words from near
where Elias was standing.

Elias had been realising all morning how many there were
who felt as Lucy did. Did they want change at any price? But
never mind what he or his workmates felt: on that morning
they were all going to use their strength to restore the sabotaged railway line to normal, and none of them could do other
than obey the commands of the foreman. They lined up and
marched to the trucks provided for them by the railways.
There were some army trucks there too.

The men were counted like heads of cattle and ordered to
get in. The trucks moved off fast to the scene of the night's
disaster. Many other truckloads of blackmen were already
there to do the bosses' bidding.

Among the people at the site of the derailment were men
who worked for the security police. These were both blacks
and whites. The explosives specialists were white; the military
bosses were white; the senior railways officials were white. The
men from the press were blacks and whites. Then there were
people from the vicinity, and others from farther afield who
had heard the morning news or read the newspapers. These
spectators were kept at a distance from the scene of the disaster.
They were not going to be allowed to spread fear, though in
fact they were all ruled by fear.

If it had been possible, there would have been a total black-
out of news from the scene of the disaster. But the press saw
to it that such news was disseminated. After all, freedom of the
press was a cornerstone and pillar of what the voting public
wished to protect: democracy. The term and the concept had
absolutely no meaning for those who were going to provide
their labour to restore the use of the railway line.

Suddenly instructions were yelled out. The police had

finished their investigations, and the engineers rushed into action. But their action depended on the willingness and ability of the gangs of blackmen to act. They, who had come to do their daily work so that they could earn their daily bread, but who had very little interest in the restoration of this railway line, suddenly found themselves with their picks, shovels and hammers, digging and hammering their way through the rubble and mess among the twisted steel and crushed timber. They followed the orders given to them. They were constantly exhorted to be careful: objects were still smouldering here and there. Explosives experts had combed the area for unexploded bombs, but they warned that no total guarantee of safety could be given.

Hours passed in this cautious and arduous work. The press had left with their pictures and news stories. The spectators had left with their own stories, based less on observation than conjecture. Then suddenly, a few minutes before midday, as the blackmen were pushing ahead with the work as defined and instructed by the bosses, a loud bang like a great crack of thunder broke across the land. The noise of the explosion was so deafening that many who were quite a distance away fell to the ground in fear and panic. The blackmen who had led the way to the scene of the new explosion were protected by nothing more than their helmets.

The foreman shouted frantically to the first-aid team, "Come this way. My boys are trapped in there."

"What happened?" asked one of the explosives experts.

"You better go and find out. Then you can tell me." The foreman left him standing, and ran to the scene of the new explosion. "Those of you who are not hurt come with me and get the injured out. Come quickly, there are many in that heap."

A blackman shouted in anger, "We had no business to be here in the first place."

"This is your job," the foreman shouted back.

"It is your job."

"We will settle that later. Now come and help. This way. They're lying in their own blood. Oh God, there are so many of them."

The teams began removing the casualties from the rubble. Frantically they searched for the injured. They came upon two men who were dead. They left them where they were and hurriedly continued looking for others who might be trapped there. They removed seventeen men, and these were rushed to the hospital in Durban. Eleven of them arrived conscious. They were able to identify themselves. The other six, unconscious, could not be identified. The blast had ripped away clothes, and no pass books could be found. The patients received all possible emergency attention. The injured men who were conscious were asked for information, but it could not be relied on.

Newsmen pressed the hospital for information, but they were only told of the eleven victims of the blast who had been conscious when they were admitted. Nothing could be said about the others, or the two dead, until they had been identified and their next of kin notified.

The hospital buzzed all afternoon with talk of the injured. The word got round, travelling from person to person, telephone to telephone, and even before the press placards had appeared, news of the injured men had permeated the townships. These areas hummed with anger, but the anger was vicarious, for the other fellow and his family. Such a disaster could not happen to me, each inhabitant thought. It had already happened to seventeen families, but they were the others; them.

Lucy heard the news from neighbours, soon after she got home. She merely said, "Oh God, how tragic." Her thoughts went out fleetingly to Elias. But then, she reassured herself, nothing can have happened to him. He is working in Durban in any case. Peter Evenmore would have come here by now. No, not to Elias. The railways have so many labourers. Trying to comfort herself, she picked up Themba and held his face close to her cheek.

She went out into the open yard and began looking up and down the street, as though she were in a stupor.

The afternoon newspapers hit the streets. With their headlines about the morning's explosion they sold as if newsprint were going out of fashion. Many regular readers failed to get their usual paper. It was the same in the city and in the townships. Those who bought the paper were in an advantageous position. They could be generous and share the news. The tragedy was going to be felt, they knew, in the townships where they lived. The news was there, and it was theirs. Eleven names were mentioned. And when Lucy realised that Elias's name was not among them she heaved a sigh of relief.

She walked away from the crowd that had gathered to share the news from her neighbour's paper. It was unusual, her neighbour buying a newspaper, and in the English language at that. But then, she told herself, this kind of tragedy affects us all.

In the hospital there was near chaos. Emergency resources were tried to the utmost. There were three very serious cases. The houseman on duty had summoned the surgeon on call. He summoned various colleagues and started his examinations without delay. An orthopaedic surgeon was sent for and together the doctors sorted the serious cases from the less serious. They confirmed that three of the six were in a critical condition. Urgent major surgery was required. They obtained the superintendent's permission, and hurried to the operating room.

The tension in the room was broken by the surgeon's whisper, "We'll amputate, just above the knee."

. . .

The train that Elias usually took had arrived at the Kwa Mashu station and left again. Lucy waited in her yard. When she saw that Elias had not arrived she hurried next door with Themba, and asked her neighbour to keep an eye on him. She made for the station, thinking Elias might be discussing the news of the explosion with his colleagues there. She reached the platform. He was not there. Then she panicked. She ran back to her neighbour's. The station was a ten-minute walk from her house. She was back in no time, but to her it seemed like eternity. As her neighbour opened the door she burst out, "Elias was not on that train. He was not there. He didn't come. Oh, my God, I wonder where he is. Dear God, please let him be safe."

Themba had fallen asleep. She implored her neighbour, "Please, I beg of you, please keep my child here and look after him. I am going to find Elias. I must find him. Will you do that for me? Please. I will be back as soon as I find him."

"But where will you go to find him?"

"First I want to go to my baas. He will help me find him."

"Are you going to go now? It is nearly night."

"I have to."

"But aren't you frightened? The *tsotsis* will get you. Township thugs come out of their hiding places at night, you know that."

"I am not frightened of them. I must find my Elias."

"Then wait!" Lucy's neighbour went to the other room and fetched her handbag. She rummaged in it and then held out a pound note. "Here, take this. If you must go, take a taxi. Themba will be fine here until you return."

Lucy looked at her neighbour. "You are God-sent. Thank you. I will pay you back as soon as Elias collects his pay at the end of the week."

"Now go!"

Lucy ran out of the house. She even forgot to kiss Themba

goodbye. She made for the taxi rank. There, panting and out of breath, she said to the driver, "Please get in and head for town. I'll show you the street."

Within twenty minutes the taxi had stopped outside the Evenmores' gate. She jumped out and pleaded with the driver, "I will be back soon. Please wait for me."

The driver agreed to wait. Lucy rushed inside, through the back door. As a familiar of the household, she knew she didn't have to knock. When the door banged shut, Mary Evenmore called from the dining room, "Who is there?"

"It's me, madam. It's me, Lucy."

"Come in here." Lucy went in. "What's happened? Why are you looking so frightened? What's wrong?"

"I don't know, madam. I want your help to find out."

"Find out what?"

"Elias hasn't returned, and there's been another explosion at Pinecrest."

"Was Elias there?" Peter put down his knife and fork.

"I don't know. That is what I want to find out. It is not like him to be late without telling me . . . "

"Are you sure he was there?"

"I don't know. Oh baas, please help me find him."

"All right Lucy, we'll help you find Elias. Now sit down and try to be calm."

"No baas. I can't do that. I want to find Elias."

"All right then, let's not waste time."

Peter got up from the table, leaving his dinner unfinished. "How did you get here?"

"By taxi. He is waiting outside."

Peter told his wife to pay the taxi man and dismiss him. He went to the telephone, dialled the non-European hospital and asked to speak to someone who could give him information about the railway casualties.

"My name is Peter Evenmore. I wish to know whether a Mr

Elias Mzimande was admitted to the hospital this afternoon after the explosion near Pinecrest."

"Are you a relative, sir?"

"No. I am a friend. But his wife is with me and she wants to know."

"In that case will you please hold on. I will find out for you."

"Thank you."

The man went away to fetch the admissions book.

"I am sorry, sir, the name Mzimande does not appear on my list."

"I see. Then that's good. I will tell his wife."

"Hold on, sir!"

"What is it now?"

"There are six men here who have not been identified."

"Are they dead?"

"No."

"Then why aren't they identified"

"They were brought in unconscious."

"Are they still unconscious?"

"I don't know, sir."

"Can you find out for me?"

"It would be quicker if you came here yourself."

"Yes, yes, thank you. I'm on my way."

He replaced the receiver and stared at Lucy.

"Tell me baas, what did they say?"

"They don't know. But there are six people who were brought in unconscious and they don't know who they are."

"Be brave, Lucy," said Mary, holding her hands. "Elias will be well. Don't worry, he will be well."

Peter said quietly, "Lucy, let's go to the hospital and see whether Elias is there or not."

"I'll come too," said Mary. The sleep-in maid was there to look after her child.

.   .   .

Peter led the way into the hospital. Mary could not keep up with his long strides, but Lucy matched him step for step. He, however, could not match her anxiety. At times she walked ahead. Then she had to pause and wait for Peter and Mary to catch up. As they entered the building, Peter beckoned to a passing sister and asked, "Sister, would you kindly take us to where the victims of this morning's explosion are."

"Yes, follow me."

"We want to see the ones who were admitted unconscious."

"Come this way."

She led the three visitors into a surgical ward and said to the ward sister, "Please help these people."

They were led to the far end of the ward where the six beds, with the six unidentified patients, were curtained off. The ward sister drew back the curtain and said, "Here they are."

"Where is Elias?" demanded Lucy.

"We don't know who Elias is," answered the sister.

Lucy and Peter moved from bed to bed. Lucy reached the fourth bed and for a moment or two was silent with shock. Then she screamed, "Elias, oh my Elias!" She leaned forward and put her hand on Elias's face. There was no response, no reaction. She wiped the sweat from his forehead. She looked down at his body. A drip was attached to the back of his hand, which was lying restfully on the turned-back sheet. Farther down, about where his hips would be, the covers were draped over a curved support. She moved to the foot of the bed.

"Oh my God!" She stood looking at Elias.

Mary moved up beside her and consoled: "Elias will be all right. This is a good hospital and I am sure the doctors here know what they are doing."

All the while Peter was quiet. He was standing with the two women at the end of the bed. Slowly he took hold of the bottom end of the covers, and lifted them so that they could see beneath the support. One bare leg emerged from it, the foot turned slightly out, relaxed. Lucy stared down at the bed. Gently Peter pulled the covers back. Lucy just stood there. After a while she asked quietly, "What have they done to him?"

"They have amputated his leg above the knee."

Outside a cold wind was sweeping leaves and litter around. It was already dark. Young black news-vendors in woollen caps were running up beside the cars that had to stop and wait for the lights to change. They were doing a brisk trade with the late editions. Peter bought a paper from a kid who popped up next to him as he unlocked his door. In the car, he glanced at the news items, and then read the editorial aloud to his passengers.

FACELESS COWARDS

Whoever was responsible for the bomb explosion at Pinecrest, the act was one of callous cowardice. There was not the slightest concern for who might be killed or maimed. Only one thing is certain, and that is that the perpetrators of this outrage, having resorted to such barbaric behaviour, deserve to be treated with neither sympathy nor mercy. Urban terrorism strikes at the roots of society by intimidating innocent people, and its purpose is to create alarm and despondency of such magnitude that the perpetrators may more easily achieve their evil aims. The objectives of these faceless cowards must be resisted to the utmost—

He stopped reading, looking perplexed. "I cannot understand what they will achieve by maiming people like Elias."

Lucy broke her silence. "They did not intend to maim Elias. It just happened."

"Surely they must know that such acts harm innocent people."

"Yes baas, we know that many of us are going to get hurt and many of us are going to die. All of us will pay for our freedom. We will pay gladly."

Peter and Mary sat silently in the car as they drove home.

CHAPTER 17

On a cold Friday morning Elias was discharged from the hospital. He was provided with a pair of crutches. The technicians at the hospital, with the assistance of the orthopaedic surgeons, had done a good job with the artificial leg attached to his thigh. It was tapered down from knee height, and ended in a circular shape. The flattened part that served as the bottom of a foot was no more than two inches in diameter. Elias was told that with the passage of time, and with practice, he would be able to walk without the crutches. This took about three months, and then he gave the crutches back as requested to the hospital authorities. He had learned to walk with just one ordinary stick. He limped, but he could get about.

He hobbled up to the office of the works foreman. He had gone back for his job. The secretary referred him to the railways office that dealt with workmen's compensation. She told him where to go and he trudged the streets of Durban until he found it. He had to find out about his job. He knocked at an office door, where he was met by a black interpreter.

"Yes, what is your problem?"

"That I am now lame."

"So what must I do about that?"

"I am looking for the office where my job is to be discussed."

"Who sent you here?"

"I was told by the secretary at the foreman's office."

"What did she say?"

"That I should come here."

"Then come in. Your name?"

Elias stood there on one foot and a stick, while the black interpreter disappeared into the secrecy of the adjacent offices. After a while he returned.

"Were you the one who lost a leg in the explosion at Pinecrest?"

"Yes."

"Then follow me."

The man led the way and Elias limped behind him. They reached an office where an elderly white man was seated at a desk. This white man, the interpreter had said on the way, had retired from the job he had done all his working life. He looked as if he were in his early seventies. The place smelt of tobacco and stale air. For Elias the non-smoker it was nauseating. He controlled himself. Officious in manner and tone, the white man asked, "Are you Elias Mzimande?"

"Yes, sir." Elias saw the deep lines in his face.

"Have you got your pass book with you for identification?"

"Yes, baas."

Elias took the pass book out of his hip pocket and showed it to the old man, who glanced at his photograph and checked it directly with Elias's face.

"Well, you look alike," he said, without smiling.

He reached for a brown file, took out three forms and placed them separately in front of Elias. Pointing at the places marked for signature he commanded, "Sign here, there and there."

"What am I signing?"

"I didn't ask you to ask me questions. Now sign here, there and there."

Elias looked at the black interpreter for some explanation,

out none was forthcoming. The white man said, "When you have signed these three papers you will qualify for a lump sum settlement for the injuries you sustained while you were on duty."

"Sir, what do you mean by injuries? I have lost a whole leg."

"Yes, I know that. Look, we have a job to do here and we haven't got all day. Now sign, and let's get this over with. Stop wasting my time! Don't you want your money?"

"Yes, but—"

"Sign before I close my file on you."

Elias told him, "Sorry, sorry sir, I cannot sign. You see, I cannot read or write."

"Then," the white man said, pulling over an ink pad, "put your right thumb imprint here, there and there. And you and I," he said to the interpreter, "will witness the thumbprint."

"Yes sir," volunteered the black man. Elias put his thumb impressions as he was commanded. The witnesses signed. With the documents completed according to regulations Elias was handed a sheet of paper.

"This is a letter about the money for you to retire on."

"Retire on!" Elias, shocked, looked with envy at the retired, old, white man.

"Yes," said the interpreter.

"But I can't retire. I am a young man. I want to work. I have a wife and a child."

"That may be," said the interpreter; and opening the door he ordered, "You may go now."

Elias left. The door closed behind him. He stood there and stared at the empty, lifeless walls of the corridor in this government building. While he bit his lip in bewilderment the door behind him opened again and the old white man sauntered past without saying a word. He gathered, with his tongue, the smelly, chewed-out tobacco in his mouth and spat it into a plastic bin, strategically placed. He was on his way out for lunch. The black interpreter followed him out, his shoulders sagging. He too was going out for lunch. When he saw that Elias hadn't attempted to move he said tauntingly, "Come now, Mzimande, you will have enough to feed me, your girl-friends and yourself many, many meals. Go out and enjoy your life. And if you don't get out fast you'll be locked in this building for the lunch-hour. We don't want to do that to you. Now get out of here."

Elias, still in a daze, left the offices without a word. He made for the station and the train to Kwa Mashu, to his home, his son, and Lucy.

He got out of the train with the help of a fellow passenger. Those around him, especially the elderly, were afraid the train would pull out before they had all alighted. An elderly woman of the township gave Elias her shoulder to lean on as he got down from the train. They managed very well and Elias was grateful, and at the same time angry with himself. He was ashamed of his condition. And to compound his shame and anger, he had in his possession a notice for his retirement at his age. He felt useless. He limped home, where he explained all that had happened to Lucy.

"Don't you think we should ask Peter Evermore for advice on what we should do about my job?"

"Not a bad idea. At least he will be able to read the letter and tell us what all that small print means. But let's leave it till Monday morning. I have to go to work in any case. We will go together."

"What is all this?" asked Peter Evenmore.

"I am retired from my job," Elias answered meekly.

"What? You are retired at this age?" asked Mary.

"They say so."

While Peter read the letter, Mary walked out onto the porch. Lucy followed her. Away from the men, the two women looked at each other. Mary asked, "Lucy, what are you going to do? I mean with Elias losing his job. And now that he has lost his leg, who is going to employ him?"

"We will have to look after that together. We don't know yet what Elias is going to do. But I do know what I'm going to do."

"And what is that?"

"Never let him believe he has lost his manhood in any way."

"You are very wise. Let's go in and see what the men have decided."

Peter and Elias were still going over the details of the retirement notice. Mary approached the dining room table, and read the letter over Peter's shoulder.

" 'Total payable for assessed percentage disability: four hundred and eighty-three rand,' " she read aloud. She read the paragraph again. "Is this the amount on which you are expected to retire?"

"That is what the letter says," answered Peter.

Mary sat down and cupped her head in both her palms. In exasperation she asked, "Elias, what rent do you pay?"

"Five rand thirty-five cents a month."

"And what do you spend on food, clothing, soap, candles, coal, whatever you have to buy?"

"We tried to keep it under fifteen rand a month."

"And your furniture instalments?"

"Two rand forty."

"And what did you earn?"

"It used to come to about nine pounds a month—eighteen rand, in this new money, if I got a chance to work overtime."

"Then where did you get the difference between what you earned and what you in fact spent?"

"We use Lucy's wages that she earns from you."

"I didn't realise . . . "

"The madams don't usually know how it is with us." Lucy picked up the letter.

"All right. We have a problem on our hands. Let us see how

best we can solve it," interrupted Peter Evenmore. "Have you read this paragraph here?" He turned to Elias. " 'The amount will be deposited in a post office savings account, and a savings book will be sent to you. When the book is in your possession you will be permitted to withdraw at any post office the sum of six rand per month.' "

"What!" cried Mary.

"We saw that," said Lucy.

"Then what in the name of heaven must you do?" shouted Peter. He went over to the window and lit his pipe.

Lucy said, "Come on. This is not the end of the world. We will manage. Yes, we will manage somehow." She came across to Elias and only fifteen minutes after their arrival at the Evenmores' she was saying, "Come Elias, we must go. There is lots to be done and we'd better get started right away."

"Wait, Lucy!" begged Mary. "You cannot go just like that as if nothing has happened."

"Don't go yet, Lucy. Elias, please stay awhile." Peter sounded almost pleading.

They sat down again. Mary broke the silence: "I want you two to know that I hate what is happening to you. If there is any way in which we can help, we will. Won't we, Peter?"

"Of course. On that score you should not have a moment's doubt."

"Then what are we going to do?" Mary asked.

"I don't know," answered Peter.

The radio had been on softly all the time. A snatch of news caught Peter's attention and he turned the volume up.

" . . . report that in two explosions that occurred in the Johannesburg area on Saturday night, when a native was killed, it has now been established that a second non-European was seriously injured. He is said to be in a critical condition. The first blast occurred at a post office in a suburb west of the centre of the city. The other explosion damaged the city council's administrative offices in one of the native townships. In both instances, sabotage is suspected. Near the sites of the explosions, pamphlets were found claiming responsibility for the organisation known as Umkhonto we Sizwe (The Spear of the Nation). The organisation concerned is connected with the banned African National Congress. Damage to property has not yet been assessed. The police will issue a further statement when investigations have been completed."

"What a tragedy!" interrupted Peter, switching the radio off.

"It's terrible," said Elias soberly, looking at Lucy.

"But why the devil can't the people of this country resolve their differences around a table?" asked Mary.

"You can't force people round a table with just words," Lucy butted in.

"What do you mean?" asked Mary.

"When the black people were weak, they wanted to talk around a table, and the strong white people refused to talk. You see for yourselves what kind of building is attacked. The post offices belong to the government. The township offices are hated, because the officials there push us around, and tell us where we can live and where we can't. You know they throw our furniture out onto the street and lock us out if we are late with our rent, or if they decide someone else should get our house. Their inspectors wake us up in the middle of the night to check our passes. Our people are protesting the only way they can. These things are just signs that we have had enough. We are not going to forget our demands, just because some organisations have been banned. New ones will always appear, and lead us to freedom. Then we may be willing to talk."

Elias noticed the sharpness with which Lucy was handling her employers. He kept his own thoughts to himself: *A bomb in a post office, secret organisations, sabotage in the townships. There must be some better way. Our own people are getting hurt.*

One man killed, another injured, and seriously. He may be maimed, he must be in pain. I know what sort of pain . . . He said suddenly, "That is enough. Now I want to go."

"Where to?" asked Peter.

"I want to go to my home."

"Why so suddenly?"

"I want to go and straighten out a few things in my mind."

"Well, can't you do it here? Aren't you going to discuss it with us?"

"No. There is no need now. I know what they wanted, the baases who brought me here. And I know how they treated me. Now I just want to think about it, and see how I am going to survive."

"What do you mean, Elias?" begged Mary.

"That's all, ma'am."

Mary turned to her husband. She was disconcerted by the firmness of Elias's tone. Both she and Peter remembered how Elias had always depended on their advice and help, and been grateful for it. Lucy's attitude was not new to them. But Elias was their blue-eyed black boy, who had come from Umzinyathi with one desire: to emulate their own lifestyle. He had seemed to be making quite a good beginning. Now he was saying, From this day on, I'll go my own way.

Peter asked, "Elias, are you certain you don't want us to help you in your present difficulties?"

"How, Peter? Things are as they are."

"But you can't even use the money they have given you."

"No. But I can draw my monthly amount. I'll take care of the rest."

Everybody was silent for a while. Lucy picked Themba up from the floor, saying, "Your father says we must go." She did not express her thoughts aloud: I want to hear what Elias has in mind. I have never seen him like this. This new trouble seems to be giving rise to new ideas. Perhaps I am going to learn something sweet from him today.

As Lucy lifted the child, Elias struggled to stand up. Peter rushed over to him, saying, "Come, let me help you."

"No, no, I will manage. I will not be a burden to anyone."

Mary was astonished. Lucy too, and she smiled so that he would feel encouraged. She was impatient to know more.

Elias said decisively, "Now let us go."

Nobody reminded Lucy that for her it was a working day.

CHAPTER 18

It was nearly midday when the Mzimandes got home. The sun was scorching in Kwa Mashu and there were very few people around. As they walked towards their house along the dusty street, they were greeted with many sympathetic cries. The women, especially, did not hesitate to call out "Oh shame!" when they saw Elias limping his way past their homes. Elias merely smiled at them and kept walking. His attention was attracted by a youth in a pair of thin cotton shorts, who came staggering out of one of the houses in his own street, carrying a paper packet. He wondered how and why such a young man, with the use of both his legs, should be staggering around as if he had lost all sense of balance. When the lad came closer it was clear that he was very drunk. As they were about to pass each other, the lad said, "Yes, you one-legged man, do you want to go in there?"

"No I don't," replied Elias, who suspected what he meant. Elias suspected, but Lucy knew.

"You better go in if you want to forget you are one-legged," the youth drawled, grinning.

"I am happy as I am."

"You can't be happier than I am."

"Maybe not. Maybe you have the use of two legs. But by

God you must be—" Before Elias could finish what he wanted to say, the young man fell flat on his stomach, and while he was licking the dust beneath him Lucy realised she had heard something shatter as he fell. She and Elias turned towards him and then instinctively stopped to help the lad. Blood was flowing profusely from beneath him.

"He must be badly hurt," cried Elias.

"Let me pick him up and see what's happened."

Lucy put Themba down and lifted the drunken youth to a sitting position. His intestines were spilling out onto his groin, and his thin shorts were a mess of blood and dirt. Lucy was horrified, disgusted, and overcome with sorrow at the plight of this young man who just a moment before had been full of pep and cocky enough to advise Elias how to be happy. She shouted, "My God! What has happened here!"

Then she saw the shattered remains of the liquor bottle. As he fell onto the packet he was carrying, the boy had smashed the bottle, and the jagged glass had practically disembowelled him. Blood was pouring from him and she and Elias were afraid he might die. People had gathered round, and someone ran off to fetch help. The police arrived, and a few minutes later, an ambulance. The attendants put the young man on the stretcher and rushed him into the vehicle. They said something to the policemen, and drove off.

Elias and Lucy walked silently towards their house. They heard the townsfolk eagerly discussing the weekend's explosions near Johannesburg. The tragedy of the disembowelled youth was dismissed among the people after they agreed that the fellow was young and deserved more from life than what he got. He was written off as dead.

Pointing to a house, Lucy said softly, "Elias, I think the young man had come out of there."

On the porch of the gaily painted cottage an obese, heavily made-up woman was standing. She was the queen of that shebeen. When she noticed them staring at her, she said quietly, in a matter-of-fact voice, "I told him he had had enough and there was no need to carry that bottle of liquor. He could have come back to drink more here, but he insisted he needed some for the evening, before he went to bed. I begged him like his mother would. But he didn't listen to me."

Feeling awkward when she received no response, she went on, "He did say he had lost his job. He was retrenched because women could do his work for a lower wage. Well, what could I have done? I also have to make a living."

She came down the steps and met Lucy and Elias on the untarred, unkempt kerb.

"You two are new here. I haven't seen either of you in my palace."

"Sorry, we don't drink," Elias retorted immediately. Lucy was a little taken aback by his high-handed answer. She wondered whether he knew what went on in there. She knew that he knew that she used to drink, and enjoy drinking. She let it pass, and was content with his handling of the situation. Elias noticed scores of empty bottles being taken away by bottle pedlars.

Looking at them, the queen said, "They make a living doing that. They don't do too badly either. You should see them over the weekends when they become my customers."

At home Lucy went about her household chores. Elias lay down, resting his leg on the bed. He stared up fixedly into the ceiling-less roof. Lucy came into the room and found her man lying there with this lost look on his face. It was only when she looked into his eyes that she realised he was deep in thought. His eyes were surrounded with pain and a kind of searching.

"I'm thinking about you," he said. "Now that I am useless—"

"You are anything but useless. I will bite the life out of anyone who says you are."

"Lucy, maybe I can sell bottles. I could also collect them from the queen. I could have a basket tied to my back."

"Elias, to make any money you would have to take dozens and dozens. And how would you manage, my love? I don't want you hurt any more than you are already. How would you walk with that weight on your back?"

He rose to demonstrate, but Lucy interrupted him: "Now you just rest and relax. There is no need for you to eat your heart out about what you are going to do. Elias my love, I thought you would rely on me for . . . I want to be, I can be, everything you need."

"Lucy, I trust you and need and want you, but I must have something to do. If I don't, how will I spend the rest of my days? I must be of some use to us. I know I can. If I fail, I will be the first to admit it."

Weeks went by. Lucy did her best at the Evenmores' to be the model worker. She succeeded. She had always been competent; now she felt she had to be doubly efficient. She could not afford to lose the meagre wage she earned. What she valued most about the job was the food provided for her there. By now she was bringing home practically all of it, to share with Elias and Themba. While Lucy was at work, Elias had gone out to see the shebeen queen. He had started collecting and selling empty bottles. Their combined earnings were not, however, enough to meet their needs, and he was working longer and longer hours, trying to make a few extra cents.

One day when Elias was on his rounds with the empty bottles, he was stopped by a black plain-clothes policeman. These police were notorious for their abuse of the authority given them; in the townships they were known as "black-jacks."

"Who are you?" the policeman asked.

"Elias Mzimande."

"Do you live in Kwa Mashu?"

"Yes."

"Where is your pass book?"

"I have it with me."

"I am a policeman. I want to see it."

The blackjack did not bother to identify himself. He took it for granted that his authority would not be flouted by any township-dweller, let alone a one-legged one. Elias wobbled on his stick and the bottles in the basket on his back clinked as if they were being thrown around. The policeman paid no attention to that. He just waited for the pass book. With much difficulty Elias managed to take the document out of his hip pocket. As he was handing it over, he dropped it and it fell next to his bare foot. The policeman did not stir to help pick it up. He waited, and Elias battled to reach down for the pass book. He had to put the basket of bottles down. Bending and struggling to pick up the document, he observed the policeman out of the corner of his eye. Elias's face was contorted with pain and hatred and he thought, You bloody bastard, you are not a man, you are a mouse and a stinking one at that. You are a mouse in a man's outfit.

"Come on. Pick it up and give it to me," commanded the blackjack.

"You must be paid very well for doing what you are doing."

"Don't give me your lip. I want your pass book."

Elias finally grasped the book and jerked out his arm, growling, "Here, satisfy yourself."

The man opened the document, and after reading and flipping a few pages, said, "So you are not employed?"

"That is true."

"I see you have been unemployed for quite a few months."

"That is true."

"But you occupy a house that should be occupied by an employed man."

"I pay my rent in time."

"But you are unemployed."

"I know that. I want to work, but the baases at the railways retired me . . . after I lost my leg."

"They retired you? Well, you can't work on the railways with just one leg, now can you?"

"Then what is expected of me? I was working for them when I lost my leg. I was there on duty when it happened."

"I got nothing to do with that."

"I have a lot to do with that."

"It is not your house. Only people who work in the city can live here."

"But there are so many who work in the city who don't live here."

"I know that."

"So why can't I live here? I am paying my rent in time."

"That my bosses will have to decide. I will go and report your case to them."

"And what is my family supposed to do?"

"I don't know them and I can't worry about them. I have a job to do and I'm not going to lose it because of you."

"But I am working. I am making a living. I am not begging. I am not stealing and I am not a burden on anybody."

"I am glad to hear that but I must go. You will hear from my bosses soon, I'm sure."

He left without helping Elias to hoist the basket of bottles onto his back. Elias wriggled and cursed himself back into his shoulder-straps, and limped his way home.

Two months later, very early one morning, there was a knock on the door. Lucy wondered who could be visiting them at that hour. Elias on the other hand had a niggling suspicion that *they* had arrived. He had not told Lucy about the altercation with the policeman. He did not want to worry her. He had felt all the time that she had too much on her mind to be burdened with more of his troubles. So he had kept quiet all along, and he kept quiet when he heard the knocking. When it became persistent, and louder, Lucy shouted, "All right, you don't have to break down the door. I'm coming."

She unbolted the door and opened it an inch or two. "Yes? What do you want?" she asked.

"If you opened the door and let us in a bit quicker, we might be able to tell you what we want and who we are," said a white man. He had two officious-looking black men with him.

Lucy shouted to Elias, "There are two black men and a white man who want to come in, and they say they have something to tell us."

"Let them in, Lucy," answered Elias.

"He is a wise man," said the white man. They came in and, without being invited to sit down, the two black men helped themselves to seats. The white man opened his briefcase and took out a file.

"Elias Mzimande lives here, doesn't he?"

"Yes."

"Is he around?"

"Yes."

"We wish to talk to him."

"He has just woken up. He will not be long."

"Tell him not to delay us."

"But he has just woken up."

"Tell him to get a move on. We have many calls to make."

Lucy left them with disgust on her face. She went to Elias in the bedroom, where he was struggling to pull on his pants over the underwear he had slept in. She said, "They want to see you."

"I was expecting them."

He held her by the wrist, and limped through to the other room. As he appeared, the white man said, "We have a notice of eviction for you. Since you are no longer employed in Durban, you are to vacate this house within thirty days."

"Where do you expect me to go?" asked Elias.

"That is not our job."

"You do your job and we lose our home. Get out of here!" shouted Lucy.

The three men left and Lucy followed them outside. Behind her Elias wobbled and struggled, trying to restrain her from losing her temper again. As the men were getting into their car Lucy hurled so much abuse at them that she attracted the attention of her neighbours, who came out of their houses and stood watching and listening from their porches. Lucy turned round to them and proclaimed, "These sons of bastards want us to leave our home. They say that because my husband no longer works he is not entitled to live here . . . the bloody bastards! They bring us here, we are crippled by them, and then they dump us."

"Oh, what a shameful thing," cried an elderly neighbour.

"Shame on them . . . shame on them. The cowards, they have their homes and their jobs. We have to suffer for their selfishness."

"Come inside, Lucy. Let them alone. Please, come inside," begged Elias.

Lucy turned to her man and for the first time that morning she saw anger in his eyes. His voice was subdued but his eyes were aflame. As he hobbled indoors, she held him by the arm and allowed him to lean on her for support. It was natural to Lucy to give support. He on the other hand had had to acquire the habit of accepting it.

"Elias, we'll survive this too. We have each other and we have our son."

He turned his face sharply to look at her. It was the first time he had heard Lucy refer to Themba as "our son." He took her in his arms and hugged her as he had never done before. All trace of worry was swept away from his face, and a new kind of self-confidence replaced it.

Within an hour Lucy and Elias had eaten, and they were

seated at their kitchen table with pen and paper in front of them. Lucy was going to list, as best she could, the unpaid-for items in their house and the sums owing on them. They considered these at some length and came to the conclusion that they would cart all the things they had to their new home. They agreed that they would have to find a new place, and not deprive the new domestic hand at the Evenmores' of her accommodation by asking to be housed there. They knew as well as any of the migrant blacks who had streamed into the city that accommodation in Durban was very, very difficult to come by.

"Lucy, it looks as if we'll have to try the landlords in a squatter area outside Durban. One of my workmates at the railways lived in a place called New Farm, about four miles from here. It's in Inanda. But if we lived there, you would have to take a bus and the train to work. Or two buses."

"I wonder if the Evenmores will pay the extra fares."

"They may. But it will be hard for you."

"Elias, I want to start making you a little like me, the me I once was. I don't want to change you, I don't want to mould you. I only hope you will become a little bit like me. A little brash, a bit cruel—to be kind to ourselves—a little pushy."

"Do I have a choice? I can't fight you. Let's not quarrel."

"For a start I don't see how we can pay this month's rent. And as for the instalments we owe on our furniture—"

"Lucy!"

"Don't let this scare you. What we can't get by pleading, we have to take, however we can."

"Do you know that we are about to tread a dangerous path?"

"What could be more dangerous than not knowing where or how we are going to live next month?"

"You have an answer for everything."

"To hell with your scruples. They only understand their own language. No other is good enough for them. We must use the language they have taught us. We must fend for our-selves. Isn't that what they constantly teach us?"

Elias relaxed, and he saw his problems, which were not of his making, in a perspective he had never seen them in before. If he had been cheated, then he would cheat too. He told himself, yes, I will do just that, but I will choose whom I cheat. For now I agree with Lucy. We must go to a place where the hire purchase people cannot find us. Yes, these people I am going to cheat.

"What are you thinking about, Elias?"

"That I am going out to Inanda this very day to look for a shack for us to live in. At New Farm, no one will know where we have come from or who we are, at least for the first few months."

"So you have begun to see things my way?"

"I didn't say I disagreed with you."

He kissed her cheek. Then in a confident voice he said, "We'll manage."

CHAPTER 19

"Lucy, while you were at work a message came from my cousin Madoda. He'll be here from Soweto this weekend. But with all this happening . . . "

"It doesn't matter. We will wait for him. Is he coming with his wife?"

"I think so. The poor, good devils."

"Why do you say that?"

"They have longed for children ever since they married, but something is wrong somewhere."

Lucy was quiet for a while, thinking how she herself had lived for years now with Elias, and had not had a child of her own. She wondered whether the loss of her first child had anything to do with her not conceiving again.

Oh, what does it matter, she reasoned. I have Themba and that is enough for me. Loving and caring for Themba and Elias is a world big enough and good enough for me. Just as well that we have only one child. God knows what would have become of us if we had more. And now this move to the squatter township. How on earth can one bring up children in such conditions? We are lucky we only have Themba.

Lucy went outside, alone. She gazed around her and pondered on the dullness of her environment. She wondered how she and Elias, with their Themba, had survived the two and a half years in the township. Themba was growing into a fine child. She had noticed that. But she had never paid much attention to the surroundings in which she had spent such an important part of her life. Now that they were going to leave, she began to look around her.

Elias hobbled out of the house on his stick. He stood near the door and kept a silent watch on his woman's movements. He wondered how much she minded leaving Kwa Mashu. They had come there together. They had rented a house and made it their home. He did not want to interrupt her thoughts, yet he wanted to know each and every one of them.

She came towards him.

"Just a few minutes ago you were full of verve and enthusiasm about tackling life in the new place. Now you are so thoughtful that I am beginning to be afraid."

"Don't be afraid, Elias. I am worried, yes. But not for me and not for you. For Themba. A squatter area is a squatter area. Here in Kwa Mashu, bad as it is, there are roads, there are trains, there are streetlights, there are toilets. The lack of hygiene in the squatter areas worries me the most."

Elias became quiet. Aimlessly they shuffled around, and then Lucy broke the silence: "Come, let us go in. We will think about all this later."

They made tea, drank it and talked some more.

"I don't want Themba to be hurt, Elias. I don't want him to suffer. I want him to be good and grow up proud, and I want him to be educated as you always dreamed for him."

"We will see to that, Lucy."

"We will, but can we see to it in that squatter place?"

"It will be a problem. But we will try our best for him. You know there are times when I think about other children: the privileged ones in this township—even the children of the baases—and I often think that the best is not good enough for Themba."

Lucy stared at him, and remembered the circumstances in which he had handed his son to her for the kind of upbringing he dreamed of. She wondered whether he would have had the same expectations if Nomsa had been alive. She didn't mention Nomsa's name, but she asked, "Do you think I will manage to bring up your son the way you want me to?"

"Of course you will!" he replied without hesitation.

That Saturday morning, Elias and Lucy got up several hours before Madoda's train from Johannesburg was expected. They took the train from Kwa Mashu and arrived in Durban station in good time. As they stared at the railway line, Elias's heart sank, and memories of the circumstances in which he had lost his leg came flooding back. He tried to suppress his emotions and look eager to greet his cousin. But Lucy knew there was something about trains that would always affect him. To distract him she asked teasingly, "Is your cousin younger or older than you?"

"Younger."

"Good."

"Why? What if he were older?"

"Then I couldn't make fun of him. As he is younger, I can. I will pull his nose for him. That is my right, you know?"

"I know. Only he has a very stubby nose."

"It will be more difficult then. But I will not stop trying."

"Good luck to you. But I hear his wife is very pretty. See that you don't overdo it; otherwise she will pull your nose off your face."

The train had come in and jolted to a stop. Scores of people clustered around the doors and windows. Elias could not push into this crowd, so he stood and looked along the train. Some three coaches away he recognised a head jutting out of a window. He shouted to Lucy, "There he is. Come."

They went down the platform. Madoda and his wife,

Serafina, had got out of the train. Only when Elias stood in front of him did Madoda recognise his cousin. He stared at him, speechless. Elias, unable to take his cousin's silence, said, "Hai! Madoda! How are you?"

"Elias, it is good to see you."

Madoda and Serafina, assisted by Lucy, carried the baggage to the other platform, where they had to wait an hour for the next train to Kwa Mashu. Sitting there on a bench, the four of them exchanged pleasantries and polite enquiries, and when it was time for Madoda to ask about Elias's leg, he did.

Workers and shoppers on their way back home had begun to mill around on the platform. Before the train was due to leave for Kwa Mashu it was already packed to capacity. Madoda said, "Elias, you shouldn't have come. We would have found our way to Kwa Mashu. This damned full train is going to be very uncomfortable for you."

"Don't pity me. I will manage. I wanted to come and meet you. After all, I am the only one you know here in Durban."

"I'm sorry." Pulling a bag over, Madoda went on, "Now here, Lucy and Serafina, sit on this; Elias can have the seat and I'll stand. We'll keep our belongings between you girls and myself. That way they'll be safe from fast fingers."

The Madodas spent four happy days with their hosts. It was on the fifth day of their stay that they discovered Elias and Lucy were troubled.

"What has happened?" Madoda asked.

"We have to move out of this house by the end of the month because I am unemployed. We have decided to go to New Farm, just a few miles from here. It is a squatter camp where nobody knows anybody, and many people who can't get houses in the townships are dumping themselves there."

"And what about Themba?"

"He, in fact, is our problem."

"Why?"

"Lucy and I have been wondering whether New Farm is the place for us to bring up our child."

Madoda and Serafina caught each other's eye; instantaneously a message passed between them.

Silence settled, and Themba burst into the room, wanting to play. He ran up to Madoda and grabbed him around the neck. In his native tongue he asked, "Why don't you use a stick like my father?"

"Your father needs one, son."

"And you?"

"I don't."

"That's funny."

Elias chipped in, "I need a stick because I have one natural leg. Your uncle has two of them."

"Oh, I see," said Themba, fingering Madoda's hair. Madoda asked the little boy, "Do you like me?"

"Yes."

"Do you like your auntie?"

"Yes."

"Will you come with us for a holiday?"

"Yes. Can we go now?"

"No, not right now. *We* are on holiday, and we still have a week to spend with you and your parents."

"Then when can we go?"

"As soon as our holiday is finished, you can, if your parents agree, start yours with us."

"Oh, that will be nice."

Elias looked at Lucy, and the glance sealed something they could not have explained right then.

That evening Lucy and Elias lay awake in bed, discussing Themba and his future. Their child would soon be six years old. They knew they had to make a decision about him.

In the morning at breakfast, Serafina and Madoda were

silent, visibly deep in thought. As they left the table, Serafina said, "Lucy, would you and Elias agree to let us take care of Themba in Soweto and educate him there?"

Both Lucy and Elias had known it would come to this. They didn't answer.

"Think about it, you two," Madoda urged. "It will be a joy for us to look after him, and it will make your way so much easier at New Farm." He added, "Elias, today we want to go to the sea. We don't have the sea in the Transvaal, you know, and we'd like to enjoy it while we are here. We'll take Themba with us." In a matter-of-fact way he continued: "That will give the two of you some more time to think over our proposal." He walked off to fetch his coat.

That whole Saturday, Lucy and Elias stayed home, debating whether Themba should go to Soweto or not. So many unforeseen things had happened to them that they wondered if the Madodas' proposition was a blessing, or not.

The same evening, after Themba had gone to bed, Elias said, "It is all right with Lucy and me. Themba can go with you to Soweto and live with you there."

Lucy noticed that he was not speaking in his normal voice, and his eyes were full of tears. Her own voice choked with emotion, she said, "Please remember that although Themba is not my own, he and Elias are the only family I have—"

"We are glad for us, we are glad for Themba, we are glad for you, too," interrupted Serafina.

A week later Themba went away with Madoda and Serafina into his new world, where neither of his parents knew what would become of him. They only knew they were sending their son away with hearts full of hope for him. As the Johannesburg train pulled out of Durban station, Elias and Lucy were weeping openly. They could not hide what they were feeling in the midst of this failure of theirs.

Elias stood close to Lucy and this time it was he, with his

one-legged balance, who stood firmly and supported her in their common grief, his arm around her shoulder.

"Lucy, you know it is more than five years since I have been to see my own parents in Umzinyathi. Now I know what it must have been for my people to lose me. Some day I must go back and visit them."

"Tell me, Elias, how often do you think Themba will visit us?"

"Often enough, I hope."

"What do you mean by that?"

"Well, what with things as they are . . . "

They had started moving across to the other platform where the Kwa Mashu train was standing. They were early, and found themselves two seats next to each other. Their fellow passengers stared at the disabled man with the young woman beside him. Dejection and their emotion over Themba's departure had exhausted them. They leaned against each other for what little comfort they could get. In moments, both were half-asleep. The train jerked backwards in order to go forward, and they were on their way home.

This was the so-called fast train: it did not stop at all the stations between Durban and Kwa Mashu. Before long they were out of the urban area and rustling past trees and shrubs that grew along the railway line. These had not been planted there, nor were they tended—human hands had touched them only to decimate them, to make way for the railway line. Gusts of wind blew back onto the trees as the train passed, bending them backwards into contorted positions. What their pain might be in that bent state, no human could tell. The railway line was progress, progress for all men. Communications were vital. That much everyone was told. At what cost, they were not told. Neither was it clear what the people might gain as the desecration of the landscape proceeded.

CHAPTER 20

When Lucy first saw New Farm, she had to use all her willpower to hide her disgust from Elias. The shanty-town sprawled on a bleak hillside and seemed to go on forever. Puddles of smelly water lay between the rows of shacks; rubbish piled up along the alleys, and the incessant wind blew it around. Mangy dogs fought for the decaying food morsels among the rubbish, and children—many of them covered in sores—played in the puddles and filth. The walls of the shack were a patchwork of corrugated iron, cardboard and pieces of plywood from broken-up tea-chests. The roof was two rusted sheets of corrugated iron. Where gaps and holes let the wind blow in, Elias hung strips of hessian, saved from his trading in Kwa Mashu. A cardboard partition gave them two rooms, each lit by a small window in a rotting wooden frame. The door hung from one hinge. On the pitted cement floor they placed more hessian. The only water supply was a well on a neighbouring property.

The first day Lucy went from New Farm to her job at the Evenmores', she asked Elias before she left, "What will you be doing today?"

"I think I will go over to the shebeen queen in Kwa Mashu and start collecting bottles again."

"I'll see you this evening."

Lucy made her way to the bus stop. There were many men and women waiting there. All were going to work. Lucy looked around her and recognised none of them. And no one recognised her. This sudden revelation sent a frightening thought running through her head, and her spine chilled with the knowledge that Elias was different. He was so easily recognisable with his one-legged limp. She ran the risk of being late for work and hurried back to the shack, hoping to catch Elias before he left for Kwa Mashu. She took a short cut, straight up over the steep hill, instead of going round by the longer but easier track. Panting, she arrived at her new doorstep. She flung open the door and shouted for Elias. He came limping from the room where they slept.

"Elias! Do you know that you can't go back to Kwa Mashu?"

"Why not?"

"You see at the bus stop, where I was, I got lost in the crowd and nobody seemed to recognise me and I did not recognise anybody. Oh Elias, with your limp you will be recognised. And if the hire purchase fellows come looking for us, if the collectors come, they will get at you so easily, or someone will tell them they've seen you. Here in New Farm it is not going to be easy for them."

"I didn't think of that. What am I going to do? I can't sit here doing nothing."

"No, but for today you just stay here and don't go anywhere. I will try to be early, and we will figure a way out. Now I must run."

Lucy ran out of the shack and the door slammed shut behind her. Standing in that poky room, Elias wondered what fate had in store for him now. He felt restless, and started sweating. He tried to rest his amputated limb. He couldn't keep still. He began to pace the room, and this tired his one good leg. He didn't know what to do. He stepped outside and looked across at the vast expanse of farm holdings. He saw sugarcane fields and vegetable gardens. In some ways the place reminded him of Umzinyathi. But the Umzinyathi that he remembered was a place of green grass, leafy trees and undulating hills. Once, one of his elders had remarked that the Valley of a Thousand Hills started somewhere near Umzinyathi. Here in front of him there were some hills, and the land stretched away to a distant horizon, but the green, swaying leaves of sugarcane filled the foreground. The foreigners had done a good job in transforming this part of the world into a beautiful garden. It struck him that their kind of monotony showed even in the lush green plantations of sugar. He brooded all day.

When Lucy returned to their shack late in the afternoon, she went into her "kitchen" and began to prepare the evening meal. Elias limped in, and said softly, "I am feeling so much at a loss I don't know what to do, what to do with all the life ahead of me."

Lucy detected a note of bitterness and an added sense of urgency in Elias's voice. Looking straight into his eyes, she saw something that had not been there before.

"You see those farms out there . . . you see them? I am going to seek work on one of those farms."

"As what?"

"As a labourer . . . as a farmhand. I think I still know how to use the hoe."

"You would want to work the white man's fields?"

"In the present circumstances, Lucy, I am willing to work anyone's fields."

Lucy stared at her man. She knew, deep down, that it was going to be very tough for him. She wanted to stop him, but at the same time she did not want to stop the growth of his self-reliance. She had learned that the man was determined to do things, that he was not going to give in. He was battling to forget his disability and she must not remind him of it. She came up to him and, clinging around his waist and leaning on his chest, she murmured, "Elias, you are strong. I am so proud to be your woman."

"You are not just my woman, you are my wife."

"But we are not married."

"A marriage certificate is just a piece of paper to say to the world that we can live together. I don't give a damn for that."

"Why are you so sure that I don't care about it?"

"If you must have the certificate, then we shall have it."

"I didn't say that."

"No, you didn't." He was quiet for a while, then he asked, "If we have more children, I suppose they must be registered as our children?"

"That doesn't worry me. They will be the children of our love and I don't care what the world thinks about that," Lucy said proudly.

"It is not what the world will think of them, it is what the world will do to them that worries me," Elias responded. "Today, without documents, we can't move. It is documents from the time we are born till the time we die. Our children will have to have birth certificates, won't they?"

"Yes, but still I don't care. Leave all that. What I want to talk about is us, and you in particular."

"What about me?"

"I still think you should not work on the farm."

"Forget that. Since I have nothing to do in this place, and I can't go to the township or the city, I have to find work near here. Look, the sooner we learn to live this kind of life, the better it will be for both of us. Now go ahead and get us something to eat, and leave the rest to me. I will do my best and we will leave the rest to providence."

Lucy quietly gathered the parcels she had wrapped at the Evenmores' and began to lay out the contents in little dishes. Elias limped towards the table. Many things were kept on it. There was nowhere else to put them. They sat down to their evening meal, and then with great misgivings about the future they went to bed.

In the morning Lucy, as usual, did her chores, dressed, and left for work. Elias had woken up with her, and he also got ready for the new day. As soon as she had left, he locked the door to their shack and followed the track to the nearest farm. There were others, blackmen like him, walking to the farms. Elias spoke to some of these men and women on the way.

"I am new here and I am looking for a job. Will you tell me who is responsible—?"

"You are looking for a job?" asked one of the women, staring rudely at his leg.

"Yes, I am."

They had reached the first farm.

"Then you must see the supervisor." Pointing to a blackman in khaki clothes and lace-up boots, who carried a cane in his hand, the woman said, "He is the one who employs and fires around here. Go and see him."

"Thank you very much," said Elias.

The regular labourers made for their allotted work places. Elias approached the induna and extended greetings.

"You, who are you and what do you want?" he asked tersely.

"My name is Elias and I am looking for work."

The induna looked him up and down. He took out a small piece of brown paper and wrapped some loose tobacco in it. He lit this, and puffed out some smoke. Through the haze he had created in front of him he scrutinised Elias. Then he said, "You will not be able to herd the cattle, because you would need the use of two agile legs; you cannot be a stablehand because you would have to walk up and down all day; you cannot cut sugarcane because you would have to stand and move; you would not be able to load the cane onto the trucks because that would require the use of both your arms, and two legs. So as I see it, the only thing you can do is hoe the gardens, or maybe the sugar fields."

"Yes, I know and I am willing."

Whether it was pity or understanding, it was difficult to tell, but the next moment Elias heard, "Come with me."

The induna led the way to what appeared to be an office attached to the west wing of a wide, sprawling mansion. There he faced a white man and said to him in simple terms, "I am employing this man to weed the fields."

"If it's OK with you then it's OK with me," answered the white man without even looking at Elias. In a matter-of-fact way he said, "His wages will be eight rand a month."

"Is that all right with you, Elias?" asked the induna. "Eight rand—four pounds?"

"It seems all right for the time being."

At this point the white man looked up and for the first time saw his new employee. He exclaimed, "But he is a one-legged man! How on earth will he be able to weed?"

"He will be able to," answered the induna.

The two black men walked away to the shed where the farm implements were stored. The white man watched them go and wondered what his induna was getting up to. As soon as they reached the shed the induna shouted to one of the farmhands to get him a hoe. He took the implement and handed it to Elias with the words, "From today this is yours, and you are expected to look after it, sharpen it and keep it in good working condition. Now join that crowd and I will allot your work as soon as I get to the field."

Elias began his first day's work as a farm labourer. While he hoed the field, he wondered whether Lucy had arrived on time at the Evenmores'. With sweat dripping down his face and his woolly hair growing damp, with the morning sun already hitting and biting his dark skin, he sighed in disbelief at what he was. He thought of the dreams that had compelled him to reject the very foundations of his protected, anchored life. But, he said to himself, I will fight all this and still be the man I wanted to be.

At the Evenmores', Lucy was at work. She had not said a word about Elias and she was so silent that Mary had to say, "Lucy, you are unusually quiet today. Are you well? Is there anything wrong?"

"Nothing much, ma'am."

"But Lucy, you are not your usual self. Is there anything wrong with Elias?"

At the mention of Elias's name, Lucy stopped her work and started to tremble. Mary came closer and asked, "What is it, Lucy? Why are you looking so frightened? What is the matter? Come, tell me."

"It is Elias, ma'am."

"Yes, what about him? Is he well? Where is he?"

"He is well, ma'am."

"Then what is it? Why don't you want to talk about it, whatever it is?"

"Ma'am . . . I don't mind talking about Elias and me. Only, I haven't told you that we have left Kwa Mashu. We were thrown out of our house."

"What do you mean? Where are you living?"

"We are no longer in Kwa Mashu."

"But why?"

"Because they said that Elias was unemployed and therefore we could not live in their house any longer."

"Then where are you living?"

"We are not in Kwa Mashu."

"The bloody devils. What do they expect you to do?"

"I don't know."

"Where is Elias?"

"I don't know."

"What do you mean?"

"He went out looking for a job as a farmhand in the neigh-bourhood."

"What?"

"Yes. And that is what is worrying me. I don't want him to work like that and yet I know I would be hurting him if I stopped him."

"What is all this? What is becoming of you two? What will become of you?"

"I don't know, ma'am." She resumed her work. Mary did not know what to do nor what was expected of her. She watched Lucy move around her house in a stupor. Lucy, who was usually graceful and full of poise, was clumsy and slow. That morning Lucy realised more clearly than ever how much Elias meant to her, and she could not bear the thought of him hoeing and weeding, handicapped as he was. Abruptly she switched off the floor polisher and turned round to look at her madam. Mary was gazing at her anxiously. Lucy asked sud-denly, "Ma'am, isn't there anything else Elias can do?"

Mary had no answer.

Fumbling for her keys in her purse, Lucy stood outside their shack and knew that her man had not returned from wherever he had gone. She unlocked the door and pushed it open. She slammed the rickety door shut behind her. She stretched out on the bed. Before long she was fast asleep. She was weighed down more with mental fatigue than physical exhaustion. She was still asleep when Elias hobbled into their home. He closed the door behind him and called out softly, "Where are you, Lucy?"

There was no reply. He limped into their bedroom and there he found his woman fast asleep. He sat beside her on the bed and gently caressed her face. With that tender touch Lucy was startled.

"When did you come home?"

"Not so long ago. I came in and found you fast asleep."

"Where had you gone?"

"I have started my new job. They are going to pay me eight rand a month. I have learned from the other workers that they also give a ration of mealie meal and beans, some salt and some sugar. That will help."

Lucy moved over and drew Elias into her arms. They found comfort for their bodies, and their tortured souls.

CHAPTER 21

For months Elias worked on the farm, and he made a point of never complaining. Together he and Lucy managed to keep the household going. They worked, they ate, they slept, they subsisted.

One Monday morning, when Lucy arrived at the Evenmores', she had a strong intuition that something terrible was about to happen—and to her. Mary seemed sad and depressed. She came up to Lucy and for the first time in her life she said, "Leave all the work. Come here and sit with me."

"What's the matter, ma'am? You are not looking well."

"Come and sit with me."

Lucy obeyed, and Mary started without delay.

"Lucy, I want you to know that we have decided to leave South Africa. We are going away for good."

"What do you mean, ma'am?"

"That we are going away. We don't want to live in this country any longer."

"But why ma'am?"

"Because I don't want to be punished by my own conscience—"

"Why should you have to punish yourself, ma'am?"

"For the likes of me, Lucy, there is a lot of money and a lot of material security in this beautiful country of yours. But for you in your own country there is nothing. I don't want to live here and suffer the ordeal of knowing that what you should have, you cannot get."

"But that is our fate, not yours."

"Yes, I know. And that is why I want to get out."

"What about baas Peter and his work?"

"He will follow me soon. But I will go first with our child. My regret is that I will not be leaving you in a secure job. Now that I am going, you will have to find another position. I am sorry, Lucy."

"This cannot be happening: first Elias, and now I too must lose my job."

"We still have two weeks before my departure."

"Then ma'am if you don't mind my saying so, I'd better start looking now."

"I know quite a few people and I will recommend you to them. I am sure we'll be able to find something for you."

"I do hope you can. The number of my people waiting in queues at the labour bureau makes me shudder to think what might become of Elias, Themba and me."

It was only now that Lucy brought in the name of Themba, but in her plight she feared for him far more than she worried about herself or even Elias.

"Lucy, work here for this week only. After that you can go out and look for another job. You will be paid for the whole month—"

"You are very kind, madam," Lucy said without looking at her. She moved away and began her work. Fifteen minutes later she exploded: "Madam I'm sorry, I can't go on. I am too anxious for myself and my family to go on like this. I wish to leave now and start looking for work. Forget this month's salary."

"But Lucy . . . "

"Yes madam I wish to go."

"But how will I manage without you?"

"Madam, I have to find some way of keeping my family's body and soul together for ever, not for just a week."

Lucy began to wind up the cord of the vacuum cleaner, and in her frantic state she got it tangled. She didn't bother to untangle it, and picking up the machine she continued, "I will put this thing in its place and if you don't mind I will be leaving."

She went to the kitchen, where the vacuum cleaner was kept, and from there she called, "Will it be possible for you to give me the names and addresses of your connections now?"

"OK, as soon as you have finished come along and I will make out a list for you."

Mary went to fetch pen and paper and sat down at the table in the dining room. Lucy sat down opposite her, without being asked. Mary wrote the list quickly and gave it to Lucy. Lucy said "Thank you," nothing more, and bolted out of the house.

She was on the roads of the Evenmores' neighbourhood—not her neighbourhood though she spent most of her waking hours there—and as she hurried along, gasping for breath, a thought struck her: I'm not the only one who is leaving and running. My madam is leaving and running too. She has so much, and she is leaving. We have nothing. We have to run from place to place just to survive. What will become of Themba and his schooling and the future that Elias and I have planned for him?

She realised that she was already in front of the first address she had been given. She paused outside the gate and waited to get her breath back. As soon as she was more composed, she went in. The gate closed behind her on its own spring. She walked briskly up to the back door. Inside the house a Pekingese, scorning its bowl of mincemeat and brown bread, gave a long, half-scared growl. Its mistress was on her feet and opening the door before Lucy could ring the bell.

"Madam, I work at the Evenmores'. In two weeks they are going away. I would like to be your domestic servant. You may, if you wish, ask Mrs Evenmore what she thinks of my work."

"Sorry, girl. I can't help you. I have no vacancy right now."

She didn't wait for Lucy's answer, and shut the door in her face. Lucy stared at the closed door.

Never mind, she consoled herself. I will go to the next one on the list. This she did. That afternoon she did not take her usual train. She went from door to door, trying to get a job for herself. It was already late when she realised that she'd better go home or her man would begin to panic. By the time she reached the station there were thousands of workers waiting for the rush-hour trains to Kwa Mashu. She wove her way among the crowd, bumping into people, being bumped into, and there were so many people it was not possible to say who was bumping whom. In the midst of all the pushing and touching and shoving, some of the men did not hesitate to pinch her on the buttocks. She knew what was happening and what the men wanted, but she ignored them and remained calm. The worst was still to come. When they all tried to board the train they pushed and they jostled, they lifted and elbowed each other. It was each one for himself. The same applied inside the train. Those who had seats had seats. The fact was that the coaches were jam-packed with tired people, and chivalry was a luxury none could afford. Lucy stood tightly pressed between men and women smelling of sweat, tobacco, liquor and perfume, and breathed in "the smell of the trains." The train jerked as it pulled out of the station, and the passengers lurched and bumped into those around them.

When Lucy arrived at her station it was already dusk. She had to take a bus to New Farm. She had a little bit of luck that day: she caught a bus immediately. As soon as the bus was full it left for Inanda. She alighted at her stop and ran all the way home. By then it was nearly dark. Elias had long returned from his work, and he was worried about her. He was pacing the front of his shack and scrutinising each group of workers making their way from the bus stop home to New Farm. He had been doing this for nearly two hours when he saw her silhouette approaching.

"What made you so late?"

"Elias, I don't know where to start. In two weeks' time there will be no work for me at the Evenmores'."

"I don't believe it. They can't fire you. They like us. We are their friends."

"They didn't fire me."

"Then why the devil did you leave them, especially now?"

"They are leaving South Africa for good."

"They are leaving South Africa? But why?"

"Because she says they don't want to be part of what happens to us blacks in this country. They feel that so many wrongs are being done to us that they will be—"

"The cowards! I thought they were our friends. I can't understand."

"There is nothing to understand. I must just go out and find another job."

"How, and where?"

"Well, I've been out looking most of the day."

"Did you find anything?"

"No."

"Never mind. We will come up with something. Now let us eat the little we have."

"Elias, I don't want to eat. I want to know what is going to become of Themba. I don't want to let him down."

"You will not let him down."

"I am frightened that I may."

Elias remembered the thoughts that had swept his mind

when he went to fetch Themba from the hospital. He remembered how Lucy had begged him to allow her to raise Themba. He remembered that she had breast-fed Themba in the hospital before he even dreamed of keeping the baby in the city environment. He remembered the joy that had filled him when he brought Themba to the khaya where Lucy lived, and the joy on Lucy's face when he handed her his flesh and blood. He turned to her and said, "Lucy, this is not the khaya and it is not Umzinyathi either. But I am happy and proud that you are Themba's mother. The few years that you have already given him are worth more than Umzinyathi could ever give."

"But Elias, I am scared."

"Don't be, Lucy. We will be all right. Themba will be all right."

He held her hand and very tenderly he continued, "Now come with me and see if you can swallow what I have prepared for us."

"No Elias. I am really not hungry. You must help me save every spare penny—I should say every spare cent, but I can't get used to this new rands-and-cents money of ours," she smiled wanly, "so that we can send it to Themba."

They were both very tired, and went to bed much earlier than usual. They had blown out the candle, and in the dark each could feel the other's body and the other's breath. But neither of them could fall asleep. When the morning was about to break Lucy got out of bed and began the day's chores.

She arrived at the Evenmores' as usual. She felt, deep in herself, that she ought to help them. Mary met her at the door, and Lucy said, "I thought I should come along and give you a hand with the heavy work. I remembered that the house has to be polished today. I will try to finish it as quickly as possible, and then I want to go out looking for a job again."

"That's very thoughtful of you, Lucy. But what happened yesterday?"

"There was no luck. But I'm going to keep trying until I find something."

"I thought of five more friends after you left. I rang them in the evening, and spoke to three, and they all said they've got suitable maids and don't need anyone. The others were out, but I'll try them a little later on. There must be someone whose maid is sick or on leave or incapable or something."

"I am grateful for your help."

"You are a real fighter, Lucy."

"What else is there to do? So many of us blacks just survive; when we are going to start living I really don't know."

She began the polishing and within a very short time it was done. Mary spoke to her other two friends. Neither needed a maid. Lucy put away the things and left the house with the words: "I hope to see you soon, madam, and I am sorry to cause you so much trouble."

"I wish you luck, Lucy, and I do hope you'll find something soon."

"I will because I must."

The words rang in Mary's ears as Lucy ran off into the streets and resumed her door-to-door knocking at the back doors of many houses. For that is where such interviews were held. The fashionable stable-doors of the white people's kitchens made an excellent division for these encounters. Only the upper half of the person inside was visible, and the whole body of the one outside was there to be seen and assessed.

For days on end she knocked at doors and pleaded for a job. With each negative reply she became more frightened, and more determined. It was on the Wednesday morning of the second week that Lucy, in her desperate mood, knocked vigorously at another door. She knocked once and there was no reply. She knocked harder the second time and there was a shout from inside: "All right, be patient, I am coming."

The voice alarmed her a little. It was the first time such a voice had answered. All the others, so far, had been female.

The man opened the stable-door at the back. He looked Lucy up and down from head to foot. He appeared to like what he saw.

"Yes, can I help you?"

"Yes, baas, I am looking for a job. I have worked as a domestic . . ."

"You look good enough to be working anywhere."

"I have done only domestic work."

"You will learn to do other work too."

"I am willing to do any work, as long as I have something to do."

"In that case, come in." He opened the bottom half of the door. At this Lucy told herself, At last I am getting somewhere.

As soon as she was inside, the man closed the door. When she turned to look at him she realised he was in his briefs, with a loose shirt hanging over them. She was a little embarrassed. Noticing her uneasiness, the man said, "Don't worry about my clothes. I am like this most of the time. I am a retired man, though I am only in my early fifties. I live alone and I am lonely . . . that is, when I am not drunk."

Lucy asked, "Can I have a job? I have worked well as a domestic."

"Sit down. By the way what is your name?"

"I am Lucy."

"That is a pretty name."

He came towards her and in a husky voice he asked, "Are you trained, and do you know any other work besides cleaning the house, washing dishes and so on?"

"Yes sir, I can do almost anything in the house."

She was growing confident that the job was in the bag for her.

"Do you do that as part of your duties or is there an additional fee for it?"

"What do you mean, sir?"

"I mean, Lucy, do you charge an additional fee?"

"For what?" she asked, but by then she had got the man's drift. For reasons she was unable to explain to herself, she kept sitting and heard him out.

"Now listen, Lucy. I have a proposition for you. If you are prepared and willing to listen to me then I will make it possible for you to earn more in one hour than you would earn in many days as a domestic."

"I still don't understand."

He came towards her and gently caressed her cheeks. "I will let you have five rand just for coming to bed with me."

Lucy was dumbfounded. She stared at her feet. She was frightened. Elias came thundering into her thoughts. Then suddenly Themba came crying and helpless into her imagination. She thought of a five-rand note. She focussed on the man standing in front of her. She could see the hairs on his thighs and the creases in his skin. She saw muscles twitch, and when she looked up at his face she saw a kind of desire that she had not seen for a long time. He said, "I will make it easier for you."

He went over to the cabinet where he kept his liquor supply and opened it.

Lucy said, "There will be no need for that. I stopped that a long time ago."

"Then you will come to bed with me?"

"Yes, if you pay me the five rand in advance."

"That will be no problem." Putting his fingers in his shirt pocket he drew out a note and added, "Since you have agreed so readily I will give you this ten-rand note instead."

Lucy kept silent. He tore off his shirt and hurriedly dropped his briefs. He stood naked in front of her. She did not move. He came closer to her and brushed her face with his penis.

"Do you like the touch of this, of what I am going to give you?"

Lucy looked up at his face and said, "Where is your bedroom?"

Waiting to Live

The man led the way. Lucy saw the affluence of a retired man who happened to be white. Looking around, she compared it with the retired status of her own man. She was in a daze. While her head spun with her loyalty to Elias, her hands were shedding her clothes, in her fear for Themba.

After it was over, the man said, "Come as often as you can. But we must take care that the neighbours do not begin to talk. I like you and I like the way you give it. Your working here will give us a good pretext to meet regularly. I tell you what, I will give you work for three days in the week. For that work I will pay you twelve rand a month. And for your additional services, I will pay you as and when. Will that suit you?"

"And what will it be for what you call as and when?"

"You name it."

"Will you be able to pay what I ask?"

"I will, if you are reasonable."

"Then it must be five rand a time."

She picked up her handbag and was making her way towards the back door when he stopped her: "Wait a minute! I have paid you ten rand already, haven't I?"

"Yes."

"Then before you go I want some more of you. I will give you another five rand if you take off all your clothes and come back to bed with me."

She obliged.

With fifteen rand in her bag Lucy left the house of the man who had offered her a new job and the temptation to return to the ways she had once walked. Only this time there was money involved. Thinking about the money in her purse she knew Themba would be cared for. Even if she hated every moment of this, she was going to do it for him and for her Elias. How she would cope with what she had just started, she did not know.

She made for the nearest post office. There she bought

225

fifteen rands' worth of postal orders and a registered envelope. On a piece of paper she scribbled a note to Themba's guardians in Soweto. She explained that she was leaving the Evenmores' and that her postal address would therefore change. She would notify them when she had a new one, but meanwhile the fifteen rand were for Themba's welfare, and any incidental expenses the Madodas might incur on his account.

On her way back to her shack and to Elias, Lucy felt remorseful and dejected, but she also knew she had started to contribute to a secure future for Themba. She tried her best to hide her guilt and depression. She was smiling and exuded confidence when she met Elias at the threshold of their shack.

Elias was also smiling. He had been paid his salary and was eagerly awaiting her arrival to hand her his full eight rand.

"Take all the money I have brought and use as much as you need," he said happily.

CHAPTER 22

Limping, Elias had hoed the white man's fields for fourteen years. Lucy, too, true to her commitment, worked for quite some time for the lonely man, and then he left Durban. Hardship aged her, and she had to turn to the black migrant workers in their single-sex hostels for extra income. That her womb was violated, time and again, she knew, yet she volunteered to violate it again and again—just so that Themba might become a man.

In the years that followed Lucy saw that her country was torn to pieces. Nelson Mandela, the "black pimpernel" had returned and he was arrested; the people's leaders volunteered, when arrested, to be hanged for their beliefs. The rulers continued to carve the country into ethnically separated "homelands." Resistance groups were brutally silenced; for blacks, South Africa had become a police state: the people could not organise. They succumbed. All this Lucy saw, and she often despaired.

And then it happened. Soweto burnt. Crowds upon crowds of young people came from everywhere. Just like the ants of Umzinyathi, the youth came together, even though time and again they were dispersed—not with whips but with guns and Saracen tanks. For the first time in more than a decade open excitement filled the air. Even as far from Soweto as Inanda, where the squatter camp of New Farm was, this excitement roused the hopes of all. Lucy said to herself, At last the vindication of the violence I did to my own womb.

In Soweto the young marched the streets singing and calling out for more to join them. For a while their elders stood and watched aghast. Still, good humour was the feeling in the air. The schools suddenly emptied of children; Themba, from his school, joined his mates. Slipping into place among the marchers he proudly held up a placard: "Down with Afrikaans."

"We are all together," a beautiful young girl called out to Themba, over the moving heads.

"At last!" he called back.

They were happy that morning. They were saying "No" to something that they did not want. They would show their elders what peaceful protest was all about.

"To the stadium . . . " The word ran back along the moving crowd. They were coming into Orlando West. All of a sudden, near the back of the huge crowd, the biggest in more than a decade, a shot was fired. Those at the front heard nothing, but the buzz ran forward: "Police! Someone's been shot!"

The leaders stopped. A wave ran backwards as if this great flowing river had suddenly met a concrete wall.

Pandemonium broke loose. A girl ran screaming. A shot was heard and a young boy fell—dead. More shots cracked out and then, in those moments, a rain of bullets fell. Another boy fell to the ground, and as Themba bent to pick him up, a searing pain burned through his own right eye. Blackness enveloped him.

The orderly march of protest had been dispersed. Joy and excitement had turned to rage. The schoolchildren, who only moments ago had marched to demonstrate their rejection of Afrikaans as a forced medium of instruction, spread out all over Soweto and they began stoning the police, burning their vehicles and attacking schools, beer-halls and administration buildings—the symbols of their oppression.

All this time, Themba's body lay slumped over the corpse of the boy who had fallen. Police vans and ambulances were parked nearby and bodies were being heaved into the vans. Among the surly crowd watching was an old woman. As the policemen threw the unconscious young man onto a pile of bodies in the nearest van, she shouted, "That boy is not dead!" A murmur arose from the bystanders and a policeman yelled through a loud-hailer, "Move off, all of you." That young man, Themba, was transferred to an ambulance.

In hospital, he had no identity; he was "another case from the riots."

The first child to be killed had been Hector Petersen, thirteen years old. His sister, howling sorrow, carried him through the streets. That photograph appeared in newspapers throughout the world.

As long as Lucy had had a regular job and a postal address, she and Elias had received news, once or twice a year, of their son. Once a photograph came: Themba, aged thirteen, in school uniform, stood at attention and stared solemnly out of the picture. But New Farm had no postal service, any more than piped water or electricity. The plan to visit Themba in Soweto or to bring him to Natal for a holiday faded slowly away: there was never enough money. Now, although Lucy sent off her postal orders from Durban at the start of each school year, she did not even expect an acknowledgement. The parents had completely lost touch with their child.

The population of New Farm swelled to many thousands. City administrations had grown even stricter about occupancy of their houses in the black townships. Drought and overcrowding, and limits set on the numbers of labourers permitted to live on the white-owned farms, forced more and more people off the land and into makeshift settlements where there was at least access to the towns and a chance of finding work.

Meanwhile other troubles intensified. For twenty years a rigid educational policy had been forced on black schoolchildren all over the country: they were to be equipped for the menial jobs they might expect to obtain when they left school. For those who, despite the limitations of the classroom, showed academic aptitude, separate "black" universities had been created. Discontent among the victims of this system mounted steadily, greatly exacerbated by the imposition upon them of Afrikaans, the hated language of the Boers, as a compulsory medium of instruction.

During that winter, when the "children's revolution" finally exploded in Soweto, Elias said, "Themba won't be involved, he must be near his final year."

Lucy countered: "He won't let his classmates down. Those children are heroic, facing the police guns with their stones and bottles, never giving in. Don't worry, he's clever enough to outwit a few policemen."

But Elias did worry: "They're not heroes, Lucy, they're hooligans. Burning down their own schools, attacking people in the beer-halls . . . "

"It's so clear, it's beautiful," said Lucy. "All their attacks are on target; they attack only those buildings that symbolize oppression. And the antidrink campaign is to wake their elders out of their alcoholic stupor, you know that."

The disturbances continued throughout July, despite many deaths and more arrests, and into August.

"I pray that boy is safe," said Elias.

"Do you want him safe and uninvolved and an outcast?" asked Lucy.

"I don't like the way they're going," said Elias. "They won't listen to their parents any more; they're completely out of control."

"And I think they may yet win."

One Sunday morning, about the middle of September, Elias answered a knock on his door. A tall young man stood there, handsome but for his right eye, which was closed and apparently sightless. He was dressed in a teeshirt, threadbare jeans and sandals.

"Is this the home of Mr Elias Mzimande?"

Elias had opened the door an inch or two; these days young troublemakers were everywhere. "Who are you?" he asked suspiciously.

"I am Themba Mzimande," replied the youth, in a surly voice.

Elias's heart missed a beat. He flung open the door, crying, "Themba, you are home! Come in, come into your house!"

"Father, I was not sure. . . . It's been a long time."

They held each other close, and then Elias, almost incoherent with joy, said, "Sit down, I'll make you some tea."

Lucy was not in; the two men sat at the kitchen table with enamel mugs of tea steaming in front of them. For a while they just gazed at each other, Elias smiling, his hands shaking, tears in his eyes. Themba did not smile, and he looked coolly about him.

Elias asked, "Why are you not at school, my son? Examinations must be starting in a few weeks."

"Father, where have you been? Don't you know what has happened? Don't you know our schools are closed? In any case I have been expelled from my school."

Elias closed his eyes in despair. With an effort, he gained a hold on himself, and said, "We were so worried for your safety, son. I thank God you are safe. But I see you are not unharmed. Your eye . . . ?"

Themba was quiet, his mouth twitching a little. He said laconically, "I wouldn't thank God—or the police."

"How is Madoda?"

"Don't know," said Themba.

There was an awkward silence. Then Elias said, "Let me go and fetch your mother. She will be so happy to see you." Leaving his son at the table, he picked his way along the alley, among broken bottles and sharp-edged fish tins, pecking chickens and puddles of filthy water, and knocked on the door of a shack farther down. There was no answer. Suddenly a shutter opened and a head and naked torso appeared. "Yes?" the man grunted.

"I have come for my wife," said Elias.

"Your wife? Oh, you can have her."

The shutter slammed in his face. Elias looked back down the alley towards his own house, and saw to his shock that Themba had followed him. The young man was within easy hearing, and could not have failed to pick up what had been said.

"She's coming," said Elias, and hobbled back to his shack.

They waited a while in silence, but Lucy did not appear. Then Elias said, "Come with me to church, Themba. I'll be very proud to show my fine son to the priest and the congregation."

"No, Father."

"What no?" said Elias. "I asked you to come with me."

"I'm not going to church," said his son. "The Church is too busy telling everyone that life will be fine in the next world, and doing nothing to improve this one."

"The Church is with us in our struggle for dignity and equality," said Elias.

"Ha!" said Themba scornfully, "is that so?" Seeing his father's distress, he relented: "But I'll walk there with you."

Elias changed hurriedly into his better pair of trousers and a worn but clean jacket, and took his Bible, wrapped in brown paper.

Waiting to Live

As they walked between the shacks, more and more people joined them, all heading the same way, dressed in their Sunday best, carrying Bibles or prayer books. Whatever these people did not have in common outside the church, they all smelled the same stench on their way there: that of vomit and hard liquor and urine that pervaded the area. At the entrance to the church a newly built gate stood open. Elias hesitated a moment, but Themba shook his head and Elias walked into the church garden without him. It was surrounded by high walls, and within the precincts there was a mixture of odours, the scent of the flowers in the garden and the stench coming from outside the walls. The morning mist had not yet dried on the flowering plants and the carefully cut and trimmed turf. Little black children on their way into the church reached out to try and touch the lush swaying palm leaves.

Father Gaba, the black priest, was standing at the church door to welcome his flock. A white priest in black robes hurried out to a large American car. The incoming crowd of shiny black faces reacted in various ways to the priests's car: some tried a smile, others spat. But most of the people walked on as if nothing had happened. The car accelerated, sped past Themba and carried away this agent of God. The priest inside the car waved, but Themba simply stared and swore at him under his breath.

From the gate he heard the first hymn start. He turned on his heel and went back to the shack. No one was there, and Elias had the key in his pocket, so Themba sat down on the doorstep and waited. An hour later, he was half-asleep in a patch of sunlight when Lucy came home.

Clutching her blouse, she was hurrying along the alley. The client had not wanted to pay, and there had been quite a skirmish. As she neared her own shack, the young man raised his head from his knees and watched her idly: a middle-aged woman, rather dishevelled, stumbling on high heels along the rutted, stony way. As she came nearer, he sat up straight and stared at her, moving his gaze slowly upwards from the veins showing on her legs, past the skirt that was too tight and too short, past the gaping blouse where the button had been torn off, to the puckered skin of her neck and the deep lines around her mouth. She had started to run. As she reached the doorway, panting a little, he stood up slowly.

"Themba! Oh Themba! I knew it was you! Oh, this is the best day!"

Unlike his father, she had recognised him instantly.

Themba allowed her to hold him close. Then he drew back, and looked away.

"Come in, where's your father? Oh yes, at church. Did you see him?"

Themba nodded.

"Breakfast, my son? We have some porridge—"

"No thank you."

Themba seemed tongue-tied. He shifted his feet on the rough cement floor, and did not seem to want to meet his mother's eyes. Suddenly he exploded: "Where have you been?"

"Oh, not far," said Lucy, not knowing how long Themba had been there.

"I know where you were, and I heard what the man said to my father. What is going on here?"

"Ah. Then you know." Lucy turned away, and held her face in her hands.

Themba shouted with scorn. "Oh you, whatever you are, you turn your face away. My father turns his face away and he walks to his church. What for? Did he go to his church to atone for his sin in doing nothing when he saw that naked man you were with? Did he ask for forgiveness? Has he already forgiven you?"

"Themba!" she implored.

At that moment Elias arrived at the door.

"Here he is," Themba shouted to his mother. "Just seeing him makes me feel sick. And as for you . . . all these years, I didn't know what you were."

Elias Mzimande slapped his son hard across the face. "This is your mother, who reared you." He crossed the little kitchen to his wife, who was standing against the wall, sobbing. "He is just a boy, he doesn't know what he is saying," he said gently, caressing the back of her neck.

Themba was baffled. He wondered what connivance, what dirt, what cheapness and what kind of love. He stood facing his parents. "I don't want to be you! I don't want to be like you! I should hate to be like you. You show me what it is to be naked, to be barren, to be dispossessed. I hate everything I see in you! You, Father, the whole world walks over you—your white masters, the men in this cesspool of a place, even your wife! I know what she does in the other shacks here: she's a slut! She's a whore! Nothing is yours, not even your wife. Oh, to me this shack stinks of shame!"

For a few weeks, Lucy and Elias saw nothing of Themba. He had left them the same day he arrived, soon after his father had slapped him, saying firmly, "I'm going now. I may see you again, I may not."

Then, again on a Sunday, he reappeared. He stood in the doorway and said, "I'm hungry."

His parents were relieved beyond measure to see him, but felt instinctively it would not do to show their relief. They were having supper themselves, mealie porridge and strong sweet tea. Lucy simply fetched a wooden crate from behind the shack and sat on it, leaving her chair for Themba. Without a word, she poured porridge from the saucepan on the stove into an enamel dish and set it before her son.

When he had eaten, he said, "Thank you."

His father said, "You are in your own home, son."

Themba said, "I was offered work on a sugar estate up the coast, but I wanted to see you again. I came back to find out if all is hopeless between us."

"That is good," said his father. "How will you find out?"

"If you permit, I will live here awhile—perhaps I can work on one of these neighbouring farms, and pay for my keep."

"You are always welcome," said his father, "and whatever we have is yours too. But I work on this nearest farm—come along with me tomorrow and we'll speak to the induna."

"You? You work, Father? On a farm?"

"Yes, Themba, why not?"

"But your leg . . . what happened to your leg? Madoda told me once, but I didn't pay attention."

"Oh, it's a long story, not so interesting."

"I want to know."

When Elias had told him, Themba asked, "Are you bitter?"

"Against whom?"

"The people who bombed the railway line."

"No. Why do you ask?"

"I thought you would be . . . "

"Are you mad? They did not mean to hurt me. They believed they were acting for me, for all of us."

"Yes, I know that. But I thought . . . you . . . "

"You are wrong. But it showed once more what violence can do. I need not tell you anything about violence, I think. Others have lost more than I lost. Some thought it was worth sacrificing their lives."

Themba was given temporary work in the stables at the farm. A groom was sick, and Themba could replace him until he was fit for work again. When he told his mother of this success, he laughed bitterly: "Of course I didn't tell them I had nearly twelve years of schooling to my credit. They never would have taken me. I had a lot of education to equip me to clean out stables and brush horses, didn't I?"

His mother laughed with him. She didn't tell him what that education had cost her.

They were all on their best behaviour. Themba did not refer to his mother's way of life or his father's incomprehensible acceptance of it. He did not rail against the Church either. But his parents knew they were in a precarious, temporary testing period. They saw how sullen Themba's face became when Lucy went out on her own. She went seldom now, but occasionally she could not avoid it.

One day, as they trudged home from the farm, Themba asked, "Where were you born, Father?"

"In Umzinyathi, over there." He gestured vaguely northwards.

"And me?"

"In Durban, in a hospital."

They had reached their shack. Lucy was preparing supper. Elias said to her, "Themba was asking where he was born."

Lucy swung round from the stove. "I am going to tell him—"

"Father told me: you had me in hospital in Durban."

"No, Themba. Your mother died when you were born."

Themba was shocked into a short silence. Then he burst out, "Oh, then I am not the child of a whore. That's something, isn't it?"

"Quiet, Themba," shouted Elias. "When you don't know what happened, don't judge."

Lucy ran into the other room and flung herself on the bed, sobbing. Elias said to his son, "Eat. And if you are ready one day to shut up and listen, we'll tell you. Good night."

For over a week there was barely a word exchanged in the shack. Themba stayed out until late in the evenings, only returning after his parents had gone to bed. On the way to work, he and Elias talked about the farm, the horses, the drought.

Then one day Themba came into the shack with his father after work and sat down at the table. "All right," he said, "I'll hold my tongue."

"After supper, my boy," said Elias.

And so they told him about Nomsa's death.

"Why didn't you take me back to Umzinyathi, to our people there?" asked Themba.

"I think my father never forgave me for that. It was disregard of his authority, and it was worse: it was a rupture in our family, in our traditions, in our links between generations. But that was what I wanted. I wanted you to be different, not like me. I wanted you to be wiser than me, better than me, richer than me, happier than me. I did not want you to grow up in those forgotten valleys, listening to your elders, learning only from the past." Elias smiled sadly. "My beliefs have not changed, my son."

"But how did you mange to look after me?" Themba was addressing himself only to his father, as if Lucy were not there. It seemed he did not trust himself to speak to her, despite his promise.

"It was so strange," answered Elias. "Both you and I were lucky. There was another woman, who offered you her breasts."

"In the hospital?"

"Yes."

"Why?"

"Because I had enough milk to feed you with," interrupted Lucy.

"*You* fed me?"

"Yes, my son, she fed you, she reared you."

"What about her own child? Where is her child?"

"My child, a little daughter, died at birth on the same day your mother died."

"And your husband? What about him?"

"I had no husband."

Themba turned to his father and asked bluntly, "Did you father her child?"

"No," answered his father.

"I didn't know then and I don't know now who the father was. Does that satisfy you, Themba?" Lucy rose and faced him. "Yes, I was that kind. I haven't changed much, have I?"

It was Sunday. Themba waited for his father to leave for church, and then he asked Lucy, "My father says he is not bitter about his leg. Are you bitter?"

"You mean towards the freedom fighters who blew up the railway line? Themba, you don't know me at all, do you?"

Themba was taken aback by her words. He had expected her to say "terrorists" or "thugs."

She did not wait for confirmation. "I think I'd better tell you a few things. Perhaps you will never understand how it was for us, in those days. It was after all the bannings. To us, it seemed our very soul had been wiped out. Then suddenly, that action proved the spirit of our people was alive! You'll never know what courage it gave us."

"But my father was so badly hurt."

"Yes. How can I explain? One thing was one thing, another was another. Sorrow and joy, together, on one day. I thought my heart would burst."

"*Amandla*,"* said Themba softly, touching Lucy's hand.

"*Awethu*,"** she responded, her mouth distorted, her eyes glistening. But she forced herself to go on. "To answer your question: yes, I was bitter about the way your father was treated. I am still bitter. That pitiful compensation, no help

---

* *amandla* (Zulu): power
** *awethu* (Zulu): to us; to the people (*Amandla awethu!*: Power to the people!)

from anywhere; we lost our house, we had no income. Oh, you know how it is with us."

"I know," said Themba. He had read about such things.

Very gently, Lucy said, "Yes, Themba, I agree with you. You must never be like your father and you must never be like me. You are trained to hate being like your father. You feel naked and dispossessed. Yes, you hate all we stand for, you hate acceptance, acquiescence. We *are* dispossessed. I for one am dispossessed of everything except the capacity to love you and your father. And ever since you were six and we sent you to Soweto, I have lived the life of one you are ashamed to call mother. Whether you call me mother, whether you think of me as mother or not, I have given you—and if need be, I will continue to give you—all I have. For me, you will always be my son."

"You mean you actually sold your body so that I might be cared for and educated?"

Lucy looked at him and could not muster the courage to say yes. Tears ran down her cheeks. Themba put his arms tightly round her.

"I have heard of parents sacrificing their very lives for their children," he said, "but Mama, I have never heard of this kind of sacrifice."

Lucy responded by holding him tighter to herself.

"Themba, my child, I love you more than I love myself."

"Oh Mama!"

"Say it again and again, Themba. I want to hear that beautiful word from your lips."

"Mama, Ma! Ma! I love you."

ABOUT THE AUTHOR

MEWA RAMGOBIN was born in Inanda, Natal, on November 10, 1932. He received a bachelor of arts degree in political science with honors from the University of South Africa. In 1971 he established and was national chairman of The Committee for Clemency South and revived the Natal Indian Congress, a sister organization of the African National Congress. For twelve years, from 1971 to 1983, he was under house arrest. He has been banned by the South African government for seventeen years.

Mewa Ramgobin was appointed national co-treasurer of the United Democratic Front in 1983. In 1984 he was detained without trial by the South African government. After making a court appeal to declare the detention orders invalid, he was released after eleven days. Five days later, he appeared at the British consulate in South Africa with various officials of the United Democratic Front and the Natal Indian Congress, to publicize before the world press the question of detention without trial in South Africa. Upon leaving the consulate on October 6, 1984, he was immediately arrested and detained without trial until December 10, 1984, whereupon he was charged with treason. He was then held without bail for more than five months. On December 9, 1985, he was acquitted of all charges. Mewa Ramgobin is married and has five children. He lives in Natal, South Africa.